A LONG WALK
TO
KNOWING

A LONG WALK

— TO —

KNOWING

ANNE FISHER

iUniverse, Inc.
Bloomington

A Long Walk to Knowing

iUniverse books may be ordered through booksellers or by contacting:

iUniverse
1663 Liberty Drive
Bloomington, IN 47403
www.iuniverse.com
1-800-Authors (1-800-288-4677)

ISBN: 978-1-4759-0982-1 (sc)
ISBN: 978-1-4759-0984-5 (hc)
ISBN: 978-1-4759-0983-8 (ebk)

Printed in the United States of America

iUniverse rev. date: 05/10/2012

CONTENTS

Chapter 1.   Escape and Survive 1

Chapter 2.   Keep an eye on the Balance...........................11

Chapter 3.   Gains and Losses..29

Chapter 4.   Healing the hole in her Soul 37

Chapter 5.   The drive out of despair.......................................42

Chapter 6.   Nothing but sand 47

Chapter 7.   Government another word for inaction.............51

Chapter 8.   A Different way to see the World 59

Chapter 9.   Travelling Companions...64

Chapter 10. Dinner with Irene..70

Chapter 11. Her return to normalcy..86

Chapter 12. This looks like home..91

Chapter 13. The second Trip South..98

Chapter 14. A Home at last...114

Chapter 15. Publication and the tightrope...........................120

Chapter 16. Companions on the horizon 132

Chapter 17. Soon to be published 140

Chapter 18. The campsite down there....................................147

Chapter 19. The Faculty Presentation 155

Chapter 20. Return to Campus..166

Chapter 21. Her trip with Buck 177

Chapter 22. Making a real home 202

Chapter 23. Back to the community 210

Chapter 24. A Completion and A Beginning.........................222

Chapter 25. The longest Wait 228

Chapter 26. Edward and his sister Elizabeth.........................239

Chapter 27. Welcome home..248

Post Script...251

CHAPTER ONE

ESCAPE AND SURVIVE

Rose rode the bus out of town, and as she surveyed the environment she knew it was time. She sat in her usual seat, near the driver, and close to the door. *The less interaction with passengers the better,* she thought to herself. If there was one thing which made her sick, it was the docility of the people in general, and especially those on the bus.

Her small frame was deceptive, one look at her no one would appreciate her wiry strength. She was an attractive person, brown hair, an attractive smile when one was available, and a quick wit, but as she was on the bus for one reason to get away from town, and the filth it represented to her. Filth was the evidence that the oligarch's had given up any responsibility in their bargain to play the capitalist game with any integrity.

The bus turned into the last terminal station on this route to the east of the city. As was her style she was up and out of her seat as the bus turned into the final station on the route, and at the door to exit into the terminal building. There was the smell of the rubbish which collected in the building, and it only got worse as no one ever attempted to contain it. She quickly passed through the Terminal building and exited onto the street. Stepping quickly, she walked up the littered street, avoiding any contact with the garbage that littered the environment; she proceeded to the small foot bridge which led to her path up the hill and out of the neighborhood

1

which surrounded the terminal building. She walked with the conviction which revealed to any who were watching that she was finished living in what her life time had turned into, a sewer. She briefly flashed on her first trip up this hill, and it had not been an unpleasant experience, but over the last year it had begun to mimic the filth and degradation of the inner city which she had left behind with her move out to the eastern edge of the city, and it had forced her to the decision she had come to reach for this night. She had to escape. By leaving the filth of what most people lived in now without realizing it was her declaration of real independence.

In her adulthood, her awareness had grown into a knowledge that now drove her to escape this vile environment, and in her gut she knew beyond any other knowledge she possessed, she could not survive in this place much longer. It had become ignored, filth, a sewer, and she wanted out.

Her facial features usually tight, and expressionless on these rides in and out of the city was now as she mounted her climb up into the hills was more relaxed. Rose, as she walked up the hill for this last time knew that she had to leave what was before her eyes, a crumbling, smelly, and corrupt world which was the result of greed. She could relax now as the decision was made. She would walk to her death, or her life, and either was preferred in her mind to the option she had exercised for a variety of reasons up to this moment.

Rose was well educated, she had several years before been awarded a Master's Degree, and it may have been the fact that she was analytical in her thought processes that her tolerance was so thin. She was too analytical to survive in a culture which required one to simply tolerate the consequences of a mindless government which was a puppet on the string of the Oligarch's who owned everything, and had over time lost any element of a social contract which had guided the Republic for now, more than three hundred years.

Over time she had been preparing to leave. She maintained her government issued apartment in the city changing lights, hauling in the bottled water which had been issued now that the water in the pipes downtown was so contaminated, she could hardly make herself open the faucets in that apartment. Had it been discovered she no longer occupied her government issued apartment she risked being fired. She had moved to the edge of the city to facilitate her escape when the time came, and she knew that time was now! Everything she had needed to do, the identification of the mole at the University who had so corrupted her plan and injured her friends, the exposure of the graft and dishonesty in her own department of the Government, was taken care of, and having settled those scores, while protecting herself was complete, and she now felt that she could leave, and leave she would this very night. Somehow making all those wrongs, right, had kept her here, enduring the growing filth, now she knew she had gotten her revenge for all that had been done to her and her friends at the University by the people for whom she worked, she was free to go and go she would.

She had broken a large number of rules herself. Moving away from the city and abandoning her Government issued apartment was a risk she felt she had to take while she finished her task of executing her vendetta on those who had made life so difficult for her, in denying her the possibility of completing the Doctorate, and costing one of the professor's her profession and threatening her other friends in the University.

When she moved to the cabin in the hills she discovered the water to be less contaminated than it had been in the city, though not clear and clean, it could be boiled and consumed with little danger and only a small amount of resentment.

Rose had been preparing for this night for many months. *I need rest before I leave,* she thought, her plan which had been finalized in her mind this last night on the bus, was to check her rucksack which contained everything she determined she would need for her walk to freedom, eat but having made the decision to leave had somehow taken her hunger away and replaced it with a kind of excitement. She made a call to her office to tell them she was ill. "I will not be in for several days" she said and disconnected lest they pick up that she did not seem sick at all. She was tired, and as she slept she felt the shock of being startled into awareness by the replay of the last earthquake which had been the primary cause of the water becoming so polluted, and left unrepaired by the owners, and upon waking, grabbed her sack, packed with everything she could carry away, and she strode away from this crumbling social order, or disorder as she preferred to think of it, and into the freedom of the night.

She headed to the east. Up the hills in which this small cabin had been hidden so many years prior, and as she climbed to the crest she looked back to see the outline of the city which had been the place of her birth those 30 plus years ago.

Images of her childhood, a single child in a society of one child families, and she could see the outline of the shore line which was giving way to the ocean coming inland with each successive day of the final melt of the ice which had capped both the south and the north poles of the planet. She remembered living in a company apartment which was issued to her father during his employment in a factory, attending the company school for her early education, playing in the park at the center of the housing area, seeing her mother whither in a way with the effects of the one worker policy of the government at that time.

Her mother was a born teacher, she would sit at the kitchen table when Rose would enter from school, and dissect her home work in ways Rose had never seen in the class rooms of her school. Yet she knew she would never use that talent because she and her father wanted to marry and have the one child they could create and the price for her mother had been life in a way it's itself.

She also thought of her Grammy her mother's mom. Grammy had a house that was in the country. It was a very big house, with a stair case in the house which led to the many bedrooms up stairs, and it was her mother's family home. The company that Grandpa had worked for was not a company which demanded that you live in a company house, and Granny, as her three children went to school and had grown, had been a teacher, and then an administrator of a school, and upon retirement she had her large yard outside and Rose remembered so many days working in Granny's garden. She grew so many of the fruits and vegetables they would consume in the meals now in her memory.

When Mom and Dad, and Rose would travel out to Grammy's for vacation times she would help Grammy with the Garden. And every bit of organic garbage would be put in a pale, and it went directly back into the soil at Grammy's yard, nothing was wasted in that house. Rose could in this moment of memory recall the smell of the earth in Grammy's garden; it was rich with a life of its own. Grammy loved to open the earth and see the black little bodies of the worms crawling through the soil and she would say that the worms were there to protect the soil for growing more of the food that would become energy for living.

Rose had climbed up the ridge as this wave of memory covered her awareness, and then she began to descend into the valley below and leave those memories behind. She looked toward the east as the sun now was just coming up on the horizon to the east and she suspected she would now never see what she had left as long as breath was in her lungs and she smiled knowing that Granny would understand, even if her parents would never have approved of her desire to find some kind of independence from the desperation she was walking away from.

This first day of her trek was both a walk away from anything she had known and as well an exploration of what could be. She walked into a new environment with much for her to learn, and the feeling her body held that first morning was only of hope. The day moved to midday and then to afternoon, she had discovered an abandoned farm and there were two pear trees with fruit available. This would be her first meal on this walk into her own freedom, she picked what she could carry, and as she strode through the valley she felt a kind of renewal that one feels when one is truly the executive of one's own soul.

She found a place up on a small hill to take her rest for the first night. It was high enough so she could see the land below for several miles, and there was a small cave which provided a bit of shelter, and kept her presence in the environment hidden. As she entered the cave she placed her rucksack on the floor and spread out her blanket. She ate one of the several tins of protein, and drank a bit of her water. Her legs ached, and though she had prepared for the trek by walking many miles each day to and from her work site, she discovered she was stressing her body in ways she had not prepared for.

This first night of a trek of many months she thought, was a celebration of freedom, but she was aware that she had no picture in her mind of what that freedom looked like, and so she let herself sleep, with the hope of some kind of picture occurring to her so she would know, but sleep was dreamless, and before dawn she was walking once again in a direction east north east, reckoning on the sun.

Day two became day ten or twelve she could not be really sure. She noted that fact that she could not really with any sense of accuracy tell how long she had walked. She had in those days discovered in a couple of places the presence of fruit trees, and she had climbed to harvest what she could, peaches, and oranges and some pear trees, bursting with fruit, and she was grateful for the bounty.

Several of the nights when she had come across the bounty of the fruit trees, she had opted to remain in the environment in order to eat, and rest. She thought though that this was not her primary task, and so she put as much as she could into her rucksack, and refocused on her goal of distance and escape.

Soon she seemed to lose the concept of past present, or future, and everything in her consciousness was an oppressive "Now". She would watch the land pass as she pressed forward. She walked through a valley of high grasses. Rose was a small woman, no more than 5 ft.' 2or 3 inches and the tall grasses now brown from heat and loss of moisture were taller than she. It felt like a protective cover as she traversed the valley, and she felt more relaxed enjoying not having to scan the environment for signs of danger. As she walked, she felt almost relaxed striding along the valley floor. Suddenly there was a sharp crack, and she dropped to hit the ground with a resounding thud. She remained motionless and wondered had she been seen and shot at by some occupant of the environment which only moments before felt so empty and safe to her.

She listened, and heard nothing, and she slowly at first crawled toward the edge of the high grasses and seeing that the trees would provide her better cover perhaps, she moved up the edge of the hill, looking behind her to see any evidence of a hunter behind where she was. She saw no evidence of life, or motion, and heard nothing which would be associated with another person in her environment, and so she took the chance of being seen, headed to the trees on a dead run to hide and reevaluate her safety. She felt a deep kind of shock. Her hands were tremulous, and her mind was racing.

In the time it took to fall to the ground she had passed through feeling a sense of safety to becoming prey on the wrong end of someone's gun barrel. In a moment she had lost any sense of dominion she had ever possessed. She worked her way to the top of the hill and at the crest of that hill she lay on her belly and surveyed the next of what we're becoming endless plains and saw below in an area close to the edge of the hill she had climbed a small one room cabin, and as she watched, there was not one sign of life in that environment. It was perhaps a half mile down the hill, and only yards from the base of the hill to the cabin's edge. It had been many days since she had eaten her last provisions, and all the fruit had as well been consumed. She had been lucky a couple of times and been able to grab and kill a small rodent, not much in the way of meat, but skinned and gutted there were edible small muscles which roasted over a small fire had sufficed to keep body and soul connected and satiated. She reckoned that it must be near sunset, the light in the sky in this setting was still impacted by the green haze of pollution, but to a significantly lessor degree than the home she had walked away from those weeks prior. The air was clearer, you could see more accurately what was between you and your next visual goal, and when she would stop and take a deep breath into her lungs the stinging which had been there in the city was no longer so present. She looked down the hill at the cabin, and she lay this night watching that cabin for signs of movement or life, amongst the cover of big boulders nestled into the hillside, as if they had been the toys of giants, tossed and then left behind.

Rose had not slept for any amount of time, she was restless, and she could feel the panic rise she had felt with the sound of the gun shot the day before. She was in a way trapped on the treadmill of do I or don't I take the risk to see what there might be to sustain me in that cabin, and finally exhaustion had its way and she drifted into sleep. She had fallen asleep amongst the big boulders on the side of the hill, and as she came awake, the sun was high in the sky overhead, and as she woke there still was no sign of life around the cabin just below her. She rose from her bedding, and after a visual survey of the hillside and valley floor, seeing nothing of a threatening nature, she walked carefully toward the cabin, approached the door, and found it to be open, and walked into a single room, a sink which she determined to have a connection to a well supply, which was clear and clean. She twisted the handle of the faucet and heard the pump kick in and looked at the water as it ran from the faucet, it was clear, utterly clear, not the tan color of the water in the city, which she had existed on for years now. There were food stuffs on shelves, a single bed, a table and one chair, and as she pulled together some of the tins of food, and grabbed a canteen filled with clear fresh smelling water, she bolted out the door, and up the hill to what she perceived to be safety. She ate that afternoon, drank copious amounts of water, and she slept in the safety of her boulders on the side of the hill. She woke near mid-night, and walked down to see if indeed the cabin was still empty, and she found it so. Her eyes adjusted to the dark she looked through the drawers to see what might be there and found a tin of what had to be dried meat, probably of a deer, and she placed the tin into her rucksack, and a canteen which she filled with water, and a back pack which she filled with the cans of food stuff which she found on the shelves in the closet by the door. She also found a pistol and a box of two dozen shells. She was ambivalent, she cradled the gun in her hand, and in a moment it too was in the rucksack along with the box of shells. She had in this visit, met her two highest needs at least for a while, clean water, and food, and in a way, another need which the events of the last days had become apparent to her in a way never before experienced, protection in a potentially hostile environment.

She had not occupied a bed in months at this point in time, and so she stretched out on the bed, and with her hand gripping the gun she fell asleep. With the sun still unwilling to make its appearance she was up and on her way, and as the sun rose into this sky this day, she was high on the next set of hills heading toward what she imagined to be, somewhere in what had been northern Nevada, as she could see ahead of her the wide expanse of flat land with little in the way of hills, and low sage brush, little for her to use for cover or protection. She walked across the flat lands and was surprised to find on her second day in this area little streams of water coursing through the otherwise arid land. She was careful to keep her water containers filled, as she came across these resources, and the tins of food and the jerky kept her energy high and she felt strangely safe in this baron expanse. She could see in the distance many days walk some more hills and to the south of her path as she walked day after day, it was as if she could in some strange way understand that her persistence in this process would in one way or another be gratified.

How she could not say, just the sense that if she kept moving she would somehow well out and find somewhere out here, where humans were so scarce, a haven which would help her redefine who she was and what she could attain.

It was in these moments she could for the first time in this escape from what she had known into what to her was completely unknown, she could just begin to taste a sense of hope. It was sweet, and she savored it in a way she had never known.

CHAPTER TWO

Keep an eye on the Balance

Rose had known for a long time, that hope for the citizens with whom she lived and worked was a lost cause. And that for her was such a significant loss, in the face of having grown up within a family which had struggled to hold onto hope over the years of her formation and independence. Her mother nurtured a sense of striving and set little goals for her to achieve throughout her younger years. She had thought at one point in her adult struggles that had been her mother's gift to her. She had qualified to go on to higher education by virtue of her excellence in the Company owned school she attended as a child. The family occupied a small two bed room apartment, which was owned by her Fathers employer, there had been a park with fruit trees growing in that environment, and as a child she had walked to and from school each day through that park area, and she would, when the trees were heavy with fruit, grab extra fruit for the family on her way home in the afternoons. She would anticipate the fruit by the flowers popping out on the trees, and the small fruit becoming present and then in the spring and summer would watch the developing produce until it was bursting with flavor and ready to be picked. She would give her Father as he left the house to go to his afternoon shift a piece of fruit to sustain his energy, until his dinner time which was provided by the company at a specific time, and of course he would eat his evening meal at 8 p.m. with his work companions. She could count on the fingers of one hand the number of dinners she had with him at home when he was working. He wanted to provide well for his family, and have enough in the account for himself and his wife upon retirement, and so he rather routinely worked the seven days of each week and pray that there would be enough when the time came to live in the retirement community to which, they would automatically be assigned.

It had become automatic in her society that the employers deducted from your account all the costs you charged on a debit card against your pay account. All of the routine costs associated with the needs of daily living were as well charged against that account and no one used money any more as it was seen as unnecessary. There was a large commissary in her neighborhood where all the employees and their families could obtain whatever they needed, and the bills for your water, and a small token charge for rent, power for your home, and communication services, was of course deducted from your balance each month. Her parents paid special attention to their account balance, and she would hear her father say that his hope was that they both died with a positive balance in their earnings account. This comment made her mother very cautious when purchasing needed clothes and food from the Commissary. Once in a great while her Father would bring a couple of roses for the family to brighten the home environment, but these occasions over the years were rare. She had been told that her mother, when she gave birth to their only child, had wanted to name her Rose in honor of her favorite flower, "then I will always have a Rose to enjoy and love" she had said, and so on the first night after her birth, her father had given her that name, and as well brought a rose bud to his wife, which she had saved pressed in one of her favorite books.

Growing up Rose knew that she would never marry. She had only to look at the emptiness faced by her mother. Yes, she knew that the love and commitment which bonded her parents was both real and sustaining to them both. Rose knew as well, she could never be happy and gain a sense of her own need for mastery, which had been carefully grafted to her soul by her Mother, a message most every day as they sat at their small table in their kitchen to complete each days learning task from the earliest of days.

As a child she was an excellent student/learner. She entered College at the state run university which was located in her state as a young woman of seventeen. For the first time in her life she lived on the Campus in a huge Dormitory for women. She remembered her last day at home, all she could think about was leaving, and moving ahead in her life, and she was intolerant of her Mothers emotions which were all about anticipation of loss. Her primary role in the last years had been so focused on this one child; she had lived and breathed mothering, and was so much at a loss about how she would maintain the closeness in the relationship. Rose on the other hand was about to step out into her own life for the first time, and could not brook her Mother's sentimentality, and her anticipation of loss. Finally it was agreed by all three that she would get on the train to go to School, and manage her transfer into adulthood by herself.

As she rode the train into adulthood she read and re-read the material about adjustments and requirements of a student embarking on advanced studies. It was a quick process, and she moved into a dormitory. She had a roommate who was equally driven as was Rose. It was a good match, they were both convinced that their lives would be quite different than the lives of their Mothers who they saw as dependent, and as Rose had said empty of choice, and possibilities.

After they obtained all the documents they needed to use the library, to have a meal ticket at the huge cafeteria, to obtain two sets of linens and personal items at the campus store. Rose had decided to work in the campus community to assist her parents in payment for this educational experience; she had heard their concerns about needing to be cautious about expenses. With that her school demands were heavy, however the harder it seemed, the more diligent she was, and she seemed to revel in the tasks of study and work, and seemed to grow and develop into a stellar student and a diligent worker.

She had always loved reading, and writing and she opted to study a major in English Composition with a minor in philosophy. And at the end of her primary year, she had been able to pay for one third of her expenses, and earn a perfect academic standing. She was becoming a stellar student, and was in her second year given a monetary award for her standing academically, which went into her own account which would upon graduation be transferred to her balance in her new employment. Both her parents were very proud of her performance, and her father wrote to her a letter which she had taken routinely, but as time passed she learned that it had contained more information than her cursory reading when it was sent. She wondered upon re-reading it in the years that came how she had overlooked his intent, and attributed it to the immaturity of a sophomore in college. "now that you have mastered what it is to be successful, do not allow that desire to succeed get into the way of our relationship with you. We are the reason you are such a good student, do not forget your Mother as you pile up your successes."

Change was happening and it was publicly talked about in the press. It was decided in the puppet congress that still met once a year that certain kinds of public endeavors would be scaled back and terminated with-in the next year. And it really hit the university campus. No more money would go to the teaching of seven fields of study, from Astronomy, to Sociology. All professors in those seven fields of study were moved out of the buildings they had occupied for years, and students in those fields of study were given one free semester in school and were required to find a more adaptive field of study. Professors and students alike had staged protests, and the authorities had responded with attacks on the demonstrators with water cannons, pungent sprays which burned their eyes and skin, and attack dogs.

Rose had joined the protests, but her parents had intervened and persuaded her to keep her head down and not risk being hurt, or recognized by any one in authority. This was hard for her to do, as so many of her friends were so negatively affected. And privately she felt as if she complied she would be giving up a large part of herself which she had worked hard to develop in these early years of her independence. "My feelings and values are important, and based in an understanding of what is fair" she had said to her parents, but they responded by cautioning her to not draw attention to herself by these values which no longer worked for the good of all.

She had decided to not speak about what was going on in her life to anyone, and she became something of an isolate even here on Campus. She understood that keeping her own counsel was going to be a hard for her as she had been relatively gregarious in her life, and she deeply resented the change that the environment was now demanding of her. "What my parents want, is for me to silently take their crap, and I do not feel honest doing that", she said to a friend.

She shut down, kept her head down, and complied, but her internal dialogue was one of commitment to always knowing what exactly was going on, and in the privacy of her own conscience she would decide for herself any issue which affected her choices.

She worked hard, studied hard, and succeeded and began her life of work for a company which contracted with the Government to produce written documents which would ultimately become standards of conduct or as she thought of them edicts. She was in the ideal place to understand and be informed about what the government really was up to, and she knew this would in fact be in her own best interests. "knowing what is in the pipeline is always better than not knowing" she said to herself as she signed her employment paper work and obtained the location of her housing unit and obtained her card to access her earnings account.

Her initial employment put her into an apartment near her work. It was actually much larger than what was described in the handout she had received, she had a small nook built in to the kitchen layout for eating, a small living room, a separate bedroom, and a bath, and

15

it was about 1000 square feet in space. She found a closet with a dry cleaning machine and a laundry with a dryer, something her mother had never had in their home. She was generally pleased with the arrangement, and she reported to work filled out the paper work for furniture, which would be delivered that very day, and she attended a brief employment educational meeting and then was escorted to her desk, and given a stack of papers she would read, re-write, and submit for publication for the public, the government, and other private companies, to distribute to their employees, customers, and public when necessary. Much of what she worked on in the early days was clearly boring and uninteresting. She did her work daily and she did it expertly. It was rare she would have her work turned back to her for more editing. She kept a low profile, and made few contacts professionally or socially.

Susan a neighbor had been a classmate in her elementary school. They were instant friends, and Susan worked in the Commissary near their home, and she would pick up things for Rose on occasion as things would be set aside to be thrown out and Rose being very cautious about her use of money from her account was grateful for Susan's thoughtfulness.

Jeff a man who worked in the Transport services for the neighborhood was the neighbor on the other side of her apartment. She did not engage him, but he told her one day he was taking a short trip in one of the vehicles he used, that he planned to travel the coast line up the edge of the ocean, and he was looking for company. "Would you like to go just for the day?" Jeff asked, and she said she would. Rose picked up some treats for the trip, and early one Sunday morning they left to travel up north.

As almost no one had personal transportation any more, the roads up the ocean highway were in terrible shape. Huge rocks inhabited the roads and care had to be exercised in passing parts of the highway. The ocean views were spectacular though, and in their conversations they found that their level of mistrust of the government and the Oligarch's who pulled the puppet strings, was about equal.

"Susan told me that we had a lot in common, she said you have very little trust for what the government puts out as information. I have never trusted those bastards, all they are interested in is their own funding and it does not matter how many asses they have to kiss to get what they want." Rose was in complete agreement with his sentiments, and over time they learned at least on these trips into the hinterlands that they could share their values and gripes about what was going on. They drove up the hills of the interior of the valleys and mountains to the east of the city, and enjoyed each other's company as frequently as they could.

Jeff was very bright, and read everything he could get his hands on from the library in the community. He had not studied hard in his preparation for college classes and had done his share of acting out as a teenaged boy, and failed to qualify for college. He had petitioned to attend a training school for Transportation services though when he exited high school, and was a talented mechanic, and he was on an upward path with in the Transport services. He had recently applied for a job as a midlevel manager taking on the task of scheduling for the various demands in Transport services. She knew he had what it took to accomplish the promotion and she even helped him study for the examination that he would have to do very well on to be considered for the promotion.

She too had felt the need to level with Jeff about her decision to not marry and remain independent in her life. "Jeff, I need to be honest with you about any future for our relationship, I like you and trust you but I will not ever marry anyone under these circumstances. I will not give up my independence as my Mother did to have a marriage and a family with my Dad, it made her an isolate, and he was over worked all the time trying to provide for us, and she ate her heart out that she had no way to help."

He seemed to understand perfectly, and he began to relate his own history. "I was raised by my Aunt, my Mom's sister. When I was two years old my father was killed in a mining accident, and the company offered an office job to my mother as a part of the agreement they reached over culpability in the accident. She called her sister who was living in another place to come and care for me to enable her to work and have some income. Jane came, and I grew to love and respect both of those women." When he had troubles with school it was his aunt who helped him work out issues, and resolve problems, and his mother would work double shifts when they were available in order to provide for the three of them.

Jeff understood that as Aunt Jane had relinquished her own life in a way for him and his mother worked at every opportunity for them; and what Rose had said made a kind of perfect sense to him, "Martyrdom, is highly overrated in my book, they are now both old and in a retirement placement, and they worry about turning on the heat in the winter for what it will cost, I just think there ought to be a better way to live." Jeff said.

"Hell I have asked that a part of my pay be transferred to them, so they can at least be warm in the winter". Rose saw in this young man a person who was loyal, and loving in his own way. "I am going to see them when I have a week's time of Vacation; I have never been down to see them". "Where do they live now?" Rose asked, and he replied," somewhere near a city called Denver," I think when we were in school it was Colorado was the state name back then." Rose stopped and closed her eyes and pictured the huge map of the United States of America her Grammy had taped to the wall in the reading room of her house. It was brown by the time she saw it but it was still colorful, and had the geographic data represented for the whole country with a little box in the ocean for Hawaii, and another for Alaska. It was a topographic picture of the whole country before the Oligarchs had decided to reallocate the geographic and governmental bodies of the states from 50 to 12.

"Why did they do that do you remember?" "I remember in school they said it was faster for 12 Senators and 12 Representatives to decide on things than it was for 509 Representatives and 100 Senators to meet and decide on what they wanted to decide on." "But as I look at it now Jeff, I think it was about not wanting to pay 609 people to make decisions that 24 could make perfectly well, and so they shrunk it down for a more selfish reason." Rose added.

She had clearly a much exercised cynicism about the governmental processes, and she was even more cynical about the oligarchs'.

The next day as she entered the large room with the desks all up against the wall with windows where she worked, she found a note on her desk to report to her supervisor's office before she attended the Lunch break. She found the note a distraction, had she done something that was out of bounds, she thought not, and she had been very careful to keep her opinions of a political nature to herself since College.

She attended to the two writing assignments she had in her work folder, and when she looked up to the clock on the wall she was surprised that the whole morning had passed, so she jumped up from her desk and walked to the single door that exited the large room, and walked to the supervisors office. She looked in and the woman waved her in and asked her to be seated. She had to wait for the woman to finish a task, and as she sat there she became more and more nervous about the wait.

Finally the woman looked up and said, "Rose you have a very enviable record here in this company, and I have a special assignment to give to you, as I know you will do it accurately and efficiently." The woman handed her an envelope, a large manila envelope, and she said, "This is a rewrite for the Governmental Complex, they sent it over and asked for our best worker to polish it and I immediately thought of you. This will be included in our annual evaluation of you and I looked at your two past evaluations and found them to be without any errors. The job is yours, and if you do well you will be rewarded with a pay grade raise and a week of vacation in addition to your regular week off. Are you willing to do the work, it may mean you might have to work through the night, but I think the reward well compensates a night in the office producing your high quality work." She agreed to the assignment.

She returned to her desk, opened the folder and found a bunch of notes, really scribbles and an outline of a program which she could see related to the notes. Then she had a rough draft of the material, and so she read through the material to understand how this should be titled.

Economy Standards for the Governmental Complex:

She passed on lunch thinking she could eat the dinner that they were sending in and she would prefer making headway on the task at hand. Her workmates passed out the door, to eat their normal lunch of a sandwich, a piece of fruit, and tea.

The room was empty for the 40 minutes of lunch break, and so she quickly wrote out an outline containing all the elements of the scribbles and the outline, she then revised the order of the elements of the outline which seemed to be more logical, and then she reviewed the rough draft which would accompany the outline of issues and edited the rough draft so that it contained no misspellings, and errors in syntax or logic.

The room had once again filled up and people were at their work stations attending to their tasks and she began to write the finished product on her computer. This would not cost her a night's sleep she thought, and when the day was officially finished she stayed to complete the work for the day thinking the task she had been given was essentially complete. At six in the evening a guard entered with a tray of food was sent in for her dinner and coffee to assist her staying awake should it take all night to finish. He placed the tray on her desk, and she quickly moved the tray away to a small table at the end of the room, sat down to eat, and take a break. "Miss, you are to give me the assignment, I will place it in the vault for the night when you are finished." "Where will I find you?" "I am on the chair just outside the room. As the building is tight, secured and locked I mean, I will need to let you out when you are ready to go."

She thanked him, and sat to take a break with a rather delicious meal of pasta, red sauce, and a salad. There was even a slice of good sour dough bread with garlic butter melting into the bread. She ate every bite and then returned the tray to the guard who looked at the clean plate with surprise, she was sure he thought he would get the leftovers. He muttered something about such a little woman, and carried the empty tray away. She took a little walk down the hall and back and had reentered the work room when he returned. She reviewed the two work products for the day, and they were both fine and she then turned her attention to the special assignment. She carefully evaluated the language usage, and then the tense, and the sequence in the outline to make sure it was all a logical flow. She discovered one error, in spelling and that was quickly corrected, she printed out the final copy and as was company policy when she was finished she erased all her work product. She put the printed copy into the envelop and returned all the background work to the envelop sealed it with a tamperproof fastener, picked up her purse, and with the sealed envelope ready to hand to the guard she exited the building in his company and discovered she had finished before eight in the evening. She remembered that as she had begun the day It had been Saturday, and so she had a day off to look forward to and perhaps a time to read, alone in her bed as she had become wont to do these days that Jeff was working all the over time he could to save up for his vacation trip to see his family in Colorado.

She knew he was working hard to be able to share with them lots of goodies he knew they loved from the commissary and could no longer afford. Living on the balance she knew was hard, she even was moved to call her parents to see how they were doing in their retirement place down south in what used to be Central Arizona. Her Mother picked up her call and was so happy to hear from her. They spoke of Rose's work, and of her two neighbors who were close friends and good supports for her, and her father joined in on the conversation, and heard about the vacation week award, and the little increase in salary. "Every little bit helps", he said and Rose asked them then point blank how their balance in the account was holding up. "Dad, I can send you a little each two weeks if it would help, I do not want you and Mom doing without things that would give you pleasure or peace at this time in your lives," And her father replied "I watch the balance and it is okay for now, maybe in the future but not now". "What are you two doing for fun; do you have an electronic Library available"? "You need to come down and spend a week with us, and see what is here. There are swimming pools and spas and all kinds of electronic games to play, your mother is quite a Chess player these days, but you know she has always been smarter than me", her Dad remarked. Her mother's voice came through and told her there was a book club she had joined and she liked meeting with the women, they would all read one book per week and on Wednesday afternoons they would meet in the common room at the activity center and give an analysis of the book they had just completed. "We should have done this kind of thing when we were still in the old neighborhood, it would have been great fun and I would have loved doing it but everyone was so uptight about the balance in the accounts we all would have had problems with the refreshments and the like". Her father pushed about when she could take vacation and come down, and Rose claimed not to be sure. "I will get back to you on that, Yes I will come down, as soon as I can, I know it has been almost three years and I need to come and see you both." She heard her mother say, "We miss you terribly", and then the call was terminated.

Rose was well aware she could have given a time to her folks, but it felt uncomfortable just to give in and provide a date certain, that was a way to set up a win for her father and a loss for her. They both sounded healthy, and her mother had made some friends and was trying new things, and her dad was just grateful not to have to go to work every day as he had for years. She hoped they both spent time in the pool and had company in for dinner once in a while. As a child she thought she loved the one child policy, but as an adult it carried with it too much responsibility, she had remarked to Jeff about it and they agreed sometimes it just turned into a mountain of guilt.

She began to feel very guilty about not going immediately to find her vacation schedule and electronically file for a time to go down to see her parents, it was cool this time of year down in the dessert and she felt that she should go this season. She could tell them that she had responsibilities to meet at this moment but she could come when Jeff had made arrangements for a week in Colorado, and then she would be home in time to meet him at the train and walk back with him into their neighborhood. She called the schedule board in her office and asked she be given the week after next to take one of her vacation weeks away. She got an instant message back that her request had been logged, and would be responded to the next working day of the week. She felt she needed to go if only for three days. And she electronically communicated she was asking only for three days week after next, and could they let her know electronically if that had been approved. She got out her smaller of the two traveling bags, packed it with casual clothes, running shoes, and a swim suit. She had a big beach towel she had planned to use on the beach some day when they drove up north, and had a picnic on the beach, it would be okay to take it down with a book or two to read by the pool and pick up a little color on her skin. She packed one business suit in case they would have friends over for a social time during her visit, and she got back on the phone to let them know she had found three days in two weeks would that be okay for now? She let it ring, and then left a message, what she had determined and asked them for a couple of days to confirm the times and the number of her high speed train on which she would arrive.

She went out on a walk as the afternoon was coming to a close, and as she re-entered her apartment there was a voice message for her and it was her Mother saying they were both so happy she would be coming. Okay she thought it is a done deal.

The week slipped by with not a hitch and she received on Tuesday her confirmation for three days off the next week and the notification that if she did not use her vacation days from her first year of employment they would lose half their value in two months, She notified her supervisor she would like to take three days from two years ago, and they complied with her request. As she arrived home she pulled up her pay window on the computer, and determined that her balance was much larger than she had remembered it would be, and so she electronically transferred 10 thousand dollars into her parents account now and make sure that they had enough for their daily living needs when she got there.

She responded by email to her parents that she would be there on Monday mid-day, and would leave on Wednesday evening to return to work on Thursday morning. Her father was delighted that she had finally made arrangements to come down, and she was curious about his reaction to the transfer of the ten thousand dollars to his account, and yet he did not mention it. "Oh well maybe he was in a situation where he was not free to discuss it."

She blew it off. She met with Jeff to help him pack for the trip and he left on Sunday night to go east through the night and be there to greet his aunt and mom early Monday morning. He had a bag full of treats for them, and had spent quite a lot over the last several days in the commissary so they would both have a really nice present. Jeff had purchased bath robes for both of them, and a warm sweater for his Aunt and a warm jacket for his mother. He got onto the train, with Rose waving him off from the station door.

She walked back to the apartment and pulled out her already packed bag, ran to the commissary to pick up some gifts for her Mom and Dad, and then returned to sleep until she walked back to the train station in the morning. She mounted the high speed train to Arizona. The speakers overhead announced that they would arrive in Phoenix by 10 a.m. and Happy Valley at 10:15. She sat down in the car which allowed her to look out at the scenery as it at first slowly passed. But more quickly she noticed that it was impossible to see any detail in things within a half a mile of the track. She watched the mountains fade away into the distance, the distant forests give way to broad deserts, and high plateaus in the distance, and she got up to purchase a cup of coffee. And by the time she reached her seat again, she heard an announcement on the overhead that Phoenix was ten minutes, and all passengers to Phoenix should walk toward their exits. Rose sat once more sipped her coffee, and watched Phoenix pass by and slow almost to a fast walk. She looked out at the desert city, and it was full of high buildings and lots of activity. They passed by the sport's arena which was a large mushroom shaped dome, and then into the downtown proper with sky scrapper's and busy streets with people movers, small busses moving people everywhere through the city. They were no longer stopped to allow for passenger's to disembark and the bells rang once again letting everyone know to be seated for the trip to the next stop. She noted that she felt a kind of anxiety building and she wondered why she was becoming anxious, she had done nothing to be worried about, and then it dawned on her awareness that her transfer of money before she agreed to the visit might have been misunderstood by her father. The train sped forward now and she felt the brake being applied and they rolled into a dusty little town with trees recently planted everywhere the eye could see. The announcer spoke on the overhead speaker, "Happy Valley Retirement Community". "We will be in the station for one half hour". She was amazed at the numbers of persons who were disembarking the train, and she stood on the inside of the train for a few moments until the crowd had dispersed. She stepped out onto the train platform and was struck by a blast of heat in the form of a light wind, and she thought to herself, *I guess this is what it is about, a desert breeze,* and with that she walked to the place where the luggage sign was lite and bags were being taken out of the baggage car. She spotted her bag, walked to pick it up and rolled it toward the Lobby of the Train Station. At the end of the train there were two big cars filled with provisions for the community, and she watched as they unloaded crates and boxes of food and wine, and beer to be sold in the commissary. Her father was just inside the station and was waving at her and she entered the door and he embraced her warmly and took her suitcase and they walked to an area where he had parked a little golf cart to transport them home. Her mother was waiting at home with lunch all prepared and so they proceeded to drive into the main entrance of the community with all the newly planted little trees down a kind of main street and around a corner to their apartment. Dad carrying her bag, she stepped into the door, to find her mother with arms outstretched and a smile on her face which she had not seen in years. "Oh Rose, my little Rose bud, I have missed you for so many years, you look tired, are you eating well you don't look like it, are you okay" "Mom", Rose said "slow down, I am fine, and you need not worry about my diet." "I am fine and I have never felt better, I am hungry and I knew you would have Lunch prepared, so let's sit and eat if that is okay?"

"Sun tea, It is all the rage down here". Her father passed her a glass of iced Tea. "You put a big jar out-side of your kitchen make sure it is in the full sun, with tea bags and water, and just let it rest in the sun, it brews all by its self and is always ready for lunch" She put a little sugar in hers and drank it down. "It is smooth that is for sure". "That is something that the Mexican women have done for a long, long time here in the desert and many of us here in the community have begun doing it too. Dad loves it and sometimes I see a second jar working in the sun after lunch". "Your mother is going to try out her Mexican cooking skills with lunch, we have Mexican style tea, and tacos and beans all mushed up into a kind of paste that you use a tortilla to pick up off the plate and eat. No silver for this meal, right honey" her father said. "That is correct" Mom said from the kitchen. "We will teach you honey, it is easy and very tasty too."

They consumed a very hearty meal together, and Rose had to admit her mother had in fact prepared a very tasty meal, and Rose was quite impressed with the how her mood and affect had shifted since she had last spent any amount of time with her parents. Her Mother's low mood had been hard to tolerate, but the shift into a kind of buoyant emptiness was difficult in a different way, Rose felt a kind of irritation as she spent the afternoon with her mother, walking to the community room to see the activities schedule, and walks with her Dad, to see the Golf Links, and the pools and the other facilities which they had access. Walking home from the Golf Links, her father explained that her mother had experienced a deeply low mood for the first year of their living in this environment. She finally agreed to enter therapy, she had joined a Group mainly women who were judged to have a significant depressed mood, and over the year of her inclusion in the Group had experienced a lifting of her perspective, and the limited degree of social activities had improved to the extent that she needed little coaching to attend activities and join with others to participate in little trips and hikes, and other activities which were designed by the program staff. She had recovered her energy, her mood was, as Rose had seen, high and much more stable, and she had recently recovered her natural curiosity, which had been a hallmark of her mother's personality in her youth. "Is she taking a medication to produce these changes?" she asked her father as they walked home. "Yes" he replied to Rose," but it is now only half of what she had taken initially."

They spent the evening watching a movie on their receiver in their home, and Rose said she was quite tired from the day's activities, and she went to bed after the movie was finished. As she prepared herself for sleep she thought about how her parents were working so hard to make this shift into a new life, and how proud she felt of the energy her mother had put into being a more positive person in the face of so many losses she had experienced through her life. She had in this day's activities, seen another element in her parents who she had over time really lost touch with and that aspect of their relationship was the degree of interdependence they shared. Over the many years of their marriage they seemed never to have lost that sense of caring and appreciation of each other.

Time passed rather quickly and Rose had become quite satisfied that her parents were quite as she had hoped, a happy and interdependent couple who were adapting to their circumstances well and seemed as they always had to love each other as their primary commitment.

Wednesday her mother carried her back in the little cart to the train station and as they waited for the train to arrive her mother assured her that economically, they were holding their own. "Mom, I live very frugally and I make a much better salary than Dad ever was able to produce, and it is important to me that you two have enough to get along without the worry of what watching the balance go down. I will be sending you money, intermittently, and I need you to be open with me about your needs as we move ahead, and I will keep you comfortable." "Rose you need not to worry" "after all we have each other and that was what we decided we wanted years and years ago".

She boarded the train, the sun was setting, and as the train pulled forward she prepared to move back into her own life and experience, and she was glad she had come down to pay a visit and see the shift and change she observed in her mother.

The economic assistance was how she would continue to be a part of this relationship, they had supported her growth, and she by contributing to ease their concerns she would make hers.

CHAPTER THREE

GAINS AND LOSSES

Rose dismounted the train as it pulled into the depot, nearest her home, and she picked up her bag, and began her walk of about a mile to her apartment. She looked at her watch and determined she would shower and eat a little snack and then go to bed and be ready for work in the morning. As she walked through the neighborhood of her home and noticed the trash collection must be running behind, as the barrels were overflowing and a lot of the contents had fallen to the ground. Everyone was charged from their earnings balance a small charge for public clean up and the company which maintained the neatness of the community was well known to have a lot of pride in the cleanliness of the public environment. And as she walked into the interior of her own neighborhood she noticed that many of her neighbors had picked up the over flow and placed full plastic garbage bags next to the trash receptacles. No one resisted the community trash charges, and had always taken the service for granted, and in its absence she could imagine that people were going to be upset if it was not resumed with some regularity.

She walked into her apartment checked the time and saw that she had lots of time to make herself a snack and take a shower, and read a little before sleep. Morning came with its enduring regularity, and she dressed, ate a piece of bread with a protein spread, drank a cup of coffee and left for work. Walking toward her employers building and she felt a shift in her energy level, and acknowledged that the three day break had been beneficial for her level of both energy and probably as well the focus she could apply to her work.

The week passed well; she had a note from her supervisor complementing her on the extra assignment she had taken on two weeks prior, and things were looking generally good. She also was well aware of the possibility of losing some of the earned vacation time if she did not take it so she determined she would schedule herself for vacation time within the time limits required and she put in the requests. She worked through the week and when Sunday came she was ready to go to the Train to meet Jeff, and listen to his story about his visit. She had planned to prepare a dinner for them, and so she spent the day reading and taking a short walk, and prepared their meal, and then when she thought she would just about be able to be in the station building to meet the train, she left her apartment, and began her walk to the Station.

Upon arriving she checked the arrival time for the train which was exactly on time, and she moved to get a coffee, and sit to wait for his arrival. She picked up a local magazine, and read some of the commentary about local issues. Rose had absolutely no interest in political concerns but she found the elements of the arguments to be interesting. She though knew the approach to resolution would be unsuccessful as they all assumed that Government had more muscle than she had observed was fact.

The announcement was broadcast in the station that the train was arriving and she stepped out onto the platform. Jeff was first at the door of his car and he exited and hugged Rose and they went to get the bags from the Baggage Rack, and walk back to their neighborhood. They shared their trips, she said she had made a new commitment to her needs to take vacation when it was available, that she had experienced a little shift in her energy level from her three days off, and she as well shared that her Mother had much improved, had been in a therapy group, and it had been a good thing to see how their lives had changed with her father's retirement. Jeff shared with Rose that his trip had been wonderful, that his mother and aunt had enjoyed spending time with him, they talked about how things really were, and that they had requested a transfer to a location which was not so cold and the people there were seemingly really working on a transfer back toward a place which was generally warmer, that it might cost a bit less, if they were able to move, and that cost reduction might just be able to get along with less stress. "My mother's health is much improved, and my aunt said that they go together for long walks when the weather is warm, and it seems to be helping her feel more energy." "How did they like the presents you took?" Rose asked. "Oh My, all the goodies were a great hit and they loved the clothes I got for them as well. I have to tell you Rose the environment in that area is beautiful, high Snow topped mountains and a big city with good public transportation, and entertainment, and culture. It is a good place for people to be, and if I am able to send them a little money each month, I think they will be able to do well even if they cannot move to a warmer climate, I told them to turn on the heat, for God's sake, and you both need to be comfortable."

As they walked the neighborhood, Rose noticed that the trash that had been strewn around on the barrels when she had returned, and as they traversed the neighborhood she noticed that the trash men had done their job in the three days since her return and the walkways were clear and the trash was not falling out of the receptacles as it had been upon her return. It had been for her though an omen of things to come, and she was still restless in the wake of her experience. Though it had been ugly and now it had been rectified, she was still aware she saw it as an omen and simply could not shake that awareness. And she could recall the stench of the smell, and it was troubling to her.

They had walked into their neighbor and Jeff went home to unpack and then he would return for dinner to Rose's apartment. She felt good that Jeff was home, and they planned a trip for the weekend after next, and thought they would like to drive out of town to the old Oregon border into the forests up north, and then come home down the oceans coast. They both looked forward to these trips out away from the valley. And the planning for Rose was just as exciting she thought as the trip itself. Jeff had the maps which were available showing passable routes, and he had them to leave with Rose who had become a navigator for their ventures. She asked him about food stuffs he would like and they agreed on foods juices and snacks, and so they were clear on what she would be doing, and he would take care of obtaining a vehicle. The evening was late and so they said their good night and Jeff went home to begin to get ready for work in the afternoon in the day which was to come.

The week proceeded as was typical she went to work and found her work to flow in a predictable and typical fashion, she had scheduled her upcoming vacation time for several weeks hence, and was happy that her lack of attention to her own needs would have resulted in losing benefits for which she had worked. She was given one more special assignment and received a note of appreciation which would become a part of her employment file, a set of documents which would follow her throughout her career.

On Wednesday evening, when she arrived home, she had a communication from her father on her device. "Rose, don't add money to our account without discussing it with me in the future. I appreciate the thought but I find it unnecessary, and I will not be dependent upon your generosity for my wellbeing." She thought about calling him and telling him he was foolish, that she would use her resources however the hell she chose and it was for mother not him, but she thought better of that approach. She sent him an e-mail message that she meant no criticism, and thought she could help, sorry for any offense. He replied that her presence was more necessary than any money would ever be, and if she could plan to come more often, it would be much appreciated". And there it was, she had long ago lost those feelings of attachment to her parents. The thought of dragging herself, down to Happy Valley on a routine basis was enough to produce a kind of dread. She felt trapped by a strong desire to do what she felt comfortable doing to assist them, and not being pulled into a trap from which there was no escape.

She tried to let it sit and not responding to her father, she even thought, perhaps if she did not respond He would let it go, but she really knew better he would wait a while and then ask her for a date certain for her next trip. Their relationship or lack thereof had become like a wad of shit that they could toss at each other hoping the other would get dirtier in the process. She had no way at this moment not to toss it back, and so on Thursday evening she responded to her father that life was kind of hectic at work at the moment and she was not in a place where she could do any planning for vacations and the like, but she would keep them posted.

She worked through the time before she and Jeff had their planned trip, and on Friday before the planned Sunday travel up north she walked through the commissary to pick up several items for snacks on the road. Rose was not the most social creature, and at first she did not pay much attention to the other shoppers, and yet she did sense a subtle difference in the environment. Finding what she had come for she walked to the exit, paying her bill with her debit card, and then walking on to her apartment. Rose reached her apartment and went in to organize her foods for the week end travels, and she heard the noise of something happening somewhere very near her location and so she went to her door, and looked out to see a couple of men from the housing authority loading furniture from Jeff's apartment onto a truck to be removed and refurbished so it would be available for someone else's use. She stepped outside to inquire. "Why are you removing the furnishings from Jeff's home?" They responded that they had been given a work order to do it, and had no more information. She re-entered her own apartment, and was aware of a kind of anxiety about what was going on, and she grabbed her hand held communication device and called the warehouse where Jeff worked now and discovered "due to our emergency condition we are not available to respond to your need. Please call us in 24 hours to allow for the handling of this situation." She called Susan and within no more than two seconds, Susan was at her door. She opened the door, and Susan grabbed her and held her in an embrace which seemed to be all enveloping. "There was an accident at the building where Jeff was working today, and all I know is that he was badly burned and died on the way to the Hospital. Someone said a battery exploded but I have no other information. I have made some calls and three others were injured, and one they do not expect to live. It is just awful Rose, I knew you needed to be told, I know you and Jeff were so close, He really did love you." Rose heard the words coming out of Susan, and she simply fell down on to the couch, in disbelief. She simply could not get her mind around such an event; it had to be a bad joke. She looked at Susan who by this time was sitting next to her on her couch, and said in response to what Susan had shared, "no it is not possible, there must be a mistake, it was someone else who got hurt," not Jeff, "how can a battery explode, they don't explode, how did it explode?" "I do not know how a battery explodes, Rose, I really did not realize that they can be dangerous like that. I just know that there will be a memorial service for him, in the morning, I will go with you if you want to attend, and you should not go alone." Rose called her office to let them know she was ill, and would not be in for work in the morning. Susan sat with her for a while and then insisted that she come to her apartment to sleep, but Rose said she would be okay alone, and if she needed anything she would call. Susan left Roses apartment at near 9 p.m. and said she would come for Rose in the morning to walk down to where the memorial was to be held.

Rose tried to sleep, but was unable. She kept thinking this must be a terrible mistake and she even got up at about midnight as that was the typical time Jeff would be getting home from work on his new schedule, but of course no Jeff. She finally achieved sleep by about 2 a.m. and was awaken by a knock on her door, Susan checking on her at 7 a.m. "The service is at 10 this morning so we will need to leave here at about 9 to get there on time" Susan said. She had some coffee, and got dressed, and walked next door to meet Susan and they walked through the familiar walking areas to get to the business district by 10 a.m. sharp. Lots of the people Jeff had worked with were there, and she looked for the Mother and the Aunt, but no one could identify them, and so she was limited in determining who they might be. She wanted to tell them that Jeff so loved them both, and had appreciated their patience and tolerance when he was having difficult times in school. They had shared so much over the two years of friendship, and she had listened to Jeff talk about each of them and how he knew he had hurt them over his growing up time. She had so much to say to these women about this young man who had so recently seen them, and now was gone. "Never to return" redundantly coursed through her mind, as she listened to people who had worked with him tell stories, funny and poignant about their time with Jeff, and what a principled guy he really was. And then it came out that Jeff would not have died if he had not gotten between the explosion and a guy who was one of the mechanics, and it was clear Jeff was dead because he wanted to save another person from harm. When this story was told, at the end of the service she felt as though she might explode, and she told Susan she needed to go home, and she walked out of the service, and began a walk that would take her to the edge of the city into an area everyone knew to be occupied by the gangs of the unemployed and hopeless of this failing society.

Rose, like most of the citizens in this city knew that there were those who were abandoned by society, that they occupied most of the old central city, which was more and more devastated by successive quakes along the fault lines in the earth. It was thought that many of them died as victims of the earth's attempts to reduce the pressure along the fault which ran right through the center of the old city, but many had escaped the terrible upheaval of the quakes, and learned to adapt to their circumstances. She had read papers in her work which purported to be evidentiary in the case of substantiating that these abandoned persons were never going to be useful in society, and they should be left without supports and they would die off over time. The evidence said otherwise though and their numbers had grown. The government kept a tight lid on those studies of the abandoned, she supposed that if they did not publicize the facts that the abandoned of society were in fact thriving then it could be argued that they had not thrived. She walked and walked. She passed up one street and down another and she arrived at the iron gates which marked the end of pedestrian traffic in the north of the reestablished community.

She walked the perimeter of the iron fencing and she arrived at a concrete embankment, which it's self-prevented her from doing anything else and so she turned to retrace her steps. She looked at her watch and she discovered it to be three in the afternoon. There was a bench up ahead and she walked toward it to sit, and evaluate her situation. She had lost her best friend, and in this moment of introspection she knew that she had loved him and had never acknowledged it to him or for that matter to herself! What would she have done at that moment, the Government was clear, one family one worker, no exceptions!

Tears streamed down her cheeks, she attempted to understand her reactions, but it was a loss, and she simply wept, and walked back into her familiar surroundings, her neighborhood, her home. The light of day had turned to dusk, and it must have been past dinner, she had no need for food, in fact the thought of putting food into her mouth was revolting. She entered her home, and lay down on the couch, and within moments she was asleep.

CHAPTER FOUR

HEALING THE HOLE IN HER SOUL

She had absolutely no sense of herself. She returned to work on Monday, and when she walked into the building she was on automatic pilot. She went to her desk, and her supervisor had placed a note to see her at 10 a.m. She went to her work file and down loaded todays assignment and rather mechanically outlined the material, and looked up some data that had been referenced, but not included, and then composed the material, and turned it in and addressed her number two, declining to go to lunch. She was finished at about 3.p.m. She had not met with her supervisor, and so she got up from her desk, and walked to see if she could re-schedule her meeting. The supervisor was standing in her door way, and seeing Rose approach waved her in.

What is wrong Rose we missed your presence on Saturday and you look like you need to go home early today, are you ill? "I am not feeling very well" Rose replied and her supervisor handed her a piece of paper and as she read it she saw that it was an announcement of a job opening for the Governmental Complex. "This is your new job she said, it fits your talents and it came to me to approve and recommend an individual if I knew one, and I do, it is you." Rose sat down and re-read the announcement and she looked up at the woman, and said, do you think I am ready? "Rose you are not well today I want you to go ahead home and take Tuesday and Wednesday off, to feel more yourself, and Thursday, when you come back in and we will decide whether or not this is your new job. I will tell you that we are in the process of losing a lot of our contract work, to the Governmental Documents office, and I think although I have not been told affirmatively that the company is near a time when we will have to lay off workers, I surely would not like to do that with you, you preform so well and I want you to feel secure in your future."

Rose had worked for this woman for two and a half years and she had never exchanged more than seven words at a time with her in that time. Now they are talking as if there was a deep relationship. Rose wondered if she should level with the woman about Jeff. She decided no, and she left to take two days to grieve, and ponder her own future as well. As she walked out of the office building she wondered if she was ready to move up or for that matter was not about to crumble into a pile of crumbs right here on the side walk. It was well known that the Government was unpredictable, but most times they took forever and a day to make up their minds about anything. She walked and read but could not retain what she had read in these days of emptiness. She returned to work on Thursday, and there was a note on her desk for her to report at 10 a.m. to the Supervisors office. She had two hours until that meeting and so she pulled up her daily work assignment. She was surprised that it was only one assignment. She read it through, and discovered it to be rather detailed and long. It was a governmental complex assignment about changes in the allocation of work outside of the governmental work staff, and it was exactly what the supervisor had implied would be happening, and in a way was a precursor of why she need to apply to the government for the editors position she had been shown. She looked up at the clock on the wall over the exit, and saw it was soon to be 10 a.m. so she closed the program she had been reading, and got some water, and went to the supervisor's office. She sat on the chair on the outside of her door as the door was shut and she could hear the woman's voice, as she waited. Promptly at Ten O'clock the office door opened and she was asked to come in and be seated. There sat one of the interviewers for the Government. He went through some questions and was writing down everything she said. She was asked if she had any questions and she asked only one, when did the position open and when it was to be filled. He responded that it opened today and it would be filled by next weekend. He folded his notes into a brief case and excused himself.

Rose was invited by the supervisor to sit and talk with her for a few moments, "are you feeling better Rose," she asked. "Some yes, I am sleeping a lot, and feel I need to for now", Rose responded. "Yes I agree if you can sleep you should to get past these health problems, I believe that sleep can help heal us and it is a blessing if we can just sleep our way through some of these illnesses". Rose just nodded in the affirmative in response. "Your interview went well I believe, and they will be back with me and I should know by Monday. Rose shut down your computer you still look like you feel poorly and you have never used your sick leave, go home and sleep. I will see you on Monday next, and I will keep you informed about the situation. Be sure you drink a lot of water that will help too. Sleep and Water"

Rose returned to turn off her computer, and pick up her purse, and left the building. She returned to her apartment and went to sleep as she was instructed to do. Rose knew she was going to have to put on a happy face before there would be one of genuine report, and so she knew she would have to address all the things she had discovered in his death, to Jeff, who at this moment, was actively living in her mind, if nowhere else on this earth.

She was a very articulate writer, and when she woke from her nap, she broke out her computer and began a letter to Jeff. She would begin by saying what she had not realized when he was alive, and as the words began to flow she wept as her fingers flew into the keys. She told him she would have had to leave him anyway had she understood how complex their relationship had become. She in capital letters announced to him what she felt, I FELL IN LOVE WITH YOU AND DID NOT KNOW IT! I SHOULD HAVE KNOWN IT, AND HAD I KNOWN IT WE WOULD

HAVE TO PART . . . I WOULD NEVER MARRY YOU, NO MATTER HOW I FELT AND THE ONLY SOLUTION TO MY DELIMNA WOULD HAVE BEEN TO MOVE SO THAT I WOULD NEVER SEE YOU AGAIN. AND IN THIS SOCIETY I WOULD HAVE NOT EVEN BEEN ABLE TO MOVE AND KEEP MY EMPLOYMENT, WHAT IN HELL WOULD I HAVE DONE. HAD WE MARRIED I WOULD HAVE TURNED INTO MY MOTHER AND I WOULD DO ANYTHING TO AVOID THAT KIND OF HURT AND FRUSTRATION. WHY DID YOU DIE, JEFF, BECAUSE YOU WERE A NICE GUY, ALWAYS TAKING CARE OF OTHERS, YOU SHOULD LEARN TO MIND YOUR OWN BUSINESS, YOU BASTARD, YOU NOW HAVE DEPRIVED YOUR MOTHER AND YOUR AUNT OF THE PEACE IN THEIR OLD AGE THAT YOU COULD HAVE PROVIDED, WHY DID YOU MAKE IT YOUR BUSINESS TO TRY TO PROTECT THAT STRANGER.

IT DID NOT WORK ANY WAY, HE STILL GOT HURT, AND YOU GOT KILLED, YOU IDIOT YOU KILLED YOUR SELF BECAUSE YOUR WERE TOO DAMNED KIND. I LOVE YOU, JEFF, BUT YOU WERE A DANGER TO ME, I WOULD HAVE TO GIVE UP MY INDEPENDENCE, OR LEAVE YOU, AND YOU LEFT ME . . . DAMN IT YOU LEFT ME—and she began to sob deep soulful sobs, and she knew she had tapped into the core of her own hurt. She kept the page, and did not know if she would return to write more, but for now she seemed to have tapped into what the core of her feelings were and she felt a little relief in the process.

Doubt that was close to what she felt and the doubt was about her. Could she know a man as a friend, and not fall in love with that person. She had some male friends in college, and had not grown to feel a romantic love for them. She would have to stay clear of men for friends. She got into the shower; she washed thoroughly and washed her hair as well, wrapped her hair in a towel, and put on pajamas for bed. She grabbed a book about history, and dove into it with all the energy she could muster. Rose went into the kitchen to get a little to eat, opened the refrigerator unit to see the snacks for the trip there and Rose gasped and once again was in tears, sweets and cheeses, she remembered purchasing them just before she returned home on the day he was killed. She had opened the door of the refrigerator and just not looked before. She went to her computer pulled up the page she had started, and now her words about she wanted to please him any way she could and she got it she had loved this man for a long, long time and failed to tell him what was going on for her in this relationship. Kindness would be her only expression of love, her independence was too important to her and by god she did not have to give up being kind and thoughtful.

What would she do with the cheese and jelly candy that Jeff had so loved as they drove out into the parts of their home where no one passed on these roads? What would she do without Jeff to share her deepest and blackest thoughts about their society which seemed to be the absolute victim of isolated wealth and ignorance? No one would understand her; no one would tolerate her wit about all this crap. What the hell would she do for the rest of her life? And the old solution was there in her mind's eye. Isolation and distance, which was how she handled her parents and that, would be her solution for herself. She knew in a part of her soul that was punishment, but it also would protect her from the pain she felt when she would be in one way or the other become aware of Jeff, now dead and gone.

In that moment it was like she shifted from a human to a computer, lots of skills and no feeling. She would not expose herself to this injury ever again, and that would just have to be that.

CHAPTER FIVE

THE DRIVE OUT OF DESPAIR

Rose wrote to her Parents: "Mom and Dad, I have been offered a new job working for the Government which looked to be not only more stable but perhaps more lucrative. Because of this transfer I might not have the vacation time I had logged with the first Company and I will have to focus quite closely on work for a time, so I will not be free to visit in the near future. I will keep you posted on how I am progressing, please know I am thinking of you both, and will be forwarding monies to your account as I am in a very good place with finances. Love, Rose." Letting her know that he had caught the shit ball, her father wrote back, "we realize that new employment is a step up the ladder of success and congratulate you, and understand you will need to focus your energy on your new situation. Please keep us informed of your situation we are very much looking forward to your return visit with us. Mom is doing well, and sends you her congratulations on your success. Thank you for the remittances, we will do something good with the monies you forward". Dad.

On Monday she reported for work, and had a note from her supervisor, to report to her office at 10 a.m. She opened her computer for today's assignment, and found a blank screen. She opened a program on her computer which kept track of her work load, to determine perhaps why there was no assignment. She saw the notation which revealed she was to report later for interviews with Governmental Employers at 11 a.m. on this date. The clock on the wall said 8:15, and so she went to obtain a cup of coffee, and returned to her desk and read on line the daily paper.

She knew she was early for the 11 a.m. appointment with her supervisor, but she went out in the hall and sat down next to the woman's door about 10 minutes early. Surprisingly the door opened, and the woman stuck her head out into the hall, and ushered her into the office closing the door behind. Rose sat down, and the woman said, well you look yourself again Rose, time away from work to sleep and drink a lot of water, must have done the trick. I am glad you are looking better. Rose thanked her for her interest and support in the possible new position. "Rose I have a vested interest in your moving into the Government, I am as well being hired away, and I want very much to take you with me. You are a diligent worker and I will continue to be your supervisor, so I need your skill and knowledge to make my life much easier as well. The days of this company are numbered; please do not say this outside of this office. I have watched you develop and you have the intelligence and good work ethic to move ahead in the Government, I want you to know that this interview really is a snap. It really is just a formality that they think they need to go through, I have talked to the man who will be my supervisor and he is very supportive to my bringing my best worker with me in the deal." They continued to chat, and Rose again thanked her for her support.

At Eleven o'clock sharp there was a knock on the door and Rose got up to let the woman in the hall come in and was seated. She introduced herself as the retiring head of communications department in the Government, Greeted Angela, the Supervisor, warmly, and then introduced herself to Rose. "I am here to see if my friend Angela who will be taking my position in the future, has made a good choice for our open position for writer in the department of Internal Communications. She began asking about her education and her work experience, and she was handed a personnel folder with Rose's name on the cover. Rose told her that she had graduated with honors from her university and had been here in this company working for now almost three years. "How many of your work products over the three years have been returned for further editing?" She asked. Angela broke in and said none. "Is that right? My, my, you are looking to make your job easier are you not? And Angela concurred. There were several more questions from the retiring Head of Governmental Communications, and the interview was completed.

You will be required to move, you know, we will open a governmental apartment for you and you will be expected to move on this Wednesday. Your salary will be determined by the personnel department but I can assure you it will be more than you make in this company and I can communicate to Angela what it will be this afternoon if you like. "Yes I would like to plan on what I can send to my parents who are in retirement at this time." "That is very thoughtful of you Rose; I will make sure Angela knows so you can make whatever arrangements you need to. We want you both on board by Monday coming if that will be okay with you both, I will consider this hire as a completed task" She rose from her seat, and was on her way back to the governmental complex to complete her days work. Angela smiled, and told Rose her work assignments were logged and marked completed and excellent. You will be expected to clean your apartment thoroughly and pack all your possessions in boxes that will be delivered to you this afternoon. I will communicate with you on your communicator, and I will see you at work at the Governmental complex on Monday at 8 a.m." Angela had a very satisfied smile on her face as the meeting ended. Rose walked to her desk, picked up her purse, and walked out of the company for the last time.

She entered her apartment, wrote a note of thanks to Angela on her instant communicator, and then went onto the computer to find any information which might be available to her on the role and function of Communications department in government. What she read was no different from what she had been doing for the past three years and she determined this was a kind of lateral transfer with a little increase in pay.

She began identifying all of her personal items. She put what was hers on the bed and within a few moments there was a knock on her door and she was asked how many boxes of what size she needed. She selected what she needed and she was given one box that was insulated to preserve perishable food to be packed on Wednesday before 9 a.m.

Each of the boxes contained a brown package of paper, for wrapping of breakable objects of which she had almost none. She loaded in only her work clothes and shoes in two of the boxes, she had some books from her mother's collection and she packed them next and placed them both on the couch next to the door. She packed her toiletries wrapping them carefully if breakable, and labeling the boxes with her name and citizen number for I.D. but not sealing them as yet, that would be her task on Wednesday when they were to pick her and all her possessions up, and place into the cold box whatever was in her refrigerator.

She thought she heard Susan come in from work, and she stopped what she had been doing and walked over to knock on Susan's door to invite her to walk into the city for dinner. They had never done such a thing in the past and Susan was curious about why? Rose announced she was leaving her current job and moving to a new job, she knew this was a kind of shock but she had known it might be coming up and she was notified today that she was accepted. The two women walked into town and found a nice eatery where they could be served outside at a table by the sidewalk, and relax with a good meal. They talked about the history of their relationship, in grammar school and here in this neighborhood. "Susan you have been such a good friend, I want to thank you for all the support you have been for me. You helped me so much when Jeff was killed, and so many other thoughtful ways, I will really miss you. I will let you know where they take me and what it is like and perhaps we can make times to get together if the opportunities present okay? Susan thought to herself out of sight out of mind, but she agreed they should try to maintain their friendship.

As they passed back in to the neighborhood, they laughed about having your whole life in five boxes, and Susan gave Rose a big hug and said let me know if you need help with anything, and they said good night. Rose felt in that moment a twinge of loss but she quickly shut down once again. That was that.

Tuesday for Rose was a sleep as late as you want day. She set no alarm, it had been packed earlier and she had no clear memory of which box it was in and relished the thought of no alarm to waken her any way.

She spent the day relaxing and reading, and in the late afternoon she began washing her appliances and bathroom down so that there would be no fees attached to this move beyond those that she would be paying for the move, itself.

Wednesday she was up early and packed her food from the refrigerator unit went to the commissary as soon as it opened at 7 a.m. to pick up a quick breakfast so eating for the day would essentially be taken care of and she decided to sit at an outdoor table, to enjoy the morning sun and relax before the pressure of the day began. She watched her former colleagues walking to work but as was typical for her no one engaged her and she did not attempt to communicate with any of them. At 8:30 she was back at her apartment to wait for the movers to arrive and change her life for this next phase of new experience in Government. An experience which would be a combination of challenge and intrigue that at this moment she could hardly have been able to conceive.

CHAPTER SIX

Nothing but sand

She found herself in a broad plain, and she had noticed that as she walked day after day the sun was both brighter and hotter, and she was aware that its position over her head over the time she had walked was now directly over her head at midday, and far more heat came down onto her shoulders now as the overcast of smog had diminished. She knew her lungs no longer ached at the end of the day and she as well could feel her general wellbeing had improved over the many months of her escape. She had learned the holes of a particular size, were the doors to rabbit dens and in the afternoons if she found a series of these holes, she would establish her home for a night and very quietly position herself to watch for one of the rabbits to attempt an exit. It was not the most efficient method, she would many times wait for a long time with no animal presenting for dinner, but over time she had snagged a number of rather big animals which she could grab and hold long enough to slit their throats, bleed them out and harvest the meat to dry or roast to consume over several days. She had as well found some abandoned former farms and had obtained some wire which was stiff enough to make a rack of wire which she could mount over her fire and dry the meat slowly to make her own rabbit jerky which was not as good as the jerky she had found in the cabin but clearly was preferred to the hunger she had struggled with at times. Several of the farms had fruit trees and her love of fresh fruit this time of year had been gratified. Her struggle for water had been more difficult of late; she found herself in low hills and little in the way of streams or small lakes which would satisfy her thirst. She had on this day only a small amount of water in one of her jars, and about half of the canteen. She parceled out the water carefully, and right now just wanted one of the rabbits to exit their hole, so that she might hurl herself at the target and trap and kill it so she would have some way to quell her hunger.

She placed herself in a place where her shadow would not be seen, and she waited. This night would be meatless, as she waited for a guest who failed to show. She had a meal of a hand full of rather dried peach, obtained at the last farm she had found. She had now no food and limited water, and ahead of her was a wide deep valley she hopped would yield something to sustain her physical needs.

Nights in this environment were cold and clear and she put on a jacket and rolled up in her insulated blanket to stay warm, and she fell asleep quickly and slept deeply. On nights which were begun on an empty stomach she would routinely waken early and this day was no exception. She folded the blanket and packed it away in her backpack, and going through her ruck sack she found a small apricot in the bottom of her rucksack and she quickly ate it and began her daily walk toward the valley ahead.

Soon the land actively headed onto a downward sloop, and as she walked she picked up her pace as her goal for this day was to try to get to the far side of the valley before her energy was sapped, and so she followed a natural path taking her walk into a slope where wild bushes were dense with a rocky path which split the bushes in a kind of natural way and as she found herself passing the bushes that they were heavy with small berries, and she kind of unconsciously put one in her mouth. Biting down on the small black fruit her mouth was filled with a taste she had not experienced in years. She flashed on her Granny's garden, and remembered the jam her Granny would make of the berries from the garden. Blueberries, she had not tasted them in years, and she was amazed and she stopped and began gathering these berries, eating handfuls at a time, and filling her back pack and pockets for her needs ahead. As far as the eye could see she saw these wild bushes and as she looked ahead she was aware of trees at the bottom of the valley and hoped these would be as fruit filled as these bushes had been. She walked slowly and ate as she passed more of the wild blue berries, and was aware that for the first time in some time she was actually feeling her level of hunger was satisfied.

She wound her way to the middle of the valley and the sun was now high in the sky. Her energy was equally high and at the base of the valley held what she had looked for miles and it was a small stream of clear and clean flowing water, and so she stooped to fill her jars and canteen to their tops. She found a pear tree but the fruit was not quite ripe, and so she walked on ahead to see if she could make it up out of the small canyon and up onto the other side. She felt a burst of energy as she proceeded up the hill. The water in the stream had been very cold and she wondered if it was snow melt from the hills to her left as she walked toward the east. The sun was at her back and drooping in the sky as she mounted the top of the valley and she looked ahead to determine how much land she could cross before her day would end. She thought to herself that each time in this walk she had been near the end of her life sustaining supplies, she had found some resource, and had only had two or three days of walks without any food or any water, and there was a sense almost on the level of her soul that she would be okay, it would be hard, but she could somehow trust this process of walking away from the filth and degrading social order she had left behind. She had no idea of where she would ultimately be but she knew it was preferable to what she had left.

She looked ahead and saw a small hill in the distance, and she thought although it looked a bit more than she might be able to reach before sundown she would push and not stop until her arrival at the knowll. She pushed herself ahead and as her energy began to wane she pushed even more toward her next goal.

Arriving at the edge of what she had presumed was a knoll she camped in the dark, falling into a sleep very easily. She woke in the middle of the night to the howls of coyote in the distance. She had walked at this time across almost a third of the continent, though she was not really aware that she had made it that far, and the wild animals which inhabited that space other than many rabbits who had sacrificed themselves for her trip and her needs had remained hidden. In a subtle way it felt comforting to her to know that others were surviving here with her, just to hear their presence in their kind of mournful howls was enough.

Coming awake to the howls of the wild dogs broke her sleep and she rose very early to again walk to her next place of rest. She walked the base of the knowll and as the sun rose she could see a wide expanse of flat terrain ahead of her. It had been her experience over her time that this meant a dearth of resources but recognizing she had enough water, and fruit to sustain her for several more days and longer if she was careful she pushed on and walked with a good even stride into her future.

CHAPTER SEVEN

GOVERNMENT ANOTHER WORD FOR INACTION

She stood in a group of Government workers at 8:00 a.m. at the Central Entryway to the main Office complex for the Governmental Activities Center. She was ready to go to work but there was some reason they were not opening the doors so that the employees could reach their work spaces and begin their work day. Her former supervisor was as well standing outside the main door and she walked over to ask if she had any idea what the problem was, and Angela reported she had no idea. Rose said she was excited about beginning again in a new setting, and Angela indicated that she had known for some time that the future of their former employer was limited and she said to Rose that at her age she was grateful for the change. "I stood to be on the market for some time at my age Rose, I would have had only a couple of weeks in my apartment if they had known I was looking, and I was quite worried until this opportunity came along. They say that they do not discriminate on age, but that is pure poppycock if you know what I mean, and I am so happy I could bring you over with me." Rose thanked her once again for her thoughtfulness, and asked if she had moved in the past week and did she like her living arrangement now and Angela indicated that her living arrangements were much improved and she had to move in only two days and it had been hectic at best. They continued to chat and the employees continued to stand in the sun which was now heating up and people were becoming faint, and overheated. The Security Guards brought out water to give to the crowd and finally after an hour and forty minutes wait, the doors were opened and people lined up to be escorted to their various areas of work. Rose lined up in the group under the sign which said Documents Composition and Angela walked independently toward her new office and a final briefing from the Supervisor who she would by the end of the day replace.

As Rose was assigned a work station in a room filled with about twenty five computer stations and was handed an outline of her work responsibilities, and the do's and don'ts's of her employment. The section which was to contain her salary agreements was left empty, and she was told that this would be settled by the end of the week and she could see the director of the department day after tomorrow for some decision. She frankly did not care much, but she had been given a figure and wondered if they intended to welsh on the deal that they had, she thought, agreed to when she accepted the job.

She reflected on the expectations she had and how several of the elements of the expectations had been denied. Her old apartment had been larger than the one she moved to, her walk to work was much farther than it had been in her other neighborhood, there were fewer conveniences available to her in her new apartment, a washing machine was available to her however the dry cleaning machine was not available, and the dryer was so small she had to take twice the time for a load of laundry than had been the case in her old setting. She missed her kitchen nook where she had spent hours not only eating but doing her correspondence and study as her computer had been set up in that setting most days. There were only small windows in this new setting and her light in her new apartment was very low requiring her to purchase lamps to read in the afternoon as she lost direct sun light coming into the environment. Her old place had been 1000 square feet and her new place as she measured was only 860. She was okay with it but she felt hemmed in and it felt kind of oppressive. And she well knew that she was where she would be and she needed to adjust.

She accessed her assignments for the day and began to address the work. It was routine work and there was no problem completing the material. At noon, they were all ushered to cafeteria where they could select a variety of sandwiches, a soup of the day for those who preferred a hot meal, and fruit and a beverage. Everyone from her unit was expected to eat and clear their space and line up in twenty minutes. There was an allotted time about five minutes, to take a bathroom break and then line up to be escorted back to their work stations.

The afternoon was predictable; everyone seemed to be working and focused on that work with almost no conversation taking place. She exchanged hellos with a few people during the lunch break but beyond that she talked with no one. At 5 p.m. they all shut down their work stations, and lined up to be escorted to the exits allowing for the end of the work day. She lined up with the others, and in a line they all walked to the exit area, and it reminded her of elementary school with all the kids in neat and quiet lines to pass the other rooms in the school being thoughtful of the needs of others for order and discipline in the school which needed order and quiet in order to function. She pondered the need for such an arrangement in a Governmental complex, and finally landed on the notion that the government would do it for the sake of compliance and probably no other reason. *The more compliance they can get the better they on top would feel,* she finally thought to herself.

After a week on her new job she spent Sunday preparing to return, laundry and shopping at the new Commissary which seemed to be more broadly stocked with many new items she had never before seen in other settings, and she bought some new and interesting things to eat and enjoy. She walking home from the commissary she thought of Jeff, he had been her reason in her old life to browse the shelves in the commissary and she felt a deep emptiness, and thought to write in her journal about those feelings as a way to move ahead and finish all of her old business.

Her first week melted into her first month and her father had written to find out how her new work setting was and she thought to engage her in planning for a next visit. She wrote back to them to let them know her new physical address, and her initial impressions of the new work site. She tried to sound as though she had more responsibilities in this new job but as well needed to spend more time in preparation on her own for security on the job. She knew she was building a wall between she and her parents, and it was intentional. She in a way wished that she missed them. She knew that Jeff had really missed his family, she could see it in his face, and he would report feelings of longing to see them again. She had no idea why she had been deprived of such feelings and really it seemed too much to ponder at times. It was a fact that she felt almost nothing for her parents, they had always had each other and their emotional attachment was obvious, she loved her mother as a child and exaggerated the role and function of her father in her early years, and over the years they had demanded that she squelch her independence. And she if she explored it she would have come face to face with the seat of her rage. And as a palliative she chose never to go there.

It would have been a lot cleaner if she could just level with them but she knew that would never be an option and so she chose to send money to their account, which in reality cost her, to her thinking nothing because, she transferred the amount of her raise into their account on a monthly basis.

As she had experienced in her old position she was called on by Angela to handle difficult production pieces and gained several letters of complement in her employment file, and had as well garnered a pay raise and was doing well in her career. She noticed as time passed that she was up to her old habits of being too focused on work at the exclusion of time off and she had no idea of anything she could do which would provide for a break in her work and please her in the way vacations seemed to do for others.

She was about to reach the end of her first year of Government employment and she had earned additional time off and she needed to use it, and she would have to find a way to do that in her style if it was to be of value to her. There was a posting on the bulletin board of a English composition workshop for persons working in Government who wished to add to their skills, and she thought about that but thought it was too elementary for where her skills were. But it planted a seed of sorts and the seed over a few weeks seemed to grow quietly into the thought that she might seek advanced studies in her old University. She really had found that her reading had been lately most focused on history and she wondered if she would be able to attend classes or do guided work independently and earn an advanced degree. Her time in the University had been her happiest and in her judgment her most productive. She knew her intellectual gifts were not being exercised by the work she found she was involved in and she needed a challenge.

She had been able to earn vacation in the amount of 6 days at this time. She placed a call to her old history professor at the University and she was surprised that he greeted her communication as if they had spoken yesterday. "Rose how have you been, it has been a long time, how can I assist you?" "Dr. Hamilton, it is good to hear your voice, I have missed being on campus since I left, and I wonder if you could help me; at minimum I would like to be able to access the library, and I wonder if there is a possibility of earning an advanced degree in History?" "Do you remember if you had enough history units to declare a major? As I remember you declared an English Major did you not?" "Yes" she replied, "and I do not remember if I had enough units in history to declare a Major." "Never mind" Dr. Hamilton replied you can test out and earn enough units I believe to begin on a Masters in History with in a couple of months if I remember you used to consume information like a thirsty sponge. I will forward to you materials to re-enroll as a distant student and I will write one of the two letters you need from faculty to be admitted, and I will locate someone else who remembers your work and we will get you set to return to Campus on a regular basis and it will be so good to be able to see you here again."

She gave him her computer access numbers, and he said he would electronically forward her materials so that the project of her advanced studies would become a reality within the week if she could complete her documentation.

She went to work on the first day of the week, and went to her office with the group as was expected. She checked her assignments and called to see if she could make an appointment with Angela to gain her support for her school plans, the message capacity was connected so she left a message she would appreciate ten minutes of her time to discuss something personal with her. She began addressing her work assignments and worked through to Lunch and went with her group to have lunch.

She checked for messages and had a request from Angela to meet her at the outdoor eatery at a particular location as soon as she could arrive after work. She sent back a message in the affirmative, and checked the clock to see it was only ten minutes of dismissal, and so she shut down her computer, and prepared to leave. She quickly checked a local map to confirm the location of the eatery, and planned her walk to that establishment, and headed out with her group to the exit location they were allowed to use.

Walking briskly she arrived to find Angela waiting at a table under an awning and she approached the table and sat down. Angela looked as though she had aged over the year, her hair was almost a different color from the auburn it had always been, and her expression was one of a tired ageing older woman but she was happy to see Rose, "I suggested we meet here as this kind of meeting would not be approved by those folks we work for, Rose, I hope it was not too much to ask you to walk all this way", and Rose responded that she had not minded, and was just happy to see her for a little visit. Angela asked her what she had wanted to share, and Rose responded that she had hoped to gain her support in doing some off campus study and perhaps earn an advanced degree. "Angela, I have been bored, I have always done better quality work when I am challenged, and I think the Government would benefit from this kind of a plan." Angela pondered the question for a moment, and then responded she would support the plan, but that Rose needed to know people in Government are chronically lazy, and clearly not into self-improvement. "I understand your desire, but I can assure you that the people above me will at least think you are crazy and possibly think there is something deviant in what you are asking to do. Some of those people are rather deeply invested in petty graft, and outright dishonesty, and as a result they will wonder what you are up to with this plan." She felt suddenly downcast, and Angela picked up on the shift in her mood. She was quiet, and Angela said I need to let you know that I am looking for other employment, for the next few years, I am sixty years old, and I have a few more years in me, Rose, but I have communicated with the former director about the management style and she says now that it was the reason she left and went into retirement earlier than she might have. She like you and I try to put in a good days work for our employer the standard in Government at least here is to find out how you can keep your own stress down, and at the same time beat the system.

"I applaud your goals, and I will do whatever I can to advance your plan, but you must understand, the culture in the work site is not supportive to personal or professional growth".

"Okay I dragged you all the way over here, now let me buy you dinner". Angela handed her a menu, and they ordered and Angela ordered a white wine to accompany their meal, and told the waiter than she would cover the bill. Rose thanked her for dinner, and they sat and ate together, and chatted about Roses idea for advanced learning. She finally asked, do you think I need to tell them that I am doing the advanced study, and Angela smiled, The university will deduct your costs I presume from your account and the employer has to approve that use, is that not true? Rose I think they need to know.

"Yes of course I guess you are right." "I will receive a request for auto deduct as your tuition bills come due, and I will of course approve them, but I do not have the final say, I believe the director is on the list, and He is the one I do not trust".

CHAPTER EIGHT

A DIFFERENT WAY TO SEE THE WORLD

She mounted the train to leave for six days off at the University. She had done everything she needed to do to become an extension student and in the meanwhile she had tested out of three classes in undergraduate history by reading and taking exams on line and she looked forward to seeing her old professor Gregory Hamilton, and felt very excited. The train pulled out of the station and sped at an amazing rate south to what used to have been central California. Within two hours she was exiting the train and into the station, to see Greg, her old professor waiting for her arrival. She was so glad to see him again and he seemed equally glad to see her. He was not alone, and his companion was a woman in her early fifties, she was a tall woman, neat but casual in her dress, and lovely brown hair swept back from her face, in a French roll style. She had the deepest blue eyes Rose had ever seen, and a smile which had the wattage of a street light, it was truly bright and welcoming. "Let me introduce Irene Franklin to you Rose, she will be your major professor." Rose shook her hand and Irene said to her, "I have looked at the work you have produced to make up your deficient of credits in history, and I am very positively impressed with your capacity to learn and then use what you have learned in creative and daring ways to reach new conclusions and suggest trends and outcomes". "Thank you Dr. Franklin, I appreciate your acknowledgement." "Dear, Rose it is Irene, you are no longer and undergraduate here, you have achieved advanced standing. We want to encourage a collegial relationship with our post graduates, and one of the ways we do that is to become colleagues with our Graduate students. Please call me Irene." "Yes, I will", and Greg suggested the same for him, and so walking back to Campus, Irene inquired about her work and her reasons for returning to school. Rose responded that she felt like she needed a challenge and indicating that for some time she had felt goalless, and needed something new to commit to and work for. Irene's response was interesting, and it stayed in Rose's head for the balance of the day. "Greg I feel we have a future colleague in our midst, you sound like a budding professor to me Rose."

Rose reported to the Graduate College to receive her meal ticket, her library pass, and her pass to the dorm which she would occupy as her home on campus when she was here. "We are scheduled for a meeting and seminar tomorrow" Irene said as they parted, and I would like to invite you for dinner on Thursday before you leave campus to return up north Saturday morning". "Yes I would be honored."

Walking into the Graduate Dorm, Rose felt a sense of renewal. She thought to herself she could endure almost anything at work because she now had a future that included an alternative, a life of study and thought, and the sharing of information and ideas. It was an environment which supported honest debate, and alternative ways of thought, and was a place of integrity. Yes the Government was out there but mostly it kept its distance, and that was a clear benefit.

She registered for her room, and picked up a pager which was used on campus as a communicator, and she slipped it into her pocket. She unpacked her suitcase, and put her personal items in her small bath room turned on the computer and communicated with Angela that she had made it to school, and had never been happier and more hopeful. She got a note back in the evening from Angela that she had asked people she trusted and had picked up no negative comments, she closed the note with the phrase, "and my best wishes for your continued study." Rose all in all felt she had embarked on a path that would yield for her the best hope for a contented existence in her future.

She was scheduled for an exam which was the final step in her acceptance into the Graduate College. She was up for the exam, and wanted to do it early in the day so she would not be late for the two meetings she had scheduled with Irene. It was 7 a.m. when she sat down with the computer in the testing unit. She read through the questions, and began to outline in her mind's eye her responses, and then she began to type, and within an hour and a half, she had completed the test, and had signed out of the Testing Center. Heading toward the location for the Irene's seminar she stopped by the refreshment center, picked up a cup of coffee, and carried it across the campus to the seminar.

She walked into the room with the seminar sign outside of the door and took a seat in the second row, and took out a note book to take notes within about five minutes Irene came into the door and took her place at the podium. She carried with her a pile of paper, and called the group to begin. She began to cover the datum for the course in General American History from 1780 through the end of the Civil War.

The material went smoothly and she asked everyone to identify a topic which for them held some sort of interest to produce an in-depth analysis of the event including the alternative outcomes if there might have been an alternative outcome and the consequences to the union.

The group was told to electronically forward their work to a specific address, which was her mailbox and she would send each of the students an individual response, and that it was her style to ask many times for expansion of their ideas. She dismissed the class, and put a due date of tomorrow morning and encouraged all the students to utilize the facilities in the Library for data development, and she would get back to every one individually discussing the strong and weak points in their material.

Everyone walked toward the Library complex, and Rose was walking toward the group when she heard her name being called. She stopped, turned to look behind her and seeing her major professor behind her and walking quickly to catch up she stopped, and then began walking back to meet her. Irene, smiled, and waited for Rose to come back. "I need to set an appointment for you to speak with you about your material, could we do that now"? "Yes, of course." Rose responded. They walked back into the building, and Irene took her to a small office just off the entry way. They entered the office and both took their seats, and Irene pulled up her schedule on her computer screen and asked Rose for her free times tomorrow. They set a time in the afternoon, and Rose excused herself to go to the Library to begin addressing the task. Irene in their brief meeting had given her an address to log her material into, and excused her with a smile, as Rose then was off to the library.

Her morning and afternoon was filled with books and new perspectives on the topic she was investigating, "the real reason for the war of 1812". Many of the Canadian based Indian tribes had been used by the Garrison of British Military in the southern parts of Canada, to create harassment raids into the northern areas of the United States; they burned fields, and raided settler's homes, killed families, and stole their livestock. Meanwhile the British Navy was intercepting sailing ships under the Flag of the United States, and impounding a number of U.S. citizens to work on the ships of Great Brittan. The loss of men amounted to about 10000 in total, and it challenged the ability of commerce between the United States, and France, a loyal supporter of the independence of the United States from Great Britain, its foe. The real product of the war was the capacity of the United States vessels amounted to its ability to sail and provide routes for commerce between the European markets, and the United States. It really had been about money, and, this generations, future oligarchs to keep the commerce going.

As she read about the war itself, she was amazed that the war went as well as it did, as the United States was in all areas of strength was out manned out gunned, and outnumbered in the naval vessels they had available. Her reading lead Rose to conclude that it was the energy and pressure brought on by the commerce needs of the business men in the Colonies which spurred the military on to the victory they won. In her own mind what resonated so clearly was the demand of who would become the oligarchy in her own time which had demanded the win.

She titled her response paper, "The oligarchs first battle" and she had it completed prior to dinner time. She transferred the paper to Irene before leaving the Library complex, and she went to the food court picked up a sandwich for her supper and retired early for the next day of activities. She had completed her first Graduate School activity, and she had a feeling of pride and accomplishment. She knew she was on the right course for herself and she would communicate this to her parents as soon as she returned to the city.

CHAPTER NINE

TRAVELLING COMPANIONS

The packs of wild dogs made themselves an ongoing presence as she walked and found each end of the day a safe place to stay the night. She would occasionally see one or several of them but they made no attempt to approach her or in any way interfere with her progress, and as she became more and more used to their presence she began to recognize that her needs were being cared for by this environment which seemed to sustain their needs as well. There were the occasional rabbits she was able to trap and kill for protein, and water as well seemed to be available as well. She was careful to maintain her supply and as long as she could sense by their night time cries, the wild dogs, she lost the fear that her needs would not be adequately sustained.

It was getting very cold in the nights at this point in her travels, and more and more she would gather wood as she came into areas where there was brush or fencing long abandoned to utilize for warmth at night. She had for the total time of this escape plotted an easterly path. She felt that she had been on this trek at this point in time for more than a year. She in her memory recalled another time of some degree of cold over a period of time, and she now utilized these memories for gauging the length of her escape from the degradation of the city. She had no real picture of where she would arrive, and no idea really of what that place would look like to her, to keep moving seemed to be her operating scheme, and move she did.

There had been a couple of places she had stayed for longer than a day along the way, but she had determined these would be places she felt safety in and would only be for a couple of days lest the desire to escape be lost in the joy of rest from the endurance test which had become her existence.

She began to notice that the water sources were becoming less and less available to her and she had to be more and more cautious about her not running out of this most precious commodity. She was also aware that fewer and fewer of her nights were serenaded by the howls of the packs of dogs, they had either stayed behind her on this trek, or had veered off in a different direction at some point in her path. She could hear them at a longer and longer distance, and then one night as she camped near a hill side she could hear their presence no longer. She had never made any direct contact with them, but their presence in a way had been a comfort. Rose had never made a connection with an animal before in her life, but the presence of the dogs had in its own way been a comfort and in a subtle way she grieved their absence. Alone now she walked on each day, headed toward she was not sure what, she just knew her hope whatever that meant was in putting one foot in front of the other and keeping her forward momentum going.

Water was becoming an issue, she was traveling across a long and dry, parched land. She was careful with the consumption of water. Five or six days passed, and she consumed only minimal amounts of water, she had consumed about half of the water she carried, and perhaps had the potential of five more days of a walk before she needed to find some source of water. In the distance she saw a single mountain ahead, but she thought that was perhaps a longer walk for her than she had resources to make. In the past there had been two episodes when she was either without food or without water. For the first time in this trek, she began to imagine what it would be to be totally without either food or water. She wondered what it felt like to walk without what her body demanded. She walked into a valley, not really a valley more a depression and ahead she saw a burned out shell of a ranch house, and barn. That setting could have some kind of water source, and she walked two days to reach it finding no presence of a well head, or any kind of resource. Wood, bricks and the corrugated tin which were probably a roofing material, were scattered everywhere, but no pump house, or water line of any sort were observable, and she had only one full bottle at this point, and began to feel a kind of low level of panic, with a dusty plain ahead and a single small mountain in her path.

A wind accompanied her on this phase of the escape, it came from the east and was one more barrier against which she had to struggle. She lowered her head and walked but she tired in half her normal walk time, and she found a place to camp out for the night before the light was completely gone this day and she felt that if all else failed she would rest, and consume the limited resources of a few berries and a swallow or two of her one containers.

Morning came more rapidly than her body needed. The sun was just a suggestion in the sky to the east and she rose pulled her things together, and she began this day almost with a spirit of lethargy. She walked and walked and her usual mental process of what she was seeing and wondering, and thought had changed to malaise. There was a line of blowing dust ahead and she did not process the source or the impact and only turned her back as it furiously crossed her path, and when it had past turned toward the mountain which was in her path and walked on. This was the first time in this trek she had lost that mental acuity which had always been her experience of herself, and Rose wondered if she had walked all this way only to die on this forsaken plain. This day would end in the burned out wreck of a truck. She circled the wreck and feeling it would provide some protection from the elements, she had been unbearably cold for consecutive nights, and needed some kind of a break in the intensity of this experience. She crawled into the cab of the truck, and finding one seat more or less intact, she crawled into the seat and fell into a deep sleep unaided with either moisture or food for her body.

Morning came quickly, but the protection of the truck had benefitted her to some degree and she thought this day would bring her close to the base of the mountain which had been her goal for days now. She had several black berries left in her pocket and she rather unconsciously ate them and as she consumed them, she set out on a walk to the base of this mountain. Her canteen contained about two swallows at this time. She opted to wait to drink until the midday, and she put her head down and did what she needed to do to survive, she walked. The day passed almost unconsciously, she walked and walked, she pushed as she could and as the sun now was behind her she began looking for some place to locate in her line of sight which would provide yet one more place of rest.

Somehow her thoughts drifted to a time in her childhood, she remembered reading about the Plaines Indians. Those peoples had survived on these very planes so many years before. They had survived because of the presence of a source of nutrition, the buffalo. She had seem pictures of their campsites, and they lived in pointed kinds of tents, which were made of the skins of these huge animals, and the bones of these buffalo had been carved to provide for arrows, and any number of other needs, and of course the meat of these large animals was consumed by the whole tribe. She remembered that the Indians would thank the buffalo for being plentiful, and she also remembered that these people never over hunted the buffalo respecting both the herd, and the environment. Speaking out loud, she thought of the Indians and their conserving of the environment and said, *that is what I will do, should I live to find a home here, I will use only that which I need,* and as she walked on toward the small mountain which was her goal for this day, she let the sound of that pledge repeat in her awareness.

Night was closing in and she had arrived at the base of the mountain. She hid herself among the boulders, and in a kind of act of trust she drank down what water she had in her canteen, not more than perhaps a mouthful. Her walk this day had convinced her that water was the single most important need she had, and rising in the morning finding water, would be her most primary need which had to be satisfied if she was to survive. It was in her mind that she had perhaps reached the limits of her tolerance. She lay trying to sleep at the foot of this mountain. She could hear in her memory the sound of a stream the stream in the valley with the dogs, and the berry bushes so abundant, and she counted back the days, since the water though not abundant was available when she least would expect it. She could within her memory hear the dogs in the background of her awareness, and know that they knew not to walk away from such a necessary resource, and she wondered what it was she was so driven to arrive at, what would it look like and as she finally fell asleep she found no answer in her dreams for this perpetual question she had asked herself for a year or more in this walk. A dreamless night gave weigh to the morning, and she was up with her belongings in tow and now walking in just the greyest of dawns up the edge of this mountain, she could see the tree line, it was no more than perhaps an hour's walk, and beyond that she had no notion of what she would find. She walked past big boulders, and rocky slopes to the tree line, and ahead she saw what looked like a foot path. It was not deeply worn by the feet of many yet it seemed to her to be apparent. She climbed the hill, following the path way, and as she climbed the memories of what she had to escape came back into her mind, the filth and the hopelessness of a social order that lived and seemed to thrive on the backs of everyone but the rich. And as she thought and felt what was in her mind it was as if energy for this climb became available to her as it had not been for many months. She lost the plodding nature of her steps, and began somehow as a final urge to survive logged in her awareness, she followed the path which seemed to be so apparent. For a moment she smelled the smell of rain, should she stop before she was under the cover of the trees, but not feeling any moisture falling as yet, she climbed on toward the hill top.

The trail seemed to curve up ahead and she redoubled her efforts to scale the next lift in the land, and she picked up on a different kind of odor in the wind. She could not tell what it was but kept walking up and again up and then around a large boulder which seemed to be between her and the top of this small mountain. As she passed the boulder and saw that the top was near, the smell became more and more pronounced and then, as she climbed the last incline, in front of her was a small lake surrounded by trees on all sides, and she dropped her things tore off her clothes, and ran headlong toward this lovely little body of water diving in, in only her boots and socks to the waters embrace. She let the water hold her in its mass, and she floated, sipping water as she would roll in the life sustaining fluid.

It was not long until she discovered that the little lake was home to fish, some very small, but some were a good size, enough for a meal she thought. The next question in her mind, just how does one catch a fish, one big enough to eat and feel satisfied with the meal. She would ponder that question for the time being, and she exited the lake to gather her belongings which she had thrown here and there in her mad dash toward the cool water of the lake.

She put her boots in a sunny area near a grassy knowll to dry, filled her containers out of the lake, and spread her blanket in a sunny spot to lay down in the grasses and rest. *This is a place I can stay for a while and re-coop my strength* she thought to herself. She was empty but she had water, and she thought after a short nap she could walk around and fashion a net or something that might pass as one to use to grab one of those fish for her dinner. She lay naked in the sun and slept as deeply and soundly as she had slept in many nights, really, since she was in the company of the wild dogs.

She was beginning to understand on a cellular level that all life could learn from all life, and it might be advisable to re-read the book she had in her electronic reader about the Indians of the Plaines, she was sure that they knew what it was she needed to learn, and she would once again take the role of a student in order to be able to survive.

CHAPTER TEN

DINNER WITH IRENE

It was her last night on campus for this first trip down, and she was arriving at Irene's door for dinner before she would depart on her return to the city and work for six more months. During her conferences with her three professors during this week they all concurred that she was demonstrating the quality of scholarship that she could in conjunction with the resources of the library staff and an electronic reader and a monthly electronic conference with each of them, complete many of her requirements off campus. She had studied the course of study for the Master's Degree and felt that with regular study she could accomplish the demands with ease. She had spoken with Greg about her assessment, and he agreed, telling her at any time he and Irene would be available to her and he knew Connie her other instructor would make herself available as support if needed.

A light rap on the door and within a breath it opened to her. Irene, had prepared a wonderful evening meal for the two of them, she offered her a glass of burgundy as she entered the rather cozy home, which was punctuated by the smell of books. Irene had a nice apartment, on the Campus; it was a three bedroom apartment, with a small sitting room, and a comfortable but small dining room and kitchen which exuded the odor of fresh baked bread. Two of her bed rooms were set up to be supports to her ongoing research and writing which was done in conjunction with her teaching responsibilities. She had recently completed a text which focused on the Age of the Enlightenment in Europe, and she had over her desk a plaque which was the award for Master teachers from the Western College Professors Guild. It was an award based on scholarship and creativity in teaching History at the Masters and Doctoral levels.

Irene asked her if she would like she was welcomed to select a book or two to carry back with her for her own interest, and as she walked the stacks in the one room she came across a book which reminded her of a book her mother had about the lives of the Plaines Indians, and she took that as a first offering from Irene's special collection. "Please do remember where it came from though, dear" and Rose told her she would care for it and return it the next trip down.

The two women sat over a beautiful pasta dinner, with French bread fresh from the oven and real butter, and cheeses and a salad. The odor of Basil was in the air, and Rose could not but help telling Irene about her experience with Grammy and the garden and the fresh basil she grew and used generously in much of her cooking. Rose learned that Irene like her mother had grown up with siblings, that her father had a large farm in the Des Moines area, that her younger brother had kept the farm and continued to run it as his father before him had run it, and when the one child policy had been adopted her brother, who had a bit of a rebellious streak hit the ceiling and said to her "no one can tell me how many children I can have, they can all go straight to hell as far as I am concerned". "Rose it has been a hard row for my brother to handle, he had his second son, and they both grew and were home schooled as I and my siblings had been, by my mother. There were two occasions when he was summoned to court to pay fines which were levied on the Farm for his parental transgressions, and he on one occasion had been jailed by the courts for having the second child. "We all contributed to a fund to spring him from jail and he has as yet to thank me for my contribution. I am sure he has not thanked my sister as well although my sister in law thanked us both profusely for our support."

They talked into the night and the conversation ranged the surface of both their lives, and at two in the morning Rose excused herself, from Irene, now her teacher, her guide in things academic, and her friend. Rose crossed the campus under the lighted walkway from Faculty Housing back to the Campus proper, and into the dorm to sleep before preparing at noon to return to the city. She had all the materials electronically loaded into her small computer, and she would be speaking to each of the three instructors on a rolling schedule, once each three week basis on Sundays when she would not have the typical time constraints which work presented.

Morning came early and she showered and packed her things for the return trip to the Bay area. She went to get a bite to eat, and she carried with her the book she had borrowed from Irene. She found a table which was in the shade in the patio area, and she sat and read with her suitcase at her side. She got up once to fetch more coffee, and she returned to find three now familiar faces sitting waiting for her return. "We had nothing else to do so we thought we could walk with you to the depot and see you off this morning." They all were interested in her impressions of the first week on campus in the program, and they all had observations to share about her performance on the three quick demand assignments she had turned in over the week. Rose shared with the group the week had been demanding but she had enjoyed meeting demands which mattered. They all had individual impressions of her work, and her scholarship, she, as they commented about their observations, felt a subtle pride in her abilities to learn and incorporate her own distilled thoughts after learning the material in the task. After all she had been doing this professionally for now a little more than 4 years.

As the time passed they all rose from the table and walked the seven blocks to the train station, and just before she boarded the train Irene gave her a small box. "It is some of the bread we enjoyed last evening, and some real butter, and a small knife for spreading the butter. It will help to keep body and soul together before you arrive at your home; I hope you will enjoy it." And with that she mounted the train, found a seat where she could enjoy the view of the scenery going back into the north, and the train moved out of the station and was up to speed within minutes.

Walking into her apartment she put down her bags and her back pack, and checked her communicator to see if anyone had called her, and found a message from her Mother on the screen.

"Rose, I wanted you to hear from me that my symptoms of sadness and poor energy have returned. I am grateful I had a period of feeling more normal for a while, I will treasure those times in my heart. Your Father wanted me to tell you that we are fine financially and he wants you to stop the automatic deposit into our account. He insisted that we do not need it, and he feels you should begin saving your money for your own needs. We are going to take a trip down into the south, of here; we will be going into Mexico, and perhaps South America. Probably by the time you receive this we will have left. I love you and Dad loves you, and we want you to know that the loss of the feelings of buoyancy I had achieved were a real gift to both of us, but all good things after all do come to an end. I am happy we are taking this trip, and our ability to do this is a product of your generosity with us, and we thank you. Always remember that we love you very, very much." Looking at the facial features of her mother as she played and replayed her communication before erasing it from the system she could see the difference in her emotions from her last visit. She wondered if there was another medication she could take, and the request that she save her money for her own needs well her father could just forget it at least for now, even with the costs of school, she was making good money and she would by damn use it as she chose, and he could just get used to it, she thought. She sent a short communication to her parents, and said she was happy they took the trip, and hoped that it had been interesting, and fun. She said she would contact them again and she had worked it out to get back into school to work on an advanced degree and she was very happy about her being able to be back on campus occasionally.

Walking into the governmental complex on Saturday morning was a little of a letdown, but she knew what she needed to accomplish to keep these people convinced that her attending a Graduate program would not interfere with her ability to keep her work load up to the standards which she had established within the first six months of her employment. She saw Angela as she was leaving and they walked to the outside together and then walked away from the building for a short way. Angela as they approached the outside of the building inquired about her time off, and she could see by Rose's expression that indeed this had been a wonderful reentry into the academic setting. "Do you think you might move toward teaching when you are finished Rose?" "I have to tell you it is a much less intense work environment down there, and I may if I can complete the Ph.D. apply for an instructor's position."

She reached her apartment and began studying, and eating what was left of Irene's wonderful bread and some cheeses she had in her refrigerator. She would spend all day tomorrow working on assignments which would be electronically transmitted to the instructors. "One week from tomorrow I will be on the communicator with Irene, and then Greg, and then Connie on the third week. *I will send the completed assignments in that order so each has time to go over what I have produced with time to spare.* She had wondered if her work would not have been an added strain to each of these wonderful instructors, but she let that go for the time being as her experience of their situations had been so affirming of her she figured that for them, this was fun.

Monday and work came and it was another week in the rat race. She had her normal three rewrites to complete each day, and the week seemed to whip by with the speed of light. As she left the building on Saturday evening, she had a day of reading and her communicator meeting with Irene to look forward to. She had submitted her assignment to Irene on Tuesday evening, after reviewing what she had produced on Monday evening. She felt she had been very complete in her articulation of the several questions

Irene had attached, and she wondered if her meeting would be a combination of an instructional phase, and then a recapitulation of their dinner together. She hoped that would be so.

Her study and production of assignments was steady, and provided her with a sense of satisfaction she had not felt since the early days of her professional work. It had become clear to her that what little acknowledgement had come her way for completeness or succinctness, with this or that assignment had not meant to her what the acknowledgement she had received in her college experience from people she knew had a basis in knowledge to acknowledge her capacity to synthesize information in logical and unique ways. She had been so happy doing the work to gain that recognition when she was young and now she had the opportunity to have that again and from people who were so acknowledging to her anyway; she just glowed, thinking about the opportunity before her.

She began her day reading for Greg's assignment in Epochs of Governmental development Course. She was engaged in her reading and had not noticed the time, and the silence in the apartment was broken by the sound of her Communication device sounding she had a contact attempting to connect. She jumped up to be able to appear on screen, thinking this must be a call from Irene. She answered the communicator contact and she saw a face on the screen that she thought she might know but was not sure. The woman apologized for the early hour, and verified her identity. It felt strange to her and she had no idea why this woman who she could not place was contacting her. "the reason for my call is very sad" she proceeded, "we welcomed your parents back from their vacation on Friday and they seemed to have had a nice trip, and this morning they were discovered in bed together after apparently consuming a poison together. They left a letter addressed to you, we can send it by mail to you, or we could save it for you when you come for their ashes, and any of their personal effects. "Would you like me to read it to you now?" "No, I will read it when I come down. Save it do not send it by mail." "When will we expect you, and we will be covering your transportation costs down to as a part of the costs which have been extracted from your father's account. You need to know that your employer has as well been notified so this will not be a surprise to them when you report to work in the morning."

So abrupt was the contact, she had not really processed the information. Your parents were found in bed together after consuming a poison. She repeated the information, and was surprised she was not really shocked. The decision to end their lives together as they had lived did not surprise her, but that they would have picked this time was shocking to her, as they had just returned from a vacation that they had hoped they could take for years that was, she thought the shock. She tried to reach Angela on her communicator, but had to leave a message. She had said she would call back with arrival information so someone could expect her arrival in the community. She called the train station and asked to make a reservation to Happy Valley Retirement Community, and then began to laugh almost uncontrollably. She apologized to the person who was on the communicator, and requested a boarding to the retirement facility and indicated that passage had been paid for in advance of her call. The man expressed his sympathy as he knew the drill about advanced payment for death in the family. "Was it your Dad, or your Mom", he asked, and she kind of in a flat way just said "both". He, not really knowing how to respond to her answer, provided her the departure time on Monday afternoon, and she disconnected.

There was a subtle feeling of unreality, about how she felt in these moments. She pulled into her awareness the picture of her mother's face as she talked with her at the train station a year ago. And the words echoed in her mind, "Rose you know your father is a proud man, and he is uncomfortable with monetary gifts, he thinks that is his job to provide for me" "But Mom, I am making twice the money Dad, ever made, and you know I just don't spend a lot of money anyway, good training from you I guess, just let me do this for the two of you." Her mother's protest had fallen on deaf ears, and she on the one hand was happy she had at least done that for the two of them, hoping it had made the difference at least for a while. And then the anger set in, all directed toward her father, who she supposed had engineered this exit from life. She stood up and began to rail at him. "Hard headed and stubborn son of a Bitch she almost yelled out. Who gave you the right to decide when my Mother would live and die" It became oh so clear, that Rose had her attachment to her Mother, even though it had been her mother who stimulated so many of the conflicts of her life, she had been so cautious.

Angela her boss at work called to return the message, and they talked briefly, and Angela felt she need not come in to the office that she would automatically be given three days off under these circumstances, and she should call when she returned. "These things are hard for single children; I think there is no one to share those moments in family history with, the ones that bring the laughter, and the ones which bring the tears. And that is so much of what we do in grieving". She asked Angela to go into her payroll and terminate the automatic deposit to her father's account, and Angela said she would do it first thing in the morning.

It was now past noon, and Rose was exhausted emotionally and she felt physically, she tried to reach Irene, to let her know what had happened, and she was unable to make a connection, and finally left the message on her home communicator. Rose needed to rest, but instead she opted to take a walk. Walking for her had always been a way to organize her thoughts, and bleed her system of stress, and so she walked and walked this afternoon, almost to the edge of the settled city, and at the end she knew that strangely she could have predicted this style of leaving this earth, that she had never for one moment doubted that they loved and were attached to each other, that their bond had been for many hard to understand, but it was for the two of them a fact. "Of course in bed together, that was predictable"

She boarded the train, and as it at first lurched forward to carry her to her next task, she felt she too was lurching forward in life, a little unsteady without the strength of her mother behind her and the steadiness of the continual sparing with her father gone, she hardly allowed herself to feel the nature of the loss she was about to confront.

Death had confronted her now three times. When her Granny had died, she remembered that Granny's body was placed into a box, loaded into the back of a big white car without any seats for people to occupy and they as her family had been placed into a big white car with a window between her Mom, and Dad and her and the driver. She remembered driving behind Granny's car way out to a place in the country far from Granny's house, and arriving at a place with a huge lawn that was so neatly trimmed it smelled like someone had sprayed a wonderful smell everywhere. There were some people already there waiting for Granny to come, and they all told stories about what good persons both her Granny and Gramps had been, they read out of a book that made some people smile, and some people cry, and then they lowered Granny's box into the earth, and within moments they replaced the earth and the grass from the top of Granny's hole, and it looked just like there was no hole at all, and her Mother took her hand and her Dad had his arm around Mom's waist, and they all walked back to the white car and went home. She thought as she retrieved the memory that she was in the fourth grade in school so she would have been about nine.

Jeff was the first time in her adult years she had experienced death, and that had been for her such a contaminated experience, as she was both angry at his generosity, and care of everyone but himself and the reality of her feelings of love for him, and her fear of loss of her independence. She felt she was still angered by Jeff, and as well tortured by the empty feelings of her loss of her companion. They had shared so many of the same values, and they were passionate, if not with each other at least about many of the same injustices their society pursued. Their values were like a symphony of matching tones in the music of their lives.

Now her parents, what was there to say about the two of them? They had been the one constant in life as she had known it, yes she was rebellious and stiff necked and they had in reality sponsored those terribly independent urges in her youth, expecting strangely that she would give them up when she grew into her adulthood. *They should have known better* she thought to herself, and she realized that they were pulling into the station at Phoenix, and it would be only twenty minutes until she would be in the place of their death. And what about their decision to die together by consuming poison, Rose thought, and in the bed, premature, and unexpected, and yet predictable, oh so predictable to anyone who had known them. She began to realize she had tears falling onto her cheeks, and she reached for a tissue, to wipe away the evidence of her love, and her loss.

She felt the slowing of the train, she felt it was kind of a metaphor for her own emotions at this moment, she was slowing down, she had expected that this would be the reason for her return, and yet she wanted in this moment to deny that was true, and so she collected herself and her things and went to the door to disembark the train and walk to her parent's home where she expected to see someone from the administration who would let her go in and as the train slowed and stopped she stepped onto the ramp and a pleasant woman dressed in a black dress met her with her extended hand, to welcome her here for the last time. "My name is Martha, and I am the director of final preparations here, and I will escort you to your Parents home. You will be welcomed to stay the night in their apartment, and we will not dispose of anything without your permission, and we hope we can make this as pain free as is possible. Many times people want the furniture, but that is all the property of the home, and will be refurbished and used by others, but you are welcomed to take any personal effects of your parents. I must say for both to elect to go together in this way is unusual, not that we don't have suicides, we have a lot, but not together. We all thought it was interesting." Rose did not follow her impulse to put her fist into this woman's well-oiled mouth, so she just silently endured the rather irritating blather, and walked quite intently to the front door she had last seen her father standing in. Rose turned and asked the woman for the key which she would return in the morning, and taking the key from the woman she engaged the lock, and went in and closed the door telling the woman it was time for her to retire and she would speak with the person who was on duty for these kind of things in the morning. She entered the apartment, and put her bag into the guest room, which looked just like it had looked when she had come down to see her parents. She then walked into their room, and looked at it as if she could bring the picture of them at their last moment, which failed, and then she went to the kitchen to find the letter her mother had written to her as her last mothering act, there in plain sight, on the kitchen table, in an envelope and still sealed. She opened it to read—

My lovely woman, Your father and I have made a choice which was an option we have discussed for many years, we have for so many years been with each other, and we have no idea what is to come, or if life simply has a terminus, and no matter what, we know you are stable in your work and new study opportunities, and with the low mood which has reintroduced itself to me, I am exhausted, and I feel a kind of hopelessness in terms of a future. I want you to understand that we, your Father and I are at the end of our lives, and choose to not have the shock of life without each other. This decision is our own and has nothing to do with your resistance to coming here, or whatever it is that you are doing. We insist that you see this as our free choice.

You have been my life, and my hope, and I am very proud of your apparent success. I do not know much of your work, but I realize you are devoted to your work, and I am honored that so many of your values which lead to your success were values we taught you, I had hoped to see you again, yet, I hold the picture of you when you left in my mind and in my heart.

Mother, with our love and hopes for your future

She folded the paper up once again and slipped it back into envelop it had been contained in. She got up from the table, and walked to the guest room to place the envelop into her purse, and came back to the kitchen and just sat in this environment which was so central to her mother's work each day preparing a meal for them, or cleaning up after a meal . . . very quickly in her memory she recalled the hours she and her mother spent learning the rules of grammar or the times tables, or for that matter the states of the union, or the Capitol cities of each of these states. Her mother would create games that could go on for hours in the afternoons after school, and they would laugh at redundant mistakes, and she would hate it when she had to do it until she could do it perfectly, yet she would celebrate when truly she had the information and it was her own.

She sat there at the table in the kitchen, the whole night, and was awash in memory and as the sun began to rise, she made herself a cup of tea, and ate a bit of bread and jelly, and waited for someone of these tenders of the old to arrive and instruct her about what exactly were her duties in this totally new situation. She did want to have her mother's collection of books, but she had really no need of anything else in this setting. At nine o'clock there was a knock at the door and she let in a gentleman who was there with boxes, and labels and she directed him to the closet in the guest room, where on an upper shelf her mother kept her collection of books, and he packed them quickly, and labeled the box to be shipped up to her address in the city, and he quickly left with the box to get it onto the train going north as quickly as was possible. At about an hour later, a woman entered the apartment, with a small box in her hands. She asked Rose if she was sure that the contents of the one box was the only one to be shipped to her, and she replied yes that she was indeed sure. "The train going north will leave within the hour, if you would like I will walk you back to the station, unless you want to remain here a while longer?" Rose replied she was ready to leave, and she grabbed the small bag she had brought from home and not used. With her purse, and the bag, she walked away from the apartment, and she was grateful that she did not have to deal with the community any longer. As they walked toward the station, Rose made polite conversation with the woman who herself was not as chatty as the woman who had brought her to the apartment.

Rose mounted the train car with the woman right behind her and as she entered the door, the woman handed her the small box. "The contents of the box are the combined ashes of your parents, you are not allowed to bury the ashes except in approved places; you will have to check with the government for those places in your area. We combined their ashes at their request. We are very sorry for your loss, and I hope you have a pleasant train passage home." And with that she felt the train begin its forward momentum, and she waved to the woman, and looked for a seat on the car she had entered.

She looked at the small box, no more than six, by six by four inches high. This was the remains of the two people in her life which had created her, and cared for her for every day of her childhood, and probably worried about her in her adult life every day of their separation. And it weighed almost nothing. There was a surrealist element to this whole process. She glanced out of the window, and wondered where these left over ashes, from their physical bodies would in fact end up, and a part of her was a little angry about being handed the box in such an abrupt fashion. But what the hell was the woman to do, she could not keep them, she had probably as few choices as Rose did.

She entered her apartment and placed the box on the window sill, where the morning sun would shine on them, and put in a call to Irene to see if she had time to have their meeting, and Irene answered right away. "Rose, dear Rose, I got your message and I was a little shocked, I am sure you were quite surprised and upset about losing both of your parents all at once, what happened were they in an accident?" "Well you could say that, they took their own lives together, Irene they were joined at the hip all their married life and I got a letter from my mother explaining their decision, and knowing them I see that it just was the way they wanted it to be." She read the letter her mother had written to Irene, and Irene was struck with the bluntness and yet the tenderness she heard from her mother. They talked and Rose told her many of her memories which recounted her growing up years and the separation and termination of her father's work and their transfer to the community. She also talked about her last visit with them, and after a while, Irene made a cryptic comment. "Mom did not know how to let go did she?" And her perceptive thought shared with Rose, put some of Rose's frustration in focus. "No she did not know how to let go, there were times, I felt her grip from miles away." "Rose the important thing to remember is she loved you, and many times love can hurt, as well as heal. Call me and tell me when we can talk about your work, but please do not feel you are on a schedule. I will call Greg, and let him know about your loss, and he will probably call you today to reschedule if you feel you are not ready. Take care of yourself, and if you do not mind, I will call you toward the end of the week in the evening just to check on you. Will that be Okay?" "Yes" Rose replied, and with that they disconnected.

She called Angela at work to let her know she would be in to work in the morning. Angela seemed to want her to take the third day and just rest, but Rose told her it would be better for her if she was distracted by the work, and Angela seemed to understand.

Rose got one of the books she had from school for Irene's class but her attention seemed erratic, and so she decided to walk for a while and she took off in the opposite direction from where she had walked upon receiving the news. She walked into the business district, and past toward the south of town, and came up against the fencing which separated the public from the water reclamation district, and the holding ponds over on the other side of the fencing which to her in this moment seemed impenetrable. And she felt the anger rise in her belly, *everything here is impenetrable here, you cannot find some place that you are able to walk through, there are no parks like there were years ago, why all these fences!* She began to try to relax her anger at seemingly being in a caged environment, and headed back toward her home.

There was a blinking light on her communication device, and she went to find that Greg had attempted to reach her. She punched the recall button and very quickly his face appeared on her screen. He had such a compassionate quality, and she felt his concern for her emotional situation, and she shared with him that she was doing okay, that this was as she thought it through, very understandable and she was doing okay. "You know most of us my age, Rose, have siblings to share our feelings with, this generation is alone when they face these things and that fact makes me a little angry at that decision. Any time you need a shoulder Rose, call me, but knowing you, I suspect you will try to do this alone." She thanked him and said she would like to have a meal with him when she got down there again. She assured him she would let him know, the fact that she had known him for so long made his offer, to her, more genuine, and she thought as she disconnected that he and Irene would be the two she would talk with if she found it a need. She prepared her evening meal, and sat to eat, and found tears rolling down her face, and she just let it happen.

She walked into the Governmental complex on Wednesday morning, and she found Angela waiting for her near the main entrance. "I have been thinking about you since you called me on the weekend. Is there anything I can do to help you, my dear? Death is always a shock to us, perhaps it is that we get absorbed in our own demands and a death has a way of snatching us out of ourselves and pulls us back to another time, and place." "Angela, I am okay, they both have been attached at the hip for their whole marriage, and really I could, if I had thought about it, have predicted it. My mother had fought with such a low mood, for so many years, she was feeling well when I saw them, but she let me know it had returned, and I know it just tired her terribly. I think they both got a little hopeless. I need to get back in the work and give myself a sense that I have a future."

They walked together up to the work area, and Rose entered her work room to begin her day at work. She, at lunch time realized she was distracted and had some trouble maintaining her focus. She ate some lunch and returned with her group to the work room, and she tried to focus and complete her assigned work for the day. Sooner than she thought the day was finished so she shut down the page she was working on and realized she would need to pick up the speed, she was falling behind her normal capacity to complete all her work in a given day.

She went home and just felt very tired and without eating she fell into bed and slept soundly for the first time since she had been contacted about her parents. She was grateful for the rest, and did not fight the almost overwhelming need to escape reality for a while. Why if she was so disconnected from these people did their absence cause such a disabling process? It was an unanswerable question, and she was left to walk through it on her own.

CHAPTER ELEVEN

HER RETURN TO NORMALCY

There was a book on her kitchen table, it was one of her Mother's books and it brought a feeling of happiness. It was one of the one' s as a child she had loved and reading it now was a joy to her, not the pain when it had arrived shortly after her parents joint suicide.

She needed to study but while she ate a small dinner she read a chapter about the Plaines Indians, how they took such care of the environment and maintained a balance in the use of resources never taking more than they really needed to sustain themselves.

She finished her food and rest break after work, and began to study the text from Greg's class. She was to send to Greg a summary of her study of his materials and some questions which arose from her reading so he could see where she was in her incorporation of the material. Each Sunday she would be in contact with the three faculty members, and these conversations were both a challenge and exciting as they always commented on how she incorporated the data, and seemed to get underlying elements which were subtle but still powerful in the incorporation of the data and spirit of the times. She had been sent a summary of her academic achievement and was over 95% in all three of her courses. She looked at the calendar and she realized she would be on campus and facing comprehensive exams for these three courses within the next few weeks, and she was excited about being on the campus once again. And she knew now in a way she could not have known prior to the death of her parents, that she had a home in a way, emotional attachments with these guides to her study and a sense of attachment with the campus which had after all been her first independent home.

As her study this evening proceeded she wrapped herself in the information she was reading, checked the notes she had taken during her initial read of a related book, and proceeded to make an outline of the material she had already read, and as she incorporated the material she once again felt so good about how she was progressing, and felt secure in her decision to return to school and give herself an option for the future. Yes, an option for the future, no one she worked with seemed to have a pride in their work, they did it because it provided a means to live, and it seemed to her at this point in time hopeless for any other reason. They worked six days out of seven, only for the benefit of being able to trust that they could continue to care for themselves and continue to breath. She had always, perhaps because of her genes or her upbringing, had held to hope. And perhaps because of this inclination toward hope she needed to see in her own future something different than she saw at this juncture in the lives of her associates. She even saw it in Angela, in the time that they had both been in the government she had watched Angela age in a way. It was a subtle process, yet her facial features had changed, her hair had greyed, and her energy level had slumped. She spoke frequently of her retirement which would be coming in the next three years. And when she had been with Angela as she spoke of her retirement she noted part of her looking forward to retirement was the hope that her sister would be able to join her, and there would be companionship at long last for this woman. There would be no such benefit for Rose, or for that matter no one of her generation. It had been against the law to have more than one child in a family for the last 40 years. She knew she needed to have that hope that she could have the option of finding a career in teaching on the University level. She would have a family of sorts, her colleagues, and that was her hope.

Her appointment on Sunday was with Connie, Dr. Connie Yang. She was for Rose, a woman who had a broad perspective. Connie had been born in China and her parents had immigrated to the States, when she was a child. Connie specialized in Eurasian History, and was relatively new on the faculty. Rose thought of Connie as a contemporary. She had absorbed much of the culture of her parents, she seemed to Rose shy at first meeting, but as she got to know Connie it was different from shyness rather reticent to stand out in the group. She had been trained in a college back east and had wanted to come west upon graduation to be close to her parents who lived in a retirement community near the hills to the east of the large southern California community of Los Angeles. Connie was engaged in the development of a core curriculum on Asian History, and had just submitted the body of work to the Government for approval so that it could be taught. Rose looked forward to the next semesters work as she thought she would be engaged in Asian History with Connie's first effort to teach this curriculum, but so far no one had heard whether or not it had been approved.

It was Sunday and the buzz of the Communicator went off surprising Rose as it was still early in the morning. She answered and there came up on her screen Connie's face and she was smiling broadly and announcing that last evening they had gotten the go ahead from the Governmental Office on Higher Education to begin the Eurasian Curriculum. "Finally I can next semester go ahead with my Curriculum. I am so happy Rose, and you are among the first to know. Of course Dr. Wellstone, the President of the University got the message from the Governmental office, and he called me, and I let Irene know and I told Greg at breakfast this morning, and now you are the next to know". "You must be thrilled Connie, I am so happy for you I know that you have really been excited to do this, and it will be so beneficial for us all I am sure. Do you want to work on the material I have prepared today, or do you need to call and talk with others, this morning?" "Oh no Rose lets work if this early hour is okay for you" Connie replied.

Rose gathered her notes and several supportive books and returned to the communicator to review with Connie her readings and responses to questions Connie had forwarded to her electronically. They discussed the implications of a treaty which had been signed with the Indian Tribes in the end of the relocation of the Tribes into reservations and how many times the government had reneged on the treaty and what the impact on the Indian communities had been. "And this was a time when the Government was fairly powerful still. The Indian Communities had no clear way to fight back." Rose exclaimed. "Yes" Connie replied, "The government by not being faithful to the letter of the treaties made a whole generation and more, into a community marked by a sense of hopelessness, which deeply affected their ability to survive." They talked about the whole string of violations committed by the government of that time, especially against the agreements with the Indian nations. "However now those treaties hold a lot of water, the reservations on which these people have been placed now are independent of the governmental actions, and they have natural resources they have managed well and are relatively independent, and the oligarchs don't really care much of course, they pay for the Coal, Copper. Silver and Natural Gas and a long list of what were referred to as rare earth minerals, whatever the tribes charge, and finally there is some justice for these peoples" "Yes," said Rose "as their land is the only place we know has these resources, and they are really careful in the production, they just do not pollute." "I wish this was true after they sell but they have no control over the rich." The two hours for the consultation had passed and they discontinued the call, and Rose again felt such a connection with this woman. And it was the information that created this bond.

The day passed with Rose studying and making her outlines of materials which related to the next contact with Irene. She checked her materials relating to this next contact and she reviewed a list of questions she would need to send by Tuesday to provide sufficient time for Irene's review. She began her outline which she would use to write out her responses for the list of questions Irene had sent to be returned before their next meeting. She knew this challenge made her have hope and she dug in to the process, with the glee of a kid and a bag of candy.

CHAPTER TWELVE

THIS LOOKS LIKE HOME

The Sun peeked over the edge of the top of her mountain, and she woke and had some fruit which she had found down the hill on a clump of wild fruit trees. She had quite by accident grabbed a fish for her dinner last night while cooling herself in the lake after her walk, and collecting the fruit which appeared to be ripe, and she found herself actually seriously considering staying in this environment. This environment was a place where she would never go without water, the one thing on the long trek that really had caused her real panic. And here she had protein and water, the two needs she knew would keep her alive and able to care for her needs. Fruit would be available in season, and she could dry some to give some variety through the winter months.

She had gotten here because of her perception of a trail up the side of the small mountain. Yet as she walked back the way she had gotten to the top, and saw no evidence of a trail which had been as apparent to her as she climbed. She wondered about this, and had in her mind no way to explain such an event, but it kind of haunted her, not in a negative manner, so much, as a puzzle.

This and the availability of the basic needs caused her to begin to think of this as a place she could stay. She had mounted the ridge behind the cabin and walked away from the degraded environment of her former home with no fixed idea of what she was searching for or if in deed she was becoming a wanderer. She had stayed in several environments, the cave with a pool of water, and a supply of rabbits just down the hill, and yet after only two days she gave in to the urge to move on and so she responded to that urge, and she walked away from that protected setting and across the flat lands of what she had guessed was what had been Nevada where water had been such a precious commodity.

She had no idea how far she had walked to find this small mountain in the midst of a broad plain. But she did know that she had found only one other place where she might have been able to sustain herself as well as she could sustain herself here. It was just too tempting to not try to establish a home in this setting. The trail, which apparently was not there, was to her a symbol somehow that this would be her home.

She did not have the shelter of the Cave and she began to wonder how in this setting she would be able to provide for herself some kind of shelter. Down in the flatlands approaching the mountain, she had noticed several burned out cabins and she wondered if there were some building materials she could scavenge to meet her need for shelter as weather changed from summer to fall and winter. It had become very clear to her that the seasons as she had walked were more and more distinct, and so today she would try to begin the process of looking for some building materials in these abandoned cabins. She followed the trail down as she had originally come up to find the small lake, and she thought she could get there within the day, gather what she could carry and return within the day. She would do this until she had enough materials to then begin the building in the fall. She would take only those things which she was sure would be useable, and keep from carrying things guessing it might be useable.

She looked for where the sun was at this moment in the sky and it looked to be still quite low in the morning sky, and she filled her canteen grabbed another piece of fruit, and headed toward where she remembered the burned out cabin had been. She walked and walked, and she saw not much that she remembered from her walk toward the mountain. She thought back to that day and remembered all she thought about was the absence of water and how she needed to find water so she let go of her not having been as observant as she had always tried to be. As she walked she noticed rabbit holes up against the boulders which seemed to have been scattered by those playful giants in their games, and she thought this place would more than take care of her needs. There was a small hill ahead, and as she reached the top, she surveyed the plain and there just to her right perhaps a half mile was that burned out cabin.

As she arrived at the site, she was surprised to find both some bricks with metal bars stuck into the holes in the brick she presumed to add stability to the wall and so she gathered some of the bricks and broke off with lots of twisting, the metal bars. She found some lumber too that was not completely burned and she made a pile of salvageable wooden boards, trying to keep the salvage lumber in piles to be carried ultimately up the hill. She also found what appeared to her to be cooking pots, and a skillet, and as she dug through the rubble she found several tools a saw and a mallet which she thought she could probably use as well.

She looked up to check the Sun's position in the sky, and it looked to her to be a bit after noon, and as she wanted to be back on top of the mountain by dark, she began to fashion a sled like carrier from wire and rope and some of the boards she had been able to salvage, and she began her walk back across the plain, dragging her loot, and as she arrived at the base of the hill she found a route up that accommodated to the sled with the materials she had gathered. She had consumed all the water, through the day and by the time she made it to the top of her new home she was quite tired, but very satisfied with her collection of materials. She ate some fruit, stacked the bricks and wood she had brought home, and took the cooking containers a skillet and a big pot, to the lake to attempt clean them. She drank fresh water from her other two containers, and felt exhausted from the day's work and fell asleep wrapped in the insulated blanket.

She woke with the sun, and felt sore from the activities of the day before and looked at the pile of materials she had been able to bring back. *"I am not on a schedule, and I do not have to complete this at a particular time, I can take my time, and not push myself into being really tired, and sore."* She ate her last peach, and drank a lot of water, and thought she would go down to the trees on the north side of the hill and just gather some more fruit, and try to fashion some fishing gear to make the process of catching fish a little more successful. Walking toward the trees she noticed that there was some thick grass growing on this side of the mountain. *Fishing line,* she thought, *I could tie it together so it won't break and make a wire hook on the end.* She gathered a bunch of it and stuffed it into her rucksack, and went to the trees to gather some peaches. She had about twelve peaches, which would more than last a week, especially if she could snag a couple of fish. She cut off a relatively straight branch about a quarter of an inch in diameter, for a pole, and returned to the top of the mountain, to see if she could snag at least one fish. The fishing presented another kind of challenge, as if she did not kind of braid the line it would break if one of the larger fish went after her bait, which were insects she had in abundance as they too had come for the water, and the hooks she had made from the wire she found in the burned out cabin were a couple of times probably consumed with the bait. The line was the only thing that did not let her down, it was sturdy and held consistently and at the end of the afternoon she had caught two small fish, and after gutting and cleaning they found themselves over a small fire in a frying pan and her mouth watered as she ate the first, it was delicious. That perfect resource of protein and the delicious taste sealed in her mind her decision to stay here, this place was home, and now she knew it.

Every other day she returned to the burned out cabin to retrieve materials. There had been a lot of wire in that environment, and she gathered it and rolled it into a ball to carry it home. There were as she looked at the pieces of wood which had been spared in the fire, and of course the brick which had really not been injured in the flames, and in the time of what seemed to be like a month she had gathered rather a large stash of building materials with which to work. She did find a piece of plywood which was about 6 by 8, which had some scorched places but was otherwise solid, and so on one day she placed that on her head and carried it back up the mountain and she thought this would be perfect for the roof of her little dwelling.

The weather was beginning to change and it was cooler in the mornings, and the days seemed to be shorter. Fall probably would be showing it's self soon. She found a spot up against a large tree which was in the north of the glen near the lake where she felt she wanted to begin the construction of her shelter. The ground around the tree was very smooth, and it seemed to be protected by the trees next to the lake its self, from winds which seemed to her to come from the east. She began by laying out the bricks on the north side of the building, and stabilizing the bricks as she had observed in the burned out cabin and she drove the re-bar into the ground with her hammer which she had found in the burned out shell of the cabin. As she piled up the brick they seemed more stable if she put another course in front and when she did she had what amounted to shelves. This would be where she would store her fruit to dry and be available to her through the winter.

This wall of bricks was about five feet perhaps a little less and about six feet in length. She tried to push it over, and it resisted her as it was well grounded by the rebar, and the trench in which she had begun the development of the wall. She next drew on the ground lines which would be the placement for the wooden walls. She had scavenged a lot of wire out of the burned out cabin, and it was her goal to wire the boards side by side to form each of the walls. Most of the boards she had collected were over six feet in height, and so she dug a trench where the first wall would go, and she wrapped the wire around the base of the boards and then around the tops, and as she got six or eight wrapped together she would lay the boards into the trench and secure them to the rebar stake she had placed at the edge of the brick wall. By night fall she had constructed one wooden side about six feet in length and the bricks.

To add to the stability of the wall she drove stakes on either side of the base of the wood wall, and then wired the wall to a piece of rebar on the corner of the bricks and to another length of rebar at the outer edge of the wooden wall. As the sun set that evening she slept inside her two sided shelter with no roof and had a real sense she could handle whatever she needed to handle in this environment, and she slept a deep dreamless sleep.

Three of the walls had been built as each day she made real progress, and she began to wonder how she would be able to mount the roof on the walls and secure it so it would not go blowing off if she had the fortune of a hefty wind storm. She thought she would somehow attach the roof to the wooden walls, but she had not found any nails with which she could do this task. She over the month of gathering the building materials she had kind of inventoried all of what she found in that burned out cabin. She wondered if she had not searched out everything in that locale, and then she became aware that there were two burned out places to the north that she could see from the edge of the north side of the hill when she went down to gather fruit from the trees. "yes, she thought, *I need to make this as stable as is possible, and so I will shop at a different place!*"

As she woke the next morning she was on her shopping trip to the closest of the cabins to the north. She had more energy for the walk out to the north, and was actually excited about the hope of stabilizing the roof. As she approached the leftovers of the fire, she was surprised to see so much useable stuff. There was corrugated tin, in pieces which were of a manageable size to carry, and as she dug through the rubble she found a part of the building which had not been totally consumed by the fire. In that part of the building which had been constructed with many rooms, she found a closet with bedding, and a pillow which smelled like it had been in a fire for sure, but she thought she could get at least some of the smell out of it with a dip or two in the lake. She in another part of the house found drawers which had been spared the direct flame, and in several of the drawers she found bolts, and a hand drill. The blade that was attached to the hand drill looked sharp and relatively new, and all of a sudden she had a picture in her head showing her how to secure the roof, so nothing short of a tornado would blow it off. In the last drawer she found some nails, not many perhaps a dozen, perhaps ten, she did not count them, and just stuffed them into her rucksack and she knew that her job now could be completed.

She was delighted with her solution, and she looked further to see if she could find a saw to cut the wood to fit the plan as it presented in her head. She did not find a saw, but she did find a long knife, and she thought in a pinch it might work. She headed back with everything she could carry, to her hilltop, and as she arrived with her things the sun was just setting so she settled herself into a couple of pieces of fruit for her meal, and as the moon rose up just on the horizon in the eastern sky, she organized her stash and wrapping herself in her blanket fell off into a very deep sleep.

CHAPTER THIRTEEN

THE SECOND TRIP SOUTH

It had been six months away from School and she boarded the train heading south. She now had almost a year of independent study completed, and she was very excited to see what was in store for her this time. She picked up in a conversation with Irene there would be a special assignment coming this time, and it was a research project, and that it was to be published in anticipation of her achieving all the requirements for her Masters exam. She now had completed twenty credit hours and her GPA was a sterling 97.5 the highest that they had ever seen in an independent study student. From what both Irene and Greg had communicated to her was that she was on the right path to set some records for her Masters Level studies, and they saw her sailing through the Ph.D. program with in a two year time frame. That translated in her mind to being sprung from Government Employment about the time that Angela retired. She could have not been happier to think she could apply for an instructor's position on any campus in the country, but what she really wanted was to stay right where she was on her old campus and at this point she would have been happy to teach freshmen just to be in a more humane environment. The Government paid well, and they had so far not objected to her use of her time off for advanced study. She had been informed by the Personnel Department that she was still employed under the BA in English degree and no matter how far she went with the Master's program she would still be employed as an English Major. That seemed to her to be the way they kind of tried to get even at least at this stage of the game, and she frankly did not give a rat's ass what they did or did not do. Just as long as she got her vacation time, to use as she chose.

The train was flying down the track and she looked out the window to see the far off plateau's pass and recognizing she would be in the campus within an hour. Irene had let her know that they would be there to meet her train, and that she had a surprise for her. Connie had said that Irene had hired a young post-doctoral student as a teaching assistant, that he was an Aussie, and that they all thought that she would enjoy this new member of the group. "He is a dry wit," Connie had told her, and she owned that he, for her, was a little hard to get used to mostly because she found herself not catching the joke until everyone was finished laughing, but that she was coming out of her shell with him around. "And that is a good thing; I am learning a little spontaneous behavior."

Irene was there at the station and Rose saw her waiting on the porch of the train station as they pulled into the station. She was at the door, with Irene's book under her arm to get it back into the library as soon as she could. She exited the train and met Irene, to walk and get her bag and her back pack as she had checked both. "Are you hungry, Rose? We thought you might be so the others are waiting for us to meet them at the cafeteria." "Yes what a good idea, I am very hungry, I did not stop for breakfast and I got a coffee on the train so there was something in there". They chatted as they walked toward the Baggage rack to get her bag and backpack, and then walked the short walk to the Cafeteria.

"I hear you hired a Post Doc, tell me about this Aussie guy" Rose said as they walked. "I met him at a conference on the east coast, he told me he was looking for a job until he got his Alien status taken care of with the government, and he thought it would be about 8 to 10 months until that problem was resolved. I read his Vita and he was well formed in European History practically from the dawn of time, and so I hired him as an assistant for myself, and then called Dr. Wellstone to see if it would be okay if I brought him home from the conference, or did we need a little time?" "So what did you do?" "I brought him home with me, and he is a grand help to me. I am working on book number 12, and he is a great research assistant, and he does some lectures for me as well, so he was a lucky find when I thought I would be doing this all by myself." They arrived at the Cafeteria, and Rose spotted the one face she did not know at the table. He stood up and extended his hand to shake hers and said, "I have heard about you girl, you are the glutton for punishment among this group, you work in Government and study all night to try to escape the boredom of the bureaucracy, Right? She shook his hand and she acknowledged she did in fact translate unreadable policy into the King's English. "And a magician as well,—My god, what a find!" They all had a great laugh and they sat and decided what everyone wanted for lunch.

Jake, the Aussie, went to grab the food that everyone was getting, and Greg accompanied him to bring drinks and napkins and condiments. Everyone was getting a premade sandwich, and a tea, or a soda, and it was rather simple to remember. "Good thing, too, this lady has about roughed up all my brain cells today and it is good it is so simple." She talked with the women at the table until the food arrived and she ate it down like it had been a week since she had feed herself. After lunch she walked to the dorm to pick up her room assignment, and checked her schedule for the week. She had three exams to take, one in the morning, one in the afternoon tomorrow, and one the morning of the next day. She had prepared for these exams and was ready for each of them. She noticed that there would be a conference with Irene on Wednesday morning, and she had lots of library time Wednesday through Friday to begin working on her next series of classes. Irene called on her communication device and asked her to save Friday night for "our usual dinner" and she said she was looking forward to having some social time with her.

She decided she would run over to the library and read for her next series of classes, and so she checked into the Library, was informed all new class materials were on her study desk, and so she went up to the fourth floor opened her study room and sat down to begin her reading. She spent the whole afternoon reading new materials, and at about seven p.m. she left the stacks and walked the mile back to the dorm showered and as she stood in the shower she reviewed in her mind all that the new reading had communicated to her. She was particularly interested in the Eurasian material from Connie's new materials, as it was completely new to her. She was fascinated by the culture of Asian countries, and being a beginning course it covered a lot of basic differences in the people today. She was particularly interested in the materials she had read this day about China. She knew she would be writing for publication something in one of the new classes this next phase and she wondered about the possibility of using Chinese culture or history as she let the hot water relax her and get her ready to sleep soundly.

The alarm woke her at 6:00 a.m. and she dressed and headed to the testing center for the first of three exams on her materials of study over the past several months. The focus was on material she had done for her course with Irene, and she felt she completed the material with skill and a great knowledge base. She left the exam knowing she had been complete in her answers, and that it read well. Comprehensive is what she had discovered about these testing sessions and that idea had been in a way the focus of her original outlines in study with everything she was doing in this new school experience. She also wanted to achieve the standing in this Graduate experience that she had achieved as an undergraduate; she wanted the Masters and Ph.D. work to be awarded with the Honors level of ranking at least.

The testing she felt had been up to her normal standards and in the two days of testing she had the sense that she had aced all three. She had met with her colleagues in the off campus study for a session which outlined the problems with away students success, and had this time for the first time shared her skill and insight with the use of outlines of the material in the reading and had been stopped by several of the students with the request that she meet with them to more actively demonstrate how she approached the reading assignments and actually do an outline to demonstrate the method of study. She agreed to follow up with them in the morning of her fourth day on campus. She felt a kind of affirmation in this additional responsibility and as she pondered the task she let herself feel the compliment implied in the request.

"I hear you are demonstrating your study skills with classmates," Irene commented as they met for their private session of review. "Yes and I am kind of honored that they should ask," Rose replied. "Most of these people are really gifted students, and it is a real honor that they have made this request of you, Rose, it is a real compliment."

"I wanted to talk with you about the publication assignment." Irene began. "Realizing that your work in the Government may make your selection of topic rather sensitive I want to encourage you to be careful in your selection of focus. I do know that people in sensitive work situations many times cannot afford to take on topics which we around here love for them to do, the more daring materials and the like, and as your major professor I want to work with you in the selection of something which will not draw unwanted notice." "I appreciate what you are saying, but I have worked in that area for years now and I know how to word things so that they will pass muster." Rose replied. Irene leaned back in her chair. And then, after a moment's thought, replied "avoid taking risks, Rose" "I have, in the experience of writing a dozen Text books, been hassled by the folks who approve them for publication, and you would not believe how many times I have had to revise how an idea is conveyed, to keep these paranoid folks from having a small hemorrhage on the spot." "Yes, I know that they can be a little anxious. I promise you I will go over every word and you can have the material to review if you like as I produce it if that will help. Would that be okay as I do the research and write?" Rose replied. "Yes" Irene replied, and the issue seemed to have been settled as Irene's next comment was about dinner, "How about we eat together on Friday evening before your return?" "That is great" Rose replied. "Oh by the way you had on your three test two perfect, mine and Connie's, and you got a 98% on Greg's exam, not too bad."

With that information both smiled broadly and Rose left to go help the ad hoc group with their study skills.

She spent the balance of her time in the Library stacks and studying the material for the next courses. Irene wanted her to identify what she found interesting in her reading that she might want to do her published paper on the this study section, and Rose quickly landed on a compare and contrast paper on the one child policy in this country to that of China. She felt that it was interesting and relevant. She also saw some distinct differences in the two policies from what she had read, and felt she could stay out of trouble with this work.

Friday ended with dinner with Irene, and she walked the mile from the dorm in which she stayed to Irene's apartment. She knocked on the door, and the Aussie answered the door with a glass of Australian Beer in his hand he had just poured for her. "Have a cool one, here my girl!" he said, and she took the beer and stepped in to the apartment, and greeted Irene and Jake. They sat in Irene's living room and talked about how her study was going, and had she come across any issues in her reading that she was interested in for her publication article to focus on as yet. "I am interested in a compare and contrast kind of article on the one child policy here and in China" she shared. "I know I will need to be the essence of tact in the writing but I think I can remain fairly neutral in the presentation, and it will be something I personally am interested in conducting the research." "Does this have to do with the process of grieving your parents, over the last year"? Asked Irene, and she noticed the Aussie, quiet, and become kind of reflective.

"Actually it does but in a kind of round about fashion, I have believed that my Mothers depressive state was exacerbated by the fact that I was never going to have children of my own, and had I had several siblings, things for her would not have just put an end to her role in life if a sibling would have supplied her with a grandchild or two. I truly believe that her 'mothering' role was a joy to her, and she was only 39 years old when I went away to school, leaving her with an identity shift that she just could not manage. She was a really good parent, and when she refocused her energy back onto my Dad, I think it was a hard adjustment for both of them."

"And speaking of them, they are still on my window sill, in my apartment. I just need to find a place to put their ashes, and I know that soon it will be illegal to place ashes into the ocean, and that is where my Mother said one time when we were talking she said that she would want to be, and she thought that Dad would not mind if she was happy with that kind of place." Jake began relating that his Dad had wanted that, and his mother wanted to be in the ground on their ranch, a sheep ranch which had been in her family for more than 100 years. "I took my mum with me and took my Dad in a small little box, and we went to the Great Barrier Reef, and put him right into the current, and she turned to me and said, 'you are not doing this burial at sea with me, me Laddie', 'I want to be near the house on the ranch so I can keep a good eye on what is going on', and so that is where we, my sister and I put her, and I felt really good about doing what they both wanted." "The retirement community mixed their ashes together at their request, they said, so they are going where ever it is they go together. Probably that was my Dad's idea; He probably did not trust me to take care with his ashes separately." There was a silence after her comment and then Jake asked, "You and your Dad had some conflict along the way?"

"You could say that Jake", she replied, and then she said," it was a lot like a power struggle over petty stuff, he would want A and I would automatically say no B". Rose thought for a moment, and then commented, "You know I thought about it, and it was like my Dad and I were in a constant competition about who would call the shots. I had to lie to them to get him to stop with the nagging about coming to see them, and I hated it, I wish he could have just treated me as an adult, but in reality neither of them could look at me and see I was an independent adult, and I was left with fighting like a kid."

Irene was listening to the two of her guests talk, and she chimed into the conversation. "Rose I think that both needed more children, they had only you to focus on and that is really why it felt to you like a power struggle with your Dad and with your Mother too. I know that your mother loved you a lot, Rose when you read that letter to me that she left you, she did not want you to put on yourself any unearned guilt over their mutual suicide, but it was so clear that she had to die to let go of you, and in a way she understood you needed your freedom to live and thrive in ways she could not understand. When you read that letter to me on the communicator, it was so clear that she had decided to confront what you needed which was independence. I think that was a very selfless act for your mom. I applauded her courage frankly, in a paradoxical way it was such an act of love for you and it gave her an escape from her long fight with depression."

This exploration of the policy which caused her parents such pain was a good thing to explore, and she was gratified that Irene supported the idea. Her parting words after a grand dinner, of salad, potatoes and pot roast, and a peach pie, "Thank you both for listening to my rational for the paper. I felt real support from you both and that means a lot to me." Jake gave her a hug, and then excused himself from the evening, and she and Irene exchanged pleasantries for a few minutes. "I will walk with you to the train, meet me for breakfast at the outside tables and we can enjoy a little time together there." With that Rose left and walked back the mile or so to her Dorm and packed her things to return home in the morning. She showered and lay in her bed to relax before sleep. As she lay there she recalled sitting in the kitchen table in her folk's home the night after their suicide. She remembered sitting there all night reviewing her whole experience with them, trying to recapture her childhood memories. And as she lay in her dorm bed, she realized that her Dad had taken so seriously his role of doing whatever he could to please her mother, and it came very clear to her in the moment, it really was not a power struggle, it had been only his way to maintain their contact with her, and she had understood it only through her own feelings, and failed to understand that it was the effect of the one child policy nothing more nothing less. She had a wish she knew she could never have, and she uttered the words hoping they could hear her, Sorry; there was no ball of shit, which was my emotions, not my head. Sorry Dad. And as she drifted into sleep she achieved a kind of peace she had not felt she thought in all of her years, and she slept a dreamless sleep.

She put her toiletries in the bag and her bag of dirty clothes in as well; she stripped the bed and dumped into the laundry shoot her sheets and towel, rolled her bag ahead of her and walked out into the sunshine and over to the outdoor café to meet Irene for breakfast. She as she walked the several blocks to the outdoor café, and she felt a real shift in her mood and emotions, she felt lighter, and more energetic this morning, and she was smiling as she approached the table to find Irene with menu's and a waiter from the café right there waiting for her to arrive. "I will have a waffle and blueberry syrup, and an order of scrambled eggs. And I will have coffee with milk." She said to the waiter as she sat down, and the check is mine for us both". And she handed him her charge card for campus use. Irene stood to hug her and she had a care package for her trip north, cheeses, sent to her by her brother on the family farm which were the first product from their newly refurbished Cheese plant and some bread made by Irene, a hearty French bread with the hint of garlic in it. "Thank you so much for these care packages, I try to enjoy them for days, and it is so thoughtful of you". Irene replied it was nothing. And then she said that she really understood why she had picked the topic she had discussed last evening, and was fully supportive of her goal. They chatted about her performance on the three exams and Irene said she thought it was her best performance yet. Rose agreed, "I felt so relaxed with the process this time, I think I have moved ahead in the process, and you know I really do enjoy

Jake, he is a good man, and I hope his struggle with the government is settling." Irene said she and Dr. Wellstone had both contacted the department of alien acceptance and she thought at least they were polite but had essentially said they were working on his case and it would be okayed in due time. "What is due time?" she asked Rose, and Rose replied" whenever they get to it". "That is exactly what it sounded like to me!" Irene replied. And they both laughed.

Jake approached their table and sat down next to Rose. "I have been thinking, you do not know me very well, but if you need someone who knows the ropes of laying our love ones to rest in the ocean, I would be happy to accompany you Rose, all you need to do is just tell Irene, and I will hop a train and we could rent a vehicle and find a private place on the ocean to finish it off." "How good of you Jake to offer, but I think I can manage. I will think about it and if I chicken out I will call you".

"Good enough", he said, and he rose to go back inside, and Irene thanked him and said she would be home to begin their work in an hour or so.

It was time to walk to the train station for one more half year of distant study and weekly contacts, and so they walked toward the Station and Irene carried her snacks and they talked about things that had come to light in the week, and again Irene complimented her on her performance in the testing environment.

The train was in the station and she was able to board the train right after checking her bag, and they said their good byes, and Irene said she would be on the communicator in a week. She had her box of bread and cheese, and vowed to keep it for a time when she would really savor the tastes, when she felt hungry and with a jerk the train began its trek up the coast line toward the City in the North.

These trips down to school, and back to put in the study to return, had now become a trek of hope. She could see she would be able to exit the government into a much more affirming environment of the University lifestyle. She would be able to read to her hearts content, and she could engage with students, and hopefully challenge them to be critical in their evaluations of what was going on around them. For just a second she had thought that she could make a difference in the lives of others and then she became very aware that it was a done deal. She remembered that as an undergraduate, she had believed that she and her student friends who protested the loss of seven fields of study on campus, and it ended in several government demanded expulsions, and lots of injuries in the group of protesters, and many of the students were labeled as trouble makers with the government who placed letters of non-compliance in their permanent files which followed them through their lives. Her protestations in fact had not led to anything but engaging her parent's strong requests for her to desist. Why would she want to teach students to injure themselves in the long term? She would not, but it still felt as though she should inform students about how the system really is, perhaps she could be subtle about the whole issue. She then recognized that she too would have to be careful as a University faculty, her first task would be to keep her own head down, just as her parents had requested when she was engaged in her political activities. She had done that in the Government as well, and she came up against the skill of keeping her own counsel, had been useful in the task of surviving and succeeding in the Government.

The train pulled into the station where she would be closest to her home, and she disembarked the train, picked up her bag, and back pack, and preceded toward her apartment, with the box of goodies from Irene which would go into her refrigerator. She opened her door and stepped into her home and went to the communicator to see if there was any communication which she would need to respond to prior to returning to work. There was one communication from Angela, and she returned the call and found her at work. "Glad you are back, I would like to see you perhaps this evening. Could we meet for a light supper at the place we went to before?" "Yes, what time?" she asked. "I think I can be there by about 6 p.m. See you there."

Rose wondered what was up, but she would find out this evening, and put it to the side of her awareness and proceeded to begin to do reading for her next appointment with Irene, as she would be forwarding her initial responses to the work by Tuesday evening. She took a break about 4 in the afternoon to unpack and do some laundry, and at about 5 she was on her way to meet Angela to see what it was Angela wanted to speak to her about. As she walked across the wide swath of apartments, and into the business district and she arrived a little ahead of 6 p.m. and sat and surveyed the menu for a while before Angela's arrival. She asked the waiter to bring two glasses of wine; she thought a white wine was what Angela had ordered for them the last time they met here. The wine was placed on the table and she told the waiter to charge the meal to her card and handed it to him to cover the cost of this meal for both. Angela arrived within about ten minutes, and she thanked Rose for meeting her here, she knew it was inconvenient as she was sure Rose would be doing school work if she were not here. "Rose, I have made a decision to resign, my sister and I will be going to a retirement facility in what used to be Oregon, when we were in school, as her work site and this governmental unit qualify for this same facility. I have just had it, and I need to consider my own needs ahead of many of the things that have kept me here as long as I have. I know who will be taking my place, and she is a long term government employee, and you will not have to deal with her much, if at all. Your editorial skill is far beyond hers and she may even be utilizing your skill to ease her level of stress."

Rose was surprised, but she clearly understood Angela's decision. "This will be good for you, Angela, and I completely understand. You look so tired to me, and the stress must be making you feel so tired. I want you to do what is best for you, and this feels like to me that it is a good deal for you and for your sister as well." They toasted her decision to leave the rat race, and ordered a good meal for themselves, and Rose told her the price of the dinner was her gift to Angela, for all her support and help over the years. The waiter approached them to collect their dishes as they were finishing their meal, and offered the dessert menu, and they both selected a sweet end to the meal, and the long relationship. "I will have my last day in one week, my sister is going to go to select the apartment for us this week, and I will be going up on the train on Tuesday next week. This has been a hard process, but we looked at our balances, and the fixed costs of this particular setting, and it looks to us like we have enough to live out about twenty years plus, so we will not have money issues unless we both get very healthy and live too long. My sister is a very gregarious person, and she figured in taking a vacation trip each year, and if it looks like we are too healthy for our budget, we can cut back on vacation trips I suppose."

Rose was happy for her friend and supervisor, and wished her well in the next phase of her life. "I am glad you will have your sister with you, it seems to me to have someone with whom you can do things, and just have around to talk with is a wonderful gift." Angela agreed, and with the dinner and the dessert gone, and the sun almost setting, they hugged each other, and Rose was delivered her card, and they left each in their own direction. As Rose walked back home she was grateful for Angela's influence and help through the last now six years, and she hoped she would be able to really enjoy her last years out of this rat race of work with a truly compatible person.

She approached her apartment, and went in and began her reading again and outlining her responses to the questions she had been given to focus her attention with, and as she read the material and developed her outline of the material for her responses, she was struck by the thought of what it would mean for her to not have such an ally in a supervisorial position at work. What would that mean, and how would she deal with the consequences of Angela's resignation. She began to feel the loss of her boss, and friend, and decided to shower and try to sleep so she could have a very productive Sunday before going back to work.

Sunday arrived and her sleep had been sufficient to provide her with a real desire to work and make headway with her preparation for her session with Irene in a week. She read, and prepared a breakfast of some of the cheese and bread that Irene had sent home with her. She began her outline of this material and as she read and typed the material into her computer, she became aware of what had been the beginnings of the one child policy in the United States, and this part of the development of the movement had been spoken of in the environmental movement of the 2050's. The U.S. had since the late 1900's had a growing sense of what over population was doing to the environment, but it was not until the middle of the 21st century that a serious effort was undertaken by the Environmentalists to limit families in some realistic fashion. Some people decided that they would only adopt, in order to have a family, and it was encouraged at first to have only two natural children in the family and it had stimulated a huge battle between the fundamentalists and Catholic Churches who did not cotton to the idea of the use of methods of birth control which most people used to restrict pregnancy, and the Environmentalists, who saw large families as a drain on the resources of the earth. As the battle developed the Environmental movement gained a foot hold by actively measuring the impact on the Earth's resources and publishing scientifically sound data of the impact of each new person born and dependent upon the resources of the planet. The Catholic Church who still clung to the doctrine of natural reproductive freedom, stipulating that any artificial interruption in the process was a mortal sin, in league with the fundamentalists who simply desired to keep women in a one down position, and insisting that woman had to be available sexually for their husbands gratification were locked together in the fight with those who were amassing much scientific data on the impact on the Earth's resources of one child were locked in a battle royal over the issue. The very rich were not asleep during these very public battles, and ultimately when they had secured control over the weakened government made their move claiming that the protection of the planet was paramount, the churches be damned, and pushed the one child policy as soon as they had a secure enough hold on the members of the shrunken government, and the policy was promulgated. Religions as an established fact very soon lost the battle and all their adherents, mortal sin or not, were confounded by the law of the land. Many very committed persons left their homes and went to other places, Canada, and south into Mexico and Central America, and were admitted to these new countries on the grounds of moral need. After a while it had become an excepted demand of the Government that there was a one child policy and as soon as the one child had been successfully delivered, the man was scheduled for his vasectomy and it happened to everyone. On July 4, 2091 the Vasectomy requirement was signed by the figurehead president, and it became law. Her question at this point in her reading was why was it so important for the oligarchy to side with the Environmentalist, if they gave not a damn about the health of the environment. They polluted the environment; the valley around her city was filled by the green haze of the discharge of pollutants from generating electric power, that the quality of the water in the city was not as fresh as it had been even since she had moved here three years ago, and though most of the houses on the western side of the city had been evacuated because the water from the ocean was coming inland secondary to the melt of the ice at the poles which was almost gone, and some people were becoming sick from lung conditions and routinely wore masks when they walked outside. And for that matter there was no Environmental movement to speak of any more. And then she got it, there was no environmental movement because all the fields of study which contributed to global awareness had, when she was a junior in college, been kicked out of the university. She remembered the anger with which the students were driven back by the police on campus, they had been sprayed with noxious sprays which burned the skin, and one of her compatriots had been blinded by the spray for a time, and how he had to undergo surgery to regain the sight in one of his eyes. Had she known what she now knew she would have seen the futility in their actions, perhaps her parents knew of the futility of the protests, and that is the reason for encouraging her to back off from the demonstrations. But how was she to know if they did not just say the truth that they knew. Now she had it figured out. And she was clear that the social order was a mess and at least her hoped for life on campus would mean a partial escape and only partial. The air on campus was clear, at least now it was clear, no big factories in the area, and no electrical generation plants nearby, and she would hope none were established there for a long time.

She looked at the clock and it was almost 6 p.m. She showered and prepared some food for a light dinner, and then went to bed with the book she was into to finish it and write the rest of her summary outline after work on Monday. There were several books on her electronic reader that she would need to get into for her research paper, and she would check them out after preparing the summary for Irene's primary questions. She read in bed for several more hours and then turned out her light and fell into a deep sleep. She dreamed that she was in a one seated car that she had rented, and on the floor of the front seat was the box of ashes of her parents. She was driving up the coast highway toward the north, and she spotted a beach area where she could walk out to the surf to deposit the ashes in the ocean. She could hear in this moment her mother's words about how beautiful the ocean was how big it was, and she in her dream state parked the little vehicle and walked out into the ocean a little way so the ashes would be pulled away from the beach and flow into the exiting tide. She in her dream saw herself deposit the ashes and recite a short poem to her parents about drifting on the tide to where ever they wanted to go, and as she proceeded back to the car to return home, she saw the face of her Granny speaking to her about now she was free to live according to how she saw fit, and could let go of childhood now completely. Granny said to her "now you must make your own way and trust yourself first". She woke to the alarm, got dressed for work and began her next phase of work and study as an escape from the Government employment which she knew would do her in as it had Angela.

CHAPTER FOURTEEN

A HOME AT LAST

On the northwest corner of her little shelter she had rigged a little fire place. The hearth was a metal sheet, and she had found a metal tube to act as a chimney stack with bricks at the base. The stack was stabilized by the rebar she had rigged to hold it in place and it was long enough to extend higher than the roof so the smoke would catch the wind and be evacuated out of the shelter. It was helpful as it was becoming cold especially in the evenings. Her first fire was a great success with the hot smoke being evacuated from the fire quickly and rather efficiently. She was very proud of her creativity and the cold was intense and she knew she would need some kind of heat the closer the winter got. She made a small fire for herself, this night, and wrapped herself in her insulated blanket which was just enough to feel relaxed no longer fighting the cold. She had as yet to completely stabilize the roof, but she knew exactly how she would do it and in fact had begun to do the task. She would dig out of the middle of one of the boards so it could be flipped over and stabilized to the boards of the wall, by wrapping the top board to link with the wire which kept the boards one next to the others, and then she would nail the roof to that stabilized board, and given how the wind would be broken by the trees around the lake she felt it would hold very well. As she thought about her design a small smile crept across her face, and she knew it would serve her needs rather well.

She had noticed that birds were nesting in the trees by the lake, she had no idea what kind of birds they were, but she thought as she had taken time to be as efficient about food gathering as she had of late that she could take a day to get her electronic reader out and see if she could recharge the battery enough by leaving it in the sun light, she felt maybe it would work. She had packed it in the bottom of her rucksack wrapped in a couple of towels and she had not removed it now for over a year and a half at least. And the thought of not being able to read out here would have been devastating to her.

She had not had time in the city to allow her curiosity to be her librarian, and out here she had time to really allow herself the pleasure of reading and to satisfy her curiosity about so many things she was now face to face with she had never before ever thought about. She placed the reader in the sun to stimulate the battery, but she after a while found there was no function available as yet. She almost felt mournful with the thought that she would not have access to her library.

It should be stimulated by the light of the sun, she was sure that was the thing to do, and she noted she was truly anxious. In looking for a way to distract herself she decided to go down to the fruit trees on the north side of the mountain, and she would focus on gathering what fruit was still on the trees, and bring it up to dry it and have it available during the coldest part of the year. She walked away from the camp site she had established, almost knowing she needed to get away from her reader and let it charge or not, she just needed to get away from it and let it be. Walking over the top of the hill and down the edge she looked back only one time, which just worked to intensify her feelings about not having the one tool she really loved and longed for now with the possibility of not being able to access. She made herself move ahead, and by the time she got to the grove of trees, she had let go of her anxiety. She had a large and very empty rucksack, and she set about filling it with the available fruit, to enable her to survive the cold months. She left to return with a full sack, and there was a little more fruit available she thought it was worth another trip to get the whole harvest. She felt she needed to put her energy toward this and ignore the reader. She returned with her empty sack and filled it again. So with the second trip she walked back up the hill with a heavy haul and felt that this task was in fact more important than she felt that worrying about her reader really was.

As she approached the reader there was no light showing that would be there if in fact the battery was charged. She picked it up to bring it in doors to protect it, thinking a little more time to stimulate the battery was what she would try in the morning and so as to have given it enough time.

The wind was whipping across the top of the mountain, and she entered her shelter and started a fire for warmth which would help her relax, and be able to sleep.

In the morning she focused on catching a fish or two, she lost several of her personally fashioned hooks, and at one point wanted to quit, but talked herself into being more tolerant of the contest and finally caught one rather large fish. She decided she had her protein, at least for this day, and she cleaned her catch, and found her skillet, built a small fire, and watched the fish prepare its self for her supper. She watched until she saw it become soft and tender, and she devoured the catch and felt full for the first time in a couple of days. This night she would sleep soundly.

Now with three days in the sun, there was a flicker in the battery light, and she felt absolutely elated. Patience was indeed a virtue, and she knew with another day in the brightest sun shine her battery would be fully functional, and this day she worked hard on making as much progress finishing the stabilization of her little shelter as she could make. She ate some of her fruit for this day not taking the time to fish and she finished the tie down of the roof, and she felt a sense that she could allow for a day of reading in the morning.

The days got colder and colder and she was grateful for the shelter, and the little fireplace with all the warmth that it put forth into her environment. Now the weather being cold, she went ahead and began drying the fruit to save, she would place it in the front of the fire place, and turn it frequently. She read her reader, just for pleasure these days now that outdoors was harsh, and she felt sapped of her energy when she had to go out for water or other personal needs. She felt though' protected in her little shelter, and she knew that she had a future here, and it was alright that she could not describe the nature of that future. This was something new in herself she had always used knowing what was next as an element of her personal grounding, now over the months of her trip across so many miles she had lost that condition for her security, and it had been replaced by becoming more comfortable with the idea of trusting the process. She did not think about it much but it did add a new dimension to her character which made her a lot more durable in this environment.

And these cold months instilled in her the desirability of being durable. There were times she would oversleep her fire and she would awaken cold and she would find the need to stoke the flame to warm the environment so she could return to sleep, and even with the insulated blanket she would find that the cold was so intense as to make deep sleep, impossible.

She noted several spots where there were significant leaks holes which allowed a lot of cold into her shelter, and so she set about sealing these places with mud from the lake, it was sticky and adhered to the wood and when it dried it sealed the air leaks very effectively, and she noted about the time she had all the leaks sealed the weather began to lose its intensity, and she woke one day to find snowflakes coming down. In truth it felt not so bitter cold, rather it was chilly, and at the same time beautiful with snow caps on the tree branches, and flakes floating down through the air. The whole environment was white and beautiful. The air was crisp but not the bone chilling cold of the recent days, and she walked through the snow to the lake to bring water back to her shelter, and for the first time on this trip away from civilization, such as it was, that she would have loved a coffee, with just a touch of cream.

She had the forethought to have some wood inside that was dry and ready to be put into the fire, and she picked up some of her stash and moved it inside to dry it out, and she had some fruit for her breakfast, and she thought she would fish in the snow as soon as she could, perhaps when the snow had stopped. In the meantime she had her reading to occupy her time, and she read about the Plaines Indians how they managed their lives on these very territories and found like the wild dogs never moving where there was not running water. Yes she understood why that was their primary need. They seemed to understand in a very primary way about environmental protection, and protecting their resources. She had very little understanding of their spiritually as any serious support of religion had been left behind socially by the time she found herself being raised or as an adult, but it was interesting to her that they had a strong belief in an omnipotent god, a Great Spirit. As she read, she began to really understand how that spirituality sustained them and enabled them to face the hardships of their lives. She also understood their response to the army which they referred to as the blue jackets. For years they lived comparatively peaceful lives until the army came to either kill them all or haul them all to reservations in a land with which they had no familiarity with, and where they had to live what for them was a tremendous loss of dignity and hatred directed by many of their leaders toward the blue jackets and their generals.

As she read about the ways in which they were poorly treated, cheated, and abused by the violation of the treaties the government had agreed to and poorly supplied. They had been herded from their native lands like cattle; many had died on the trip into the most god forsaken lands that were thought to be of no real value. History would prove this wrong but it would be many generations until they got their due, in natural resources which put them in the position of finally getting their justice.

She thought it remarkable that their dispositions enabled them to generation upon generation wait for fairness to prevail. She had read about how many of the Indians of the Navajo Nation had joined in during the war with Japan, to play such an amazing role using their native language to outsmart the enemy with their communication in their native language. She wondered how they could participate to support the nation that had so violated their ancestors, but they did and it worked.

She read most of the day, and the snow fell all day and just as the sun set toward the west, the snow ceased, and it began to warm just a bit, and she went out to gather enough wood to make it well into the next day, and had more fruit for an evening meal, and settled into sleep, warm and dry, and contented with her reading.

CHAPTER FIFTEEN

PUBLICATION AND THE TIGHTROPE

This phase would be intense, as she had the regular load of three classes, but as well the task of writing an article which would be published in the History annals, available for public consumption. And if it was published she knew she would have to exercise care as her employers would for sure read what she was doing and they could cause trouble if there was anything that in any way was questionable or provocative in what she had to say, she had to be the essence of care if for no other reason to protect her continued education. She spent some time finishing her outline to prepare work from for Irene's assignment, and then prepare her response to Irene's questions. The rest of the week she would read about the issue of the one child policy in China's history. She began to address the questions Irene had forwarded to her electronically. She read one resource again, and as she was sure that she had incorporated the essence of the material and then began writing the material to be sent. As the evening went along, she typed the material out and when she reread what she had produced she added one element which filled in elements of the implications of the policy and after she felt she had fully responded she hit the key to send and it was done. It was Tuesday evening and she went to the material she had gathered for the special assignment. She read and read the evening away taking occasional notes, on the Chinese one child policy. She was clear at first that the roots of the policy, was about preventing a calamity. The ruling had to be established due to the fact that food production without interfering with the birth rate would have caused famine across the nation, which would have been a calamity which would have crippled the nation. This had to be avoided, and the program took on a draconian dimension with the approach of enforcement. Many in the hinterlands did not comply, due to the fact that many children had always been a benefit. Many hands to work in the fields had always been a sign of the stability of the family and their success. The success of the program in the cities was almost universal as there was much fear about parents being jailed and punished. Female children were left as foundlings as the value culturally of son's was higher, at first with the institution of the policy. And one of the secondary problems were few women were available for marriage with the super abundance of young men of marriageable age early on, outstripped the number of women. As time went on the attitude of potentially abandoning the girl infants lessened and the people moved off the Farms in the rural environments and though for the uneducated the degree of poverty remained high, famine was averted. After about 30 years there were some changes made to the policy, for example, two married persons who had no siblings were for a time were allowed to have two children legally which was culturally more like the population development of the period prior to the period of the early 1980's.

She read about the internal politics of maintaining the policy as against the efforts to go back to another version, balancing the worker/retiree ratio to two workers to one retired person which was thought to be the ideal, and over time it was maintained by careful manipulation of the persons who would qualify to have two children. For the ones who defied the prohibition there were riots and mass killings especially in the rural provinces, which had never fully accepted the governmental intrusions in their reproductive freedom. As she read about the history of the China policy, it had nothing to do with a ruling class that was simply acquisitive, rather it had to do with management of resources, maintaining a population which would be adequate to fulfill the needs of business, and commerce, and allowing for support for those in their later years who would need social support systems to allow for a dignified end of life care.

She had been since she returned from Campus reading some about the policy's history in this country. It had long been talked about that the worker class having too many children was tasking the employment base to provide for reasonable levels of employment. The more workers society generated the more the oligarchy was called on to provide appropriate levels of employment. Employment was dependent on particular job based skills, and educational advancement to fill particular job roles which ultimately would add to the wealth of the ruling class, and for some time it was felt that a one child policy would need to be established until a kind of population tipping point was reached. All those who could not sustain the educational preparation were put out of the general social order and left to make it without any supportive services, and so every city had their abandoned roving gangs of youth who attempted to one way or another sustain themselves and their associates and families by way of theft, or extortion, or whatever other methods they found at their disposal. The oligarchs found that the expulsion of the unemployable was a convenient safety valve, and had for a time put the one child restriction on hold. Someone in a government role had done a complex study about what would predict the need for such a policy to limit the birth rate of the worker class. The point of limiting the birth rate among the working class was to actively manage the class of persons who were most suited to sustain the organized businesses which provided the ongoing wealth to the oligarch's who called the social and political shots in the nation. As she read more and more of whatever she could get her eyes on, and there was not much written on the subject, as most had been censored out of the information stream, she did get ahold of a legal document which outlined in great detail the original one child policy. She found to her surprise that the one child policy in its legislative form only applied to one group. The abandoned were not identified in the document, nor were the wealthy who called the shots for everyone, but only the working class, who could be controlled through being fired and put into the abandoned class simply by way of loss of income, and thereby loss of middle class identity. It was cleaver in its design, since most everything now was owned by the ruling class, with a few exceptions, if you lost your job, you lost your housing, and you lost your access to what you had earned, and you lost, with being abandoned by your former employer what few choices you could exercise. The only exceptions were people who had within their family's control agricultural lands to which their families had title, and had kept even with the now ' much higher tax base that was levied for the purpose of driving them off their family farms, which would be bought up by the oligarchs at tax sales which were of course rigged by the county agents to sell to them at a song.

All of a sudden she saw the meaning of what Irene had told her about with her brother, who had dared to violate the one child policy and who ran the family farm in what had been Iowa in the Midwest. Since the tax base had risen over the years both she and her sister who worked in a state government job in the east, had had the taxes taken out of their earnings balance especially at times the Farm could not sustain the tax base, especially when the crop harvest would not capture the top dollar in the markets. Irene had said that they both would return to the family home upon retirement, and they both felt it was their responsibility to sustain that place and keep it in the family free and clear of any debt.

Rose began to boil at the acquisitive nature of the oligarchy. And the words which came out of her mouth were "the bastards are like a cancer that just will not stop taking everything for themselves." She felt so angry she had to stop her work for a while and she opted to take a walk to cool down her anger. Returning to her home she saw it was close to mid night, so she showered and retired to sleep a few hours prior to returning to work. She tossed and could not find a comfortable place in her bed to fall asleep and so she turned on the light to read a book from her mother's collection and at least relax.

She did achieve sleep and woke to her alarm at 6:30 on about three and a half hours she would have to stay especially focused for her work for this day.

Once in the work environment she settled down to check her work for the day and began to get a handle on the material she would focus on for the next ten hours or so. She reviewed her material and began making outlines which would help her compose coherent documents. At about ten in the morning she saw a note for her to report to the supervisor's office come up on her screen. She got out of her chair, and moved to the door. The replacement for Angela, who by now was on her way up the coast to her new home, was in her first full day in her new position, she must want to meet her employees today, Rose thought, and she exited the work room, and moved down to the supervisors office. She was greeted by a woman who introduced herself by saying "Hello, I am your new supervisor!" No name, but standing in front of her desk was a name plaque, Sarah Wilson. Rose waited to be seated until the woman sat and requested that Rose be seated. She had Rose's personnel file in her hands, and she opened it to look at the contents and then said "well some people think you are a very skilled writer, is that what you think? Suddenly Rose was fighting the almost overwhelming need to reach over the desk and slap her snotty face, but she resisted the urge, and replied that she had no control over what people write about her in her personnel file, and dropped the urge to do her violence.

Then there were several more questions with several more aggressive comments, and she was informed that she knew that she was in school working on an advanced degree in something other than English Composition, and as a result her work would be subject to close scrutiny. This clearly was coming from somewhere other than this picky little woman, and it became clear in this moment that there was someone up stairs who was irritated with the fact that she had chosen to use her vacation time to return to school. Angela must have had a number of fights in her behalf. Suddenly she understood the shield Angela had been for her. And this little twerp of a woman was now the blunt instrument that they intended to use on her. She explained to the woman that she had always loved history and she was making herself happy with the vacation time going to good use for the time being. "You do know that raises are based on your production here and have nothing to do with study in another field, don't you? Rose responded in the affirmative, and with that she was excused. She returned to her work station, and was glad to exit the office leaving that small little person behind. She thought to herself she should be very careful in this educational venture, and this interaction was just one more reason to be careful in the publication of her study.

Upon returning home she got on the communicator, and called Irene to inform her of the interaction with the new supervisor, and get a reading on her solution which was to keep a low profile and stay out of the woman's way. Irene was quick to answer the communicator, and there her face was on Rose's screen. She shared the story, and Irene was a little shocked by the woman's attack on something that really was none of her business. "It seems to me how you choose to use vacation time is really not something they should get involved in Rose, why do you think she decided to make it an issue?" "I think that it is yanking someone's chain, in an authority position, upstairs and she is carrying his or hers water for them". "I want to talk with our President about the problem and see if he has any solution for us to consider." "That would be okay with me if you share this with Dr. Wellstone. You have told me he has some influence with people in Government and if he has any advice I would be willing to do what he thinks best". "Good, then I will speak with him in the morning and get back to you on Thursday evening". "You know, Irene, don't get back to me tomorrow evening as we are scheduled for Sunday for a conference we can speak about it then" "Are you sure, Rose?" "Yes" "Okay, talk to you on Sunday".

She opened her book that had contained limited history of the one child policy here, and as she read she became more and more aware of the fact that if the wealthy business owners could really limit the workers they could not only keep them very dependent, but as well harvest more and more of the profits for themselves. Also as she read the document of the one child policy it was clear that two groups were unaffected, the disenfranchised and the oligarchy. They were able to have two or ten children as there was one simple tax paid at the time of birth, which was to them a simple fee and of no consequence, in a feeble attempt at fairness, and there was no way to water out of a rock so whatever the penalty to the poverty class was moot. Further she wondered if the disenfranchised even knew they had a debt for each child they produced, she doubted it.

She did more reading and the more she read she understood that she would have to search to get more history, about the origins of this policy as there was a real paucity of data available, who wrote it or who had lobbied for its passage, there was little or nothing written about how it evolved into law. She went on the internet to determine if she could locate in that vast data base any information about the evolution of the idea over time, and found only two articles and one had been blacked out and was unavailable. She read the other and found nothing in it that she had not found in other sources. She got once again on the communicator, and called the University Library. She spoke with the young man who had been very helpful to her in her two trips back and after they chatted a moment he inquired of her how he could be helpful. "Brad, I need information about the one child policy which was made Law in the late years of the last century." "Yes I am familiar with some of the data, but the government stopped by and took all our reference material about that subject, and I presume that they burned it". "Why did they remove it from you, do you know?" "Of course I know, they do not appreciate having their dirty laundry out in the public!" "Somehow I thought you all might have been exempted, silly Me." she replied. "I have a good reason to know a lot about it, as I am a second child. My folks have paid fines, and my father was removed from his work, briefly as a punishment, and my mother luckily had an opportunity to work to keep the family afloat while the government had its way with my father. They are retired now but I send them money from my account as does my brother, so they don't run short in retirement. You know the story Rose, Irene mentioned last year that your folks were retired, so I know you know what I mean. Those bastards cost my parents their peace of mind, and when they came through and took all the reference materials about the policy I flipped out, and had to leave for a day as my boss thought I was going to deck the two bastards they sent."

"Brad I need to let you know that my folks are both dead, their solution to the whole dilemma by way of suicide, at first it was a shock, but I really get it now, it was their way of saying to the government that they could all go screw themselves. And any way they were joined at the hip, and I do not think if my mother had died first it would not have taken him a second to do himself in just so he would not have had to face one morning without her." Brad expressed his concern for her process of getting past the loss, and she told him she was doing well. "So Rose why are you asking for the references for the one child policy, what are you up to?" "I am writing a paper comparing and contrasting the one child policy in China and us. I just need to make sure that I am absolutely accurate in the paper, and I need all the references I can get my hands on. Do you know any libraries they have left alone?" "Actually as I think about the issue, Dr. Wellstone had made some copies of the material from another library in the east, and I will need to get Dr. Wellstone's okay to let you see the stuff, I am sure you can get into the special collection stuff, I had forgotten that we did that, it has not been looked at since it arrived. Let me call him and I will get back to you".

She re-engaged with her reading, and waited for Brad to call her back, but no call came for some time and she assumed he could not find Dr. Wellstone. It was getting late and so she went to the shower, and got ready for sleep, and went to sleep. Thursday and Friday passed and Saturday morning before work her communicator sounded and she answered. It was Brad," I have put together a packet which will be on your computer within the hour. I must share with you that Dr. Wellstone requested that you not make copies and then delete the material when you are finished, he wants you to know the material but not cite it in any way directly in the final work. It, I think illegal for us to have it, and since this paper will be a publication he just wants to keep you out of trouble". "I understand, Thanks Brad."

She went to work and there was a notice on her computer, that the peewee supervisor wanted her to be in her office at 10 a.m. She reported at 10 a.m. and was surprised by the topic. There was another woman standing in the office with the peewee supervisor, and clearly she was compliant toward this woman, and it was the strange woman who conducted the meeting. "Hi Rose, My name is Lucy, and I am an employment supervisor here in this building of the governmental complex, and I have been asked by Dr. Wellstone to be your ombudsman relative to your advanced degree work, I will be available to you to help with any conflicts which come up for you here, Dr. Wellstone is a longtime friend of mine, and he has made this request of my boss who has approved this to be a part of my responsibilities. First I want to be informed about any flack you are taking because of this out of work activity, we consider if it is done on your own time, it is perfectly okay,(and rose noted that she glanced at the supervisor) for you to use your own resources any way you want, and as well I would love to read your work I am interested in history as you are, and will be available to you in case there are issues here that need to be taken care of. Rose shook her hand and thanked her for the support, and she noticed that the supervisor was beyond subdued by this meeting. Lucy handed her a business card, and encouraged her to call any time she thought that she needed some support for her educational endeavors.

Rose left the meeting knowing that her call to get some help from the President of the University was heard and responded to by the appointment of a person who would protect and defend inside the government and she felt that would help. At least it was evidence that someone listened to Dr. Wellstone, and she appreciated the gesture. She also smiled as she pondered the crestfallen look on her supervisors face. She could imagine that she had experienced a talking too about her attitude toward employees who wanted to improve themselves.

Rose understood what the absence of hope would do to the human soul. And she saw it in the faces of her colleagues, although everyone professed they were happy to be employed and would do about anything to remain so, they all wore the mask of adjustment, to cover the depressive lack of feeling, and blunting that came without hope. Somehow she had with the support from Dr. Wellstone and now Lucy she could walk through anything because she had it now if she did not have it before. She had hope. It was hard for her to trust, but for a moment she knew she had felt it. Walking back away from the meeting she was sure she felt it. As she passed the activity of the rest of the day she hardly felt the normal sense of boredom of the typical day, and as she walked home she hardly felt that she had done a full day's work. She closed her door behind herself and went immediately to the material that Brad had forwarded to her, and she read the material rapidly and took notes especially noting the individuals who had seemed to participate in moving the legislation of family size limitation, as it was known pre passage. There had been many incarnations, it was proposed that two children would be an initial limit, in order to ease the population into the idea that this could be a kind of appropriate intrusion into their lives, and the argument that government could do whatever it deemed appropriate, and easing the population into the idea was not necessary. "They will be coerced into whatever it is we demand" the majority responded. It clearly identified those persons in the various coalitions, and she noted that the members who came directly into the government body from the oligarchy were the most rigid in the process. She read the transcripts of the deliberations and was shocked that they could legitimate pay levels. The pay levels could be trimmed by the business owners the day this policy went into effect simply because it would cost less to raise one child over many. What that really meant was more profit for the business owners, and there were even several suggestions that with smaller families they would be open to the idea of increasing prices even in the light of reduced salaries. There was so much talk about how they could, as business owners, make a killing on this legislation that they failed to vote for over a year. As she finished reading the transcripts she really got why they had come around to destroy the documents. She would have to find corroboration for anything in these notes and cite those sources, but it gave her cues about what to look for. So she had a previously Communist government who instituted a policy to make illegal a second child, to protect their society from starvation, and another presumably free democracy did it to protect the wealthiest in their social order. Wonderful!

She had to get all this out of her awareness, and it was almost mid night, and a walk would be a foolish idea, so she headed to the shower, turned it on as hot as she could stand it, and tried to relax, and prepare to sleep.

Her dreams were laced with fantasy about taking over one of the centers of power and changing laws and punishing the really wealthy. It all related to the drivel she had spent her evening reading. And as she woke, she was tired and felt as though she had not slept at all. She walked to the commissary and picked up some breakfast. She sat in the morning sun, ate her food and then returned to her home to begin her day. Irene would be calling at midday, and she felt that she was ready for the content of the consultation, so she returned to her data development for her publication assignment. She began to read several of the additional resources she had picked up in the library, and was surprised to find some corroboration of the philosophical split in the deciding group of appointed legislators. She however did not find any corroboration of either the delay, or the issues surrounding the fight. She heard the buzz of the communicator, looked at the clock and saw it must be Irene as it was about 1 p.m. She answered and after some chatting, they proceeded to discuss her assignment and written response. Irene was very complimentary about her capacity to synthesize information, and then they talked about her work on the publication.

Rose spoke about the help she had received from Brad in the Library, and Dr. Wellstone, and Irene was surprised Dr. Wellstone had retrieved the 'stolen' materials. "As you get to know him, Rose you will be amazed at how committed he is to learning and making every effort to help students who show promise." "But I have never met him and I am surprised he made these materials available and he trusted me with some of the most sensitive stuff in the whole library system." "Trust me he knows who you are and what a good potential you have. In fact, I should tell you we meet monthly just to focus on off campus students who demonstrate excellence in their work."

"Oh I had no idea he even knew my name", she responded, "I am shocked." "Several of our faculty, have joined the faculty after off campus completion program."

"So there is hope for me to be able to apply after I complete the Ph.D.?" "For you My Dear, it is a given that you will be offered a post with us."

If she had been hopeful after her meeting with Lucy, she was on a cloud now, and as they ended the conversation after her two hours she now felt that she really needed a walk just to get grounded so she would not waist the whole rest of this day.

She walked and walked and she could not suppress the grin and feelings of buoyancy she felt for her own future.

CHAPTER SIXTEEN

COMPANIONS ON THE HORIZON

It had been bitter cold for several weeks and she had needed to walk each day to accumulate fire wood to keep her warm, but she could see it was changing. The nesting birds were still occupying their nests up in the densest parts of the trees, and she could in the nights hear them making chirping and clucking noises to each other, and it made her decision to stay less lonely. She walked down the north side of her mountain home to collect fire wood and she saw dust in the distance. It was different from the occasional vehicle passing across the plain down below. It was just the suggestion of a trail of dust being blown up from the movement of what she could not say. As she passed the grove of trees she noted that the blossoms on the trees were abundant and she knew next year there would be a great harvest. It was like seeing the potential harvest in the form of little buds which would turn into fruit, which she would have available to sustain herself for yet another year.

She looked into the distance and she saw fresh dust rising into the morning air, and the tiny clouds of dust now became a focus of her curiosity. The wild dogs would run occasionally but they would not throw the dust up that she was seeing, and this was a puzzle. Whatever was doing this she estimated it had to be maybe ten miles or more away? She had collected lots of wood which was her task this morning, downed wood from trees and some dried out pieces of discarded wood which she would occasionally find. She had a good load and she returned to head down the west side of the mountain to see what wood was available down there so she would have a good supply. She needed dry wood, and there was in reality an abundance of this resource in the environment. She had started piling it on the roof of her shelter, it kept it dry and her access was almost instantly available, all she needed was to open the door which was just a hanging cloth a large towel, on the south side of the shelter, and it was instantly available to stoke her flames.

She headed down the west side of the hill and from where she walked she could as well see the cloud of dirt out on the plain to the north. Now she was really curious, and she dropped off the wood and headed down the north side of the mountain, to be in a place to see when the dust makers came into view. The sunshine was warm today, and she thought she would be back before she needed to stoke her own little flames. She could from where she was see the little trail of smoke rise from her fireplace. With the sun out today, she enjoyed the warmth of the sun on the environment. And it made her hope for the spring to come rapidly so she could get back into the water of the lake and really feel clean again. She found a place where there were some of those giant boulders and so she climbed up on top of one in order to see into the distance and now she could see large brown animals heading her way at a gallop; they were horses, she remembered as a child seeing the Plaines Indians mounted on these beautiful animals. As a child she wondered what it felt like to be mounted on these beautiful animals, which would carry you on their strong backs where ever you needed or wanted to go. And they were headed toward her. A kind of excitement filled her, she could not imagine that she would ever see one and here they were four or five of them she could not be sure exactly how many but it was a small herd, and perhaps they knew they could find water here, and they were headed toward her. As the sun set she could see that they were bedding down at the base of the mountain, in a grassy area and she headed for her shelter to grab some of the drying fruit for her evening meal, and sleep, and to return in the morning.

She had a few sparks left in her fire place and so she added some kindling to the coals which caught quickly and she put some of the more substantial pieces of wood on the flames and she ate and tried to sleep but her excitement about the horses made that difficult to accomplish and she was up as soon as the sun was up. As she walked down the hill, and she could see the little herd walking slowly, grazing as they came up the hill. And when she found a place to sit and wait for them to come up toward the top where she suspected they knew there was a source of water. They walked slowly toward the mountain's crest, not in a particular hurry as she had been, and she watched them graze and make a little headway at a time. They were now no more than half way up the side of the mountain, and she could see the individual qualities of each of the small herd, and the stallion who was behind the group and nudging the three mares and it looked like two youngsters in his little herd. They finally walked right past her, paying little or no attention to her, rather he pushed them on to the top and they rather quickly went to the lake and began a long process of drinking in the precious water. He waited for the herd to get their fill and then one of the mares stood watch over the group as he drank. She decided to slowly walk toward the group. She could not keep her eyes off the group, but tried to not to be so very direct in her gaze. She slowly moved up the hill, and she finally stopped near the crest, and the stallion moved toward her in a surprisingly direct fashion, and he stood looking directly at her and then he moved slowly to make contact, and he approached her and she spontaneously reached out to touch his forelock. She made contact and he did not move allowing her touch for she was not sure how long and then he backed away from her contact and one of the mares then approached her. She reached out to touch the mare, and she too was calm and allowed her touch. They seemed to move away then to the opposite side of the lake and they bedded down to stay here and the two youngsters drank from the lake and then lay down on the grass on the other side of the lake. She could not take her eyes off the little herd; she had really loved the birds coming in to stay for however long they needed, but the horses; that was so exciting to her; it was almost like having company when she had none other than the distant companionship of the wild dogs. She had never thought of herself as particularly social, as a kid she had had some friends, and since college she had never worried about maintaining friends especially since Jeff's death, and she knew people but had never felt a dependency on others. The trek was not hard in its isolation. But she had to admit the presence of this small herd was a real gift to her, and she was engaged in what they were doing, and how they seemed to communicate with each other. The stallion was clearly in charge and the mares kept him in view the two young ones were bonded to and watched their mothers.

She grabbed her stick for fishing, and thought she could try for a fish and keep her eye on the herd. She secretly hoped they would stay, but did not know how to help with that so she just watched them. She had no luck with the fish, but it was like she really did not care, she could try again in the morning. And she just watched. As the sun set, she noticed that the horses had bedded down on the far side of the lake, and she hoped they would have remained in the morning, and so she too bedded down. This night she fell into a deep sleep, she had not slept well in a couple of nights and it caught up to her and she could let go of her excitement this night knowing from her observation they would sleep here in the glen and they would still be there in the morning before heading out on their trek. But as they had now for two days, their needs were met just fine here and they stayed here night after night they would bed down on the other side of the lake and in the morning one or another would approach when she awoke in the morning, and she began to think of them as individuals. She began to call the stallion Handsome, and he would approach her perhaps by accident when she would call his name. He would always come as she called first thing in the morning, and as the day would pass and as she would call the three mares, named after friends in school, she thought as she repeated their names Abbey, Willa, and Frankie, that they would hear that and respond, and the two youngsters little boy and little girl. The stallion began a process of pushing the young male out of the herd. She guessed that he was about to become an adult and therefore a challenge to his dominance and the young male began to move into her space, and he would bed down next to her shelter at night. Handsome would make a point of pushing him closer to her each day; it was as if this was the point of being here. The main group was moving down the eastern edge of the mountain and little boy was left with his access to the lake on her side and his new sleeping area next to her shelter. She had the feeling that he was kind of bonding with her and she made a special attempt to make contact with him several times during the day. If she had to go get wood he would follow behind her and if she had to sit by the lake he would stay close to her and it was clear the presence of the herd was that she got a buddy out of the deal, and Handsome got rid of the competition that was a potential of Little boy's presence in the old herd. Little boy was her loyal buddy, and he seemed to understand why he had to leave. And he did the best with the situation as it was presented, and he did not have to face a life alone, he had her and it was kind of obvious that he was fine with that.

As the weather warmed the fish were more available and she had found in the process of roving the mountain that down near where the herd had established itself there were a lot of rabbits who lived in holes around some of the big boulders on the edge of the mountain where the grass was plentiful and she had jumped several of them big ones, and had even had enough meat, from her haul, made jerky over the flame and so she had a backup and the dry fruit, and her fish. Now that it was warm again, the fish were plentiful and once again interested in snagging a bug or two for their personal enjoyment. She would occasionally get into the lake to kind of bathe, and little boy would on occasion go into the lake and get thoroughly wet and come out and shake himself until he was almost dry. She thought he was imitating her when she would go for a swim, and she was in the lake one afternoon and he followed her right into the lake and came in with abandon. She was actually swimming at that moment and had no footing and he jumped into the lake and floating toward her she tried to stay clear of his thrust, and with forward momentum she wound up straddling his back. He was as surprised as she was, and he headed for the land and got out of the lake with her still mounted on his back. He stood still to let her dismount, and then as she did he very quietly walked to a sunny spot and he lay down to dry. She had her first experience riding on a horse, quite by accident, and she knew somehow, it would not be the last. She walked over to where the little colt had lay down, and she stretched out next to him to relax in the sun, and they seemed to understand that this was a shift in their relationship and she knew it.

She spent a lot of her days, mornings fishing for dinner, and reading in the sunshine in the afternoons. She would occasionally walk down to the herd and try to trap a rabbit. There were wood gathering trips, and he went with her on all but the trapping of the rabbits he would walk part of the way and be there when she would return, but Handsome had somehow communicated to him he was out of the herd and he should not approach too close. She was impressed by his behavior, and knew that he really got it.

She attempted several times to mount him and one of the times she entirely missed his back. He stood by her as she picked herself up, as if to say go ahead and try again. She did and was mounted and he walked back up to the shelter and stopped to allow her to dismount.

This year food had been good, and between the fish, and the rabbits she was storing rabbit jerky for the winter, and the cold to set in once again. She also had a good supply of wood and had returned to the burned out places down in the flatlands and made a sled to drag her wood back up to the mountain. She had also found a shower curtain in the burned out place to the north, and she used it to put under her wood pile to protect it from moisture in the ground. She had amassed quite a large pile and knew it would more than cover when the weather got cold. She wondered if she needed to build something to keep the little colt warm in the cold, but she did not know how exactly how she would construct such a shelter. And then as she thought about it he seemed to be okay and it was not really cold as yet. So she dismissed the problem.

The fruit was ripe on the trees down the hill and she harvested at least once a week, for her needs, and she hoped that the weather would not be as harsh as the last winter. But whatever came she was better prepared for the cold this year, and so she felt she could handle it now. She wondered if there were some way to preserve the fish, but had not a clue about how to do that so she let go of that idea.

She had last year gone without much in the way of protein in the coldest part of the year, and so she made more trips down the eastern edge of the mountain and was diligent about making a real stash of jerky out of the rabbits she caught. She had noticed a truck, a big one driving across the valley but it was far enough away so it caused her no anxiety, she thought it looked like it had a cargo of some kind she could not make out what it might have been and it was heading toward the east, the cargo she thought that it was covered by a tarp, or something. She thought she had maybe seen it before, but she was not sure. It did not cause her any distress as had some early in her time on the mountain, and she felt established here and if need be she did have her gun on the shelf of her little shelter and she had no problem at least brandishing it to establish her safety here, and she would if need be, get it and demonstrate her dominance.

The big truck returned after about a week. And the driver seemed to be establishing a camp site on the western side of the mountain, she walked down to a spot where she could protect her presence and she watched him set up a tent and unload things out of the cab of the big truck. There was a cold box presuming the box was holding food stuffs and there was a lantern, and a sleeping bag, and something like a backpack, and a suitcase probably containing clothing. And a tool box a bucket and a canvas bag which held who knew what. He carried everything out of the cab of the big truck and then mounted the truck the big one, took off the covering of the load on the back of the big truck pulled down the covering and put it into the cab.

What was under the tarp was another vehicle, like a small truck or a jeep kind of vehicle. He tried to start the smaller vehicle, and it would not turn on. He opened the back of the small vehicle and left it open so it was in the direct sun light, she knew he was charging a battery in the smaller vehicle, he dismounted the back of the big truck, and left it to charge. He built a small fire, and heated some food in a skillet, ate, and as the afternoon passed he sat in a camp chair and read his electronic reader. There was some kind of lettering on the big truck, but she could not read what it said. And since he looked like he was just camping for a while she walked back up the hill with the pony just behind her. She read for a while and ate some fruit and as the sun set and she went to sleep as the pony settled into his place just to the east side of her shelter.

Early in the morning she heard something like a whirring kind of sound and she got up and walked down to a place where she could see below, and she saw the camper backing the small vehicle off the back of the larger truck which had a ramp off the back of the flat bed and as the small vehicle backed off the bigger truck she watched him drive away in the smaller vehicle toward the east. She walked down to the camp and looked inside the tent, and it was very neat and clean, she noticed that he had put all of his stuff into his tent, and the environment was well tended. She walked over to the large truck and she was amazed, San Francisco City Water Company was painted on the side of the truck and she was absolutely floored they had for some time lived in the same city, and yet here they both were on this same place apparently accidentally, but already something very big in common. She at first got a feeling in her gut, anger and confusion, apparently him not doing what he was paid to do, was the cause in the final analysis of her long and arduous escape from the foul tasting water and, oh yes, the filth. She almost stomped back up the side of the mountain. And she was in touch with an anger that she felt rising from her gut, and in her mind he had become a cause of her distress and the target of her peak.

Yes indeed she was in a rage by the time she made it to the top.

CHAPTER SEVENTEEN

SOON TO BE PUBLISHED

Rose was finished with her paper, and she walked it to the post office to put it into the mail to the address she had been given. It went to an office on campus which managed the first phase of any published material which was produced and it always went in printed form to this publication office. She was happy with the material, and it had become much longer that she originally thought it would be. She could have kept it terribly focused but opted to include what she could about the historical background which she felt added interesting depth in her presentation. She explored how it was in China, how they made the food availability concerns and how accurate those estimates had been and she understood that the oligarchs knew well beyond the time the legislation was signed that they would see their wealth grow in very specific terms. Year by year they could and did see their incomes grow from the legislation years before it was enacted.

She remembered that her Granny always when she still worked received a check every two weeks and she took it to the bank depositing it into her own account and she would carry cash to purchase groceries, or a new book or some clothes, she felt credit cards were a pain in the ass, as she put it, and a problem for people who would run big balances. She on the other hand would always pay for a service that cash purchases protected people from those, what she called hidden costs. When she saw in her retirement that pay was withheld and the card payment from the account was instituted she cautioned Mom and Dad to check the purchases and make sure that there was no charge was levied against their account as it had been heralded as a way to cut banking costs. Granny did not trust the oligarchy, she thought they were in it for themselves and would make a buck, as she would say, any way they could. And she was right. Her Dad soon saw, that each month there was always a dollar difference from his accounting and his balance. Granny was right.

She walked into the Post Office and asked how much this would cost to mail, and the fellow behind the counter weighed it and took her card to pay for the postage, a charge for insurance that it should not get lost, and she took her card back and walked away. It was gone, and she would not hear anything for several weeks. She wanted to hear that it was wonderful but she decided to try to put it away and not think about it and she discovered that alone was a gargantuan task.

She needed to attend to her other tasks for school as she was due back on Campus in two months and she was coming down to the time she would devote herself to studying for the exams at this point in time, and she had really done little of her normal review of material. She had some more specific assignments to do as well and she would have to get a move on it to tie everything together neatly so she felt ready for her two days of exams. She walked into her home, and began to read. She had this Sunday without a contact from school so she knew she would not be disturbed and she felt a little hungry so she ate a sandwich and sat at her table with her book and her food and poured into the reading as if she was swimming in the deep lake of knowledge.

Rose was diligent and she read until late in the evening and had reached the end of one of her text books and began another without being really aware that it was approaching her normal bed time.

She was so engaged and was amazed that she had spent every waking hour since she had returned from the Post Office, and it was now almost mid night. She put a marker in the book and headed for the shower, and to bed.

The week went well and she had a contact with the administration about scheduled vacation time to arrange for specific dates for her next trip to school. She kept a schedule in her purse and as soon as she had the vacation time she would apply for the time off, and even wait a while for the confirmation to come through so she would be clear she did in fact have the free time to go south to school.

Wednesday she walked into her home, and the buzzer on the communicator let her know that she had a call through the day. It was Irene, and she let her know that her publication had in fact been delivered and she assured her it looked very good. She asked her to call her at home any time after 6 p.m. Rose returned the call and Irene had a friend who worked in the publications department and her friend had done a quick read and told her it was great quality and beyond fascinating. Rose knew she had lucked out with Irene's friend being the one to receive the article. Irene said she knew she would be interested in the feedback, and she had given the heads up to her friend to pick through the mail and try to find her submission.

She thanked Irene, for understanding that the feedback was so important and it really gave her a boost for the work week. She had pages and pages of notes and had developed almost forty pages in the final draft, Irene retorted that most submissions for this task are much less detailed, but she knew that she would be complete in her presentation. They agreed that she was due on campus soon and Irene was glad to know that she had begun the application for vacation time. They talked for a while and then disconnected the communication and Rose made a sandwich and she began her nightly study session.

She met with Lucy during her lunch on Monday, and she assured Lucy that she had received no hassle from her supervisor, and she had applied for vacation time but as yet had not received any confirmation from the people who did the schedules. Lucy said to give her a heads up when she got the confirmation, there is no reason this is not a 24 hour turnaround.

Lucy had the same attitude about the governmental laziness that Rose had, and Rose mused about how she had gotten the status in this place without blowing her lid about the built in inefficiency in the ways it worked. Must be a lot of patience, she thought. Rose returned to her work station and quickly she saw the flag come up to report to the supervisor's office, and she got up and walked down the hall, and knocked on the door. She waited a moment and then heard her supervisor call her into the office and she closed the door and sat. "I just wanted to complement you on your work, and let you know that your vacation request just came through." "Oh" Rose responded, "did they confirm the dates?" she asked and the woman replied in the affirmative, and Rose thanked her and she started to stand in order to return to her work station and the supervisor asked her to sit she had a question. Rose started to stiffen but she sat once again and waited. "I saw you speaking with Lucy Williams in the lunch room, and wondered what problem you were communicating to her, perhaps I could help?" Rose thought for a moment, her natural response was to deny that there was an issue, because that was in fact the truth, but there was an issue that she had with this woman and thought she would play it safe and just say that Lucy saw her and approached her to inquire what had been happening. She responded" Lucy saw me and inquired how I was doing." "Is that all?" "Yes", "Now may I return I have a lot to get done before the end of the day?" "Yes, yes, that is all." And Rose thanked her again and got up and walked back to the workroom. She sat down, and resumed her work with little thought about the excessive thoughtfulness she had just experienced. Lucy must have really gotten on her when she met with her the day she assigned herself as my ombudsman.

When she got home she had a communication on her screen from Lucy and she returned the call at her home communicator, and Lucy's face appeared on Rose's screen, and when Lucy saw her face she began to laugh. "I understand that you had a call from your supervisor today after our meeting today, what was the issue, was it that your vacation had been approved?" "Yes, I just want to know how long had they sat on that information? Do you know?" "As a matter of fact she has known for a week. It is 24 hour turn around on that, I am always informed the next day, and I could not understand how it took so long for you. The problem is that woman, what is her problem?" "Lucy she is on a power trip." "Well that makes sense, because her promotion was made by someone who has been her mentor, she had no qualifications to speak of for the job she must spend her time polishing her name plate, or something."

They chatted a while, and Lucy mentioned that she had received today her publication and" I was just reading it. Boy a great topic and I see you were sensitive to not getting into what could look like bias."

"Yes I was instructed by the Library to stay away from controversy!" "Well it reads very objectively, you did a great job, but knowing you I know you know the dirt in the process as well." "A little of it" she replied. "Well I know you have worked to do so I will let you go, thanks for returning my call."

She signed off, and made herself a sandwich and began her study. She felt that she was heading for the finish line but she wanted to review each night one of the courses until she went to the testing sessions. She read her question responses over which had been forwarded for her weekly contacts with her instructors, and it was like she had really mastered the material. But she had always worked right up to the deadline so she thought that there was no real reason to let go of a method that worked.

Another call came in, it was from Irene. She saw Irene's face on the communicator, and she was surprised as this additional communication was unpredictable to her. She asked if everything was okay, and Irene assured everything was good. I just finished reading your work, and I wanted to call and compliment you on your sensitivity of the material, you did a wonderful job, and this will be a great publication. Dr. Wellstone read it this afternoon and then forwarded his copy to me to look over. He thought it was a skillful presentation, and I agree, this is one of the most skillfully done works on a controversial topic, and you nailed all the process of its development and you did it so objectively. I just wanted you to know it is an A+ level job.

Rose thanked her for the feedback. "We are planning for the presentation of the article for several other of the faculty who have expressed an interest, and I want you to know that we will meet at the Faculty Club in one of the meeting rooms, and ask that you review your work with the faculty that are interested in hearing about the research, so try to prepare for this. It is a response to interest from faculty members and it will be very informal, and give some people the opportunity to question you about what you have learned with this project". Do not get anxious about this it is really a compliment.

Rose thought about what Irene had said, and then replied she would try to relax and try not to over react to what was meant as a compliment, but it did feel like there was extra pressure. She was assured that everything would be fine. "You have nothing to worry about."

She called and made her reservations for the train, and had shared her date of arrival with Irene before they ended their communication. She had a week and a half before she went to school, and so she thought that she would read for pleasure this night and she would give up the study time to try to relax.

The time went by rapidly before she left for school, and she reviewed the article for the presentation. And Sunday arrived and she boarded the train to go to school. She was now of a different mind about the presentation, and felt the compliment, that it indeed was a compliment and that Irene had been telling her the truth.

Irene and Jake were there to greet her upon her arrival and they got coffee to chat before she went to her dorm. She picked up her activity schedule, and went to bed early to prepare for her testing sessions.

Everything went smoothly and her test results could not have been better. She had her post testing conference with Irene, and rather than reviewing her exams, which had been perfect, they discussed her preparation for the Doctoral level of study, "I do not expect that doctoral work will present any difficulty to you, however there are some elements that may tempt you to choose independent work and publications activities, and I wanted to let you know you have some options to be thinking about elements of the number of options which will be available. I think there are some elements that may be problematic relative to your work within the Government; I want you to be careful. You need to know that you are the only one of my graduate students I cook dinner for and I decided to do that because I had a sense that you would never divulge my library, or anything personal to anyone else. And you haven't, and I encourage you to be cautious in the process. The government that we live with as you well know is devious, and you have to be cautious.

Rose left her office and wondered why she had been so cautioning to her. But in a few moments she decided that she would let it go and just as she had said, be cautious.

CHAPTER EIGHTEEN

THE CAMPSITE DOWN THERE

She had kept a watch out for the guy in the small vehicle, and finally not seeing any dust which would indicate his return, she walked down to see if she could find anything in his stuff to determine his identity, and then thought better of going through his stuff. She was still angry that he had been an employee of the company which through its ignorance had caused the illness and death of people she had known, and it would be a while before she got past that attitude. She walked back to her own campsite and occupied herself with her own chores, and she fished in the afternoon for her dinner which this time was two small fish which were more than sufficient. She and little boy went down and collected more grasses for fishing line, for in the morning. And she read some in the afternoon. She was relaxed in the evening, and as she had not slept particularly well in a while she decided she would try to get to sleep early this night. The harder she tried to relax and fall asleep, but sleep would not come, and she sat up and watched her small fire until very late. She must have finally fallen asleep at some point in the morning before sun rise and she woke with the sun high in the sky. She stretched and started to go out and she saw that camper with a bucket dipping it the lake. "Hey what are you doing here?" He looked at her kind of over his shoulder and said, "Sorry I was so noisy, as to wake you". "You didn't wake me!" then she said, "You work for those greedy bastards or are you a member of the family?" "You should know that I hate that family for what they did to the city!" "What city" he replied. "The whole bay area, you remember where you stole the truck?" "Oh that city" he replied. "Where are you from anyway?" "Why do you ask?" "I am trying very hard to get this conversation in to a less accusatory place, actually we are neighbors and we ought to make an effort to get along." She realized that he seemed to be a nice guy, He was downright handsome a man, and she thought about apologizing, but she did not want to go that far, quite so soon. "Okay, I just need you to know that I hate your bosses, they are money grubbing bastards, and caused the illness and death of some people I knew." "You know they caused my mother's death. And she was very careful to only drink the bottled water, and she must have poisoned herself in the shower. I loved that woman, and she was so sick for so long it broke my heart." By now he had moved closer with his filled bucket, and he in telling her the story of his mother's illness his expression changed and he looked so soft, he really did love her she thought.

"Who owns the little horse?" "He is my companion" why do you ask? "It is hard to find food out here, and I have had little if any meat in a while, I buy some provisions by swapping work in a town not far from here but I would rather live independently from the town so I could just read, and look at the environment and be glad I do not have to work for the bastards who fucked up your home. I know what you mean I did work for them as my father had in fact he got me the job years ago. We worked to replace the pipes, up across the mountains where the rich folks live with their private army which protects them from the rabble, and we replaced the lines to several of the big buildings in the place where the Government is housed and I like a fool asked if we would soon work on the lines for the people and they laughed in my face, they told me they were coping okay, and since they were double dipping with the bottled water and the regular basic water charge they would not approve the work orders that were sent to the mountain retreat where they live, and that was the final straw. I went to work the next day and picked up the truck and it had been set up with the little truck, and you know it was running okay and you know I thought that it would run better if it did not have to live under this smog and crap in the air, and I decided I would drive off the work site, and get away and be free of this crap. You think you hate them, I worked for them for 20 years, I really hate them. I drove for two days to be out from under the green haze and all I had to eat was my lunch that I put together so I went back to my commissary and spent almost everything I had on the card on a tent, a new reader, and lots of camping stuff, and food and then I drove for the two days I had driven before, until I knew I was safe from those bastards. And you know I am at peace now, I refuse to worry and I do not worry about almost anything. Mostly it is where I can find some protein".

She had listened to his story, and she invited him for dinner this evening. "We will have fish if I get lucky, and my other source of protein is rabbit, which really makes good jerky, I live on the stuff during the winter, and I dry fruit for the winter too". "I have some fresh veggies I can contribute to the dinner and some bread and some jam, too". And with that he thanked her for the water, and down the hill he went.

He stopped and yelled back to ask when dinner would be ready and she yelled "about dinner time". He waved to her and proceeded down to the hill to his camp.

She had to admit she thought he had decent values, and as a neighbor who hated who she hated that was not a bad deal.

She wove her fishing line, and attached the hook she had fashioned for today, and tied it to her stick she used for a pole. She reached over her head, and snagged a dragon fly and threaded it on to the hook and put it into the lake. She felt a fish which was trying hard to steal the bait, but had gotten snagged instead. She hauled it in and she put it in a bag re-baited her hook, and went after another. She got another after about an hour and the sacrifice of two bugs which were stolen right from her hook. She bagged the second and she cleaned the two fish, and she put the heads and entrails where she was burying all of her organic garbage, just as she was taught by

Granny. She had been preparing an area in her mountain top home, to plant a garden, but all she had to plant were peach pits, which were dry, but she had not been successful in finding other seeds, and she really dreamed of having a garden. The camper would be up for dinner, and she wondered how long he would camp at the bottom of the hill, and how she could kind of motivate him to move on. It was not that she was afraid of him that left when she expressed her vitriol about the oligarchs, and their inhumane business practices. And it seemed good to her that they could agree about that one fact, and she did not really know why she preferred isolation when her response to the horse herd had been one of hope for some kind of change in her isolation. She as she thought about it having a neighbor would not be too hard to get used to but there would for sure not be any more skinny dipping in the lake. She would be less spontaneous and she would not swim any more while he was on the mountain. She thought she could just ask him what his plans were for the time ahead, just conversational stuff during the meal. And she hoped that this neighborhood would drop half its population soon. She went to pick up her skillet, and prepare to get some good coals going in her outside fire pit. She got the fire started in an area she had begun cooking in when she first got there, and she tended the fire until the coals were beginning to get ready to cook the two fish. Just for good measure she put a couple of more pieces of wood on the fire to burn down to create coals, and she pulled out her electronic reader, went through the contents and picked a book to read as she waited to begin her part of the dinner.

As the afternoon proceeded she checked the position of the sun in the afternoon sky, and she threw a couple more pieces of wood on her fire, and thought the coals now were really soon to be ready. Her guess was it was about 5p.m. and so as soon as the flames turned to coals she began the cooking process, and within a half of an hour she was ready for him to come up the hill, and no sooner than she thought that thought, here he came up the hill carrying some tomatoes and some celery, and a loaf of bread and a jar. Her mouth began to water as she looked at the loaf of what appeared to be French bread.

She said hello, and asked "do you have a name, mine is Rose, and if we are neighbors it seems to make sense to at least know each other's names". "Yes my name would be good to share with you, Rose, my name is Bradley but I go by Buck". She extended her hand to him, "good to know you Buck" I might have to say to you that all afternoon I have been thinking about being social once again, beyond talking to a pony. I was here for a long time and before he got here, and I must say that I missed some kind of contact. Really I had a few friends, but I was not as social as I could have been. I worked and I studied, when I was in school again, and I lived for a while up in the hills where the water was not so awful, and then I left and did not see a soul for, well, until you were grabbing a little water". "How did you get to the south west corner of Wyoming?" "Is that where I am?" "Yes, that is what I reckon". "I walked." "How the hell did you do that?" "I did not have a vehicle, all I had were my feet, so I walked" Buck looked at her with a kind of a look of amazement and said nothing for a moment and then said, "I guess you really wanted out in a big way. I have to say you are amazing, you must have the determination to live free of those people." "Yes many of them I worked for the Government as a supervisor in the publication department". "Oh you wrote propaganda, right" "Yes, for many years I wrote propaganda, in perfect English." Buck smiled and said, "Yes I can imagine!" And they both laughed, probably for different reasons, and Buck put the food he had brought up for the meal on the roof of her little shelter, and asked if he could help with food preparation, and she showed him the two fish she had snagged for their dinner this morning cooking in an old skillet that she had brought out of one of the burned out cabins in the valley. "Where did you learn to build, you are an English major not a carpenter?" "Necessity is the mother of invention Buck, I knew I needed to have some shelter, after it really got cold and I scavenged the materials from some burned out places in the valley". He leaned into the shelter, and saw the brick storage shelves and the fire place in the north west corner, and he turned and asked if she mixed mortar to stabilize the brick, and she laughed "I used rebar in the holes and drove the rebar into the ground to stabilize the shelves, and if I do say so myself it is as stabile and I am very proud of it."

The Vegetables got cut, and put on a board which Rose used for a plate, and the two fish, Buck cut the bread into chunks, and the two of them sat in the sun, on the grass near the lake, ate and chatted and she felt fairly relaxed with him. It did not feel to her like it had in the morning, and she even told him she wanted to apologize to him for the poor way she welcomed him into her environment. He said to her he fully understood and for her not to worry. They saved some of the seeds out of the tomato and she explained that she had longed for a garden, and he responded by suggesting to her that if she wanted a garden, he could obtain some seeds for her garden the next time he went to the independent community to pick up supplies, and do work in the community in exchange for his purchases. She asked him about where these people were from and he thought he had heard from them that they were from somewhere around St. Joseph's but he knew that they all had known each other through their former work, and when they left they left together. "They are a real community, those people love each other and they have decided when they get old they have committed to take care of each other, and they get supplies from people who are still in the regular society actually I think they have a person who diverts regular commissary deliveries to them and cooks the books to show the delivery as received . . . They never know when one of the trucks will come and what it will contain, so their commissary is a variety of things all the food goes to the common kitchen and when it is full of material the women get together and make quilts and clothes, they have a common kitchen and eat all their meals together as a way to support a sense of community".

They continued talking near the lake, and as they chatted, Rose dipped the board into the water to clean it of the crumbs and little bits of the fish which were left, and she commented to Buck that she felt a kind of surprise that a whole community of people had in masse left a city and had successfully arranged a caravan of escape. As she thought about her own escape in that her taking her leave, hers had been isolated, and very much secret, she was too fearful to share her plan, as someone would have blown the whistle. "They must have shared a lot of trust amongst themselves to have that degree of trust." "I understand that they had been friends for a long time, and the community is made up in reality of about three factions which joined together each faction bringing to the group particular people with specific skills that the group as a whole felt were necessary for the success of the community. I have listened to their history which they shared with me, and they worked hard and when they left they had a strong commitment to each other and to the process of working together to support each other. Several of the community have broken the one child rules, and had to get out or face some kind of awful consequences. So the pressure to get out was high." "How did they avoid the automatic vasectomy rules Buck, where we were they did not let any man get past the automatic appointment?" "I think the babies were not born with the help of medical care, that must have been how they pulled it off, but I think that must have been scary for the mothers. You know they have a doctor in the community, and he is training a couple of the kids, they are learning anatomy and physiology he is teaching them to be able to replace him for the community. He is a pretty young guy but pretty realistic too." Rose thought about the community, and then said to Buck, "What do you do when you go there?" "Oh I help them with water problems, and I have helped with some of the plans for building on top of the land. They did their original building in big dug out places. When they originally went the idea was to stay out of sight, so they constructed all their homes underneath the ground. It was really cleaver how they developed the underground homes, they dug out septic tanks and water supply from the well they first dug. They sent up about four guys, with heavy equipment a couple of earth movers, and they built a big dorm kind of place one big room, and some sanitary facilities, and then some people came behind who had the skills they needed, a couple of furniture makers and a couple of people who set up a natural gas heating system, that they still have problems with. They did the whole building thing before everyone came up and everyone then pitched in and the women remarkably were just as good at some of the hard labor jobs as were the men. There is one lady who now spends as much time in the building trades kind of work as she does in the garden, which she loves. They are building on the surface now as they have not had any problems with people coming and trying to mess up things, but at first they were very afraid."

"I think I would love to go and meet these folks. They sound like they are real survivors, and very gutsy too." "I will go back to see what I can do to help them in about two weeks. I would be glad to take you in with me if you are serious." "I will think about it" Rose replied.

"Well while you think about coming with me, I will cook dinner for us tomorrow night. Come down to my camp site about the same time in the evening". "I will bring the fruit, some peaches, okay?" "Good" Buck replied, "see you tomorrow", and with that he got up and headed down the hill.

He had left behind the about a half loaf of bread, and the bottle of jam which had only a spoonful in the bottom, and she thought rather than trying to catch him tonight, she would just carry it down tomorrow. She cut off a small piece of the bread and ate it just before she went to bed, and it was so good she just savored each bite. She had not had any bread in so long it just was such a treat.

CHAPTER NINETEEN

THE FACULTY PRESENTATION

On Thursday evening she walked to the Faculty Social Club, which was located next to the Administration building and as she walked in she was waved to a particular room which was at the back of the building. As she walked in she noticed that there were about fifteen people already there to hear her presentation of the soon to be published work she had spent the last six months preparing. She recognized about six of the people in the room the other nine she did not know as yet. Irene saw her walk in and waved to her to join the group at the refreshment table. There were drinks, and snacks set up on a table, and she determined that Irene had been busy that afternoon setting up these snacks. There were two loafs of her wonderful bread, trays of cut fruit, several kinds of spreads for the bread, and wine, and iced tea for everyone to enjoy. She was introduced to several of the faculty members she had not as yet met, and after chatting a while, Irene stood at the front of the room to introduce Rose to the assembled group, and handed out copies of Rose's presentation on the "One Child Policy, U.S. Vs. China" and the group all sat down and became very quiet to hear her presentation. She began her presentation, by outlining the elements which were common to the two policies, and then she rapidly began describing the differences. She approached the origins of the two policies from both the political and practical consequences, and then explored the impact on particular social and political consequences. She as well looked at the styles of implementation undertaken by the two very different political systems, and she ended her talk by exploring the attitudes of the populations involved.

She spoke about all of this in about an hour's talk, and then asked for questions from the group. She fielded about six questions from faculty members assembled, and then a gentleman in a suit and tie stood up and asked her the final question. "You have been very clear in the articulation of the reason the Chinese reasoning in their implementation of their policy, but I have not really heard from you the reason for our implementation almost a century later of the same policy, could you help us to understand why, the real reason why we instituted the same policy?" She hoped that she was not talking to the enemy in this moment and that he was not a governmental guest at the presentation.

She looked at the questioner, and thought she had to be frank. "It is a plan that strongly favors the Oligarchy's management and control of the system in which we live, it is all about money". He remained standing, and he said, "Ladies and gentlemen, she nailed it, it is all about their money." And with that everyone clapped and began rising from their seats to congratulate her on a great presentation. The gentleman in the suit approached her and Irene joined her to introduce her to Dr. Wellstone the president of the university. "I have heard that you are a crack student, and I look forward to being able to interview you for a post here when you finish your doctoral work" he said as he shook her hand. Irene was smiling like a proud mother, and she said to him, "One of the best master's level people I have had in a long time".

Everyone was complimentary about her presentation and how she had managed to remain factual in her presentation, and in its publication form. Jake then approached her and said it was one of the best presentations he had attended, and she was a perceptive and skilled researcher. She thanked him, and as everyone left the room except her small group of colleagues, Jake said he would have put money on the bet that she would be as insightful as she had been.

"She is a good student and a great researcher" he said to the five of them there in this small group. Connie complimented her on her writing style, and all in all Rose felt she had scored with the entire presentation.

Irene and Jake bundled up the left overs, and Irene said to her "dinner tomorrow at my place at 5 p.m."?

"You have two classes to work on before your Master's Degree is complete, it will be, I am sure, downhill for this next semester" Irene said. "I want you to think about either taking it easy this next 6 months or perhaps if you like we can give you an initial Ph.D. class to begin work on, do not decide right now, we can discuss it tomorrow evening."

She thought through the idea of having only two courses to do in the next 6 months, and when she was really honest with herself, she knew this last half year had been arduous, and when she thought about it she honestly felt she could use the reduced pressure. She wanted to begin the next degree, but she also wanted to have energy to be able to perform well. By the time it was time to walk to Irene's apartment, she had decided to do only the two courses that were left on her Master's degree, and she felt settled with her decision. She knocked on Irene's door, and she heard Irene say, "Rose come on in". She entered and she saw Irene pulling a pie out of the oven, and placing it on the counter to cool. There was a glass of white wine on the table in the living room, and she entered and Irene came in and they sat to talk. "I asked you yesterday to think about your course work for this next session, and I hope you will give yourself a break, and finish the Masters work only". "I have thought about it and I agree with you, coming to school this time I noticed that I was really tired, and two will be just fine. I have planned to remain in the governmental system for three more years, and you know if I need more I will just take it. The real issue is that I have a way out, and that will be enough to get me through." "Good, I know working in that environment must be taxing at best, but you did get an invitation to apply last evening here, from Dr. Wellstone and he did not need to offer that if he was not genuinely interested he did not have to say anything. He could have just congratulated you on a great paper, and that would have been all he needed to do".

Irene refreshed their wine, and then thought the dinner was probably ready and she cut the pie made of many vegetables, chunks of white meat chicken and a light sauce, baked in a beautiful pie crust. There was a loaf of Irene's wonderful bread, and butter, and a fruit tart for dessert. Rose always felt well fed by these meals, and Irene's company and conversation, the two women cleaned up after dinner, and sat and talked the evening away. When Rose left the dinner she walked away not having a clue of what was about to transpire and for her she could hold onto the pleasure of a kind of mother replacement person in her life, who different from her own mother who had not a clue of Rose as an independent person functioning in the real world, could feel the pride of sponsorship, in her success. She walked into the dorm in the flush of nostalgia, thinking of her parents and hoping they could on some level know of her achievement and felt the pride and relief she had felt just the night before. She retired to sleep and slept like an infant which she found a restorative for her return to her current reality.

The train stopped at her station, and she disembarked the train, and walked to pick up her bag and walked home. She saw the box of ashes on the window sill, as she entered, and thought to herself that she really should place the ashes in the ocean soon, to complete her duty to her parents. She puzzled why it had taken her so long, and she thought it was because she was so busy with school and she reasoned now that she would have only two classes this term, she would be more able to find the time.

She read a bit as it was only three in the afternoon, and got into the first of her classes, which she was due to speak to Connie on the coming weekend. It was the U.S. Constitution course from the arguments about styles of governance and the writing of the Bill of Rights and all the internal discussion and arguments about its composition in the first body of the Constitutional Congress, and then the process of adding and defeating both suggested and existent articles of the Bill of Rights. As she read she got into a very detailed development of the history of the first ten of the articles. Rose was clearly curious about the material, and was so deeply engaged she read right past sun down, and it was almost ten in the evening she looked up to see it was time for her to sleep.

Morning was announced by the alarm clock and she was on her way to work within the hour. She spent a routine day at work, and in the evening she thought she could get into the initial questions and she could begin to compose the questions she would be sending back to Connie in the evening tomorrow. She felt she had read most of what she needed to cover in the responses to both questions but rather compulsively she read on before she began to compose her responses, and she realized she had covered the material necessary for the material in the questions, so she put the book down and began outlining her responses. By the time she finished she put her materials away and ate a little soup, and went to bed at her typical time. She had become very efficient in this study style, and was very pleased with her ability to do this as effectively as she had demonstrated thus far in this process. And nothing made her happier than these study sessions which were for her evidence of her skill level for continued study.

Rose was genuinely happy as she addressed these studies, and she tolerated the time at work which provided the money and the possibilities of continuing the study which would free her from the kind of work which she had thought would give her not only a way to make her way in the world but had proved to be just too much control, and very little chance for advancement. In returning to school she had discovered a place where her talents and intelligence would be appreciated, and for that she was very grateful.

The week went slowly as they always did at the beginning of each of her six months independent study. She came home on Saturday evening and she felt the lift she always felt when she had a tutorial session on the communicator to look forward to, and she went to the refrigerator to put together a light super and then out to take a long walk before it got too late. She decided that a sandwich would do, and she made it and carried it with her. She walked to the center of the housing district where there were some chairs and she could just sit and read until it became hard to read under the lights. She took her current book on the electronic reader with her, and she walked and walked until she arrived at the little park. There were some trees but none of these were fruit bearing kinds which she had so enjoyed as a child. She sat in an area where the light was best. And she noticed that the level of smog was higher than she had been aware of recently. As she read, she became uncomfortable, breathing was hard, and she noticed the discomfort, a kind of burning in her lungs was hard to ignore. She got up and proceeded back to her apartment which provided a filtering system for the air coming in to her environment. She thought about people who had to work outside all day, and she thought to herself that they must all be at risk for lung problems.

Her return was rapid as she wanted to be out of the smog and filth in the air. And as she walked toward her apartment she could feel the effect of the filthy air and as she made it to the door, she could feel the shortness of breath taking hold of her, and she went in and she began to cough and cough to try to clear her lungs. This event would stay with her for years, and never again did she take a walk after work, she got home as quickly as she could, and she began to become aware that this experience did nothing for her attitude toward the owners of these industries which was causing the pollution to become so evident.

That evening she did a slow burn about the environment, and her next trip to the commissary she purchased a box of medical face masks, to wear when she had a long walk to do especially at night.

She had become aware of many people wearing them, and at first she had wondered why they did this, but now she understood, and never failed to have one in her purse if the air was particularly bad she did not hesitate to put it in place and not go through what she had on that walk.

Sunday began and Connie was on the communicator by 9 a.m. and they met and talked about her material which she had sent in and Connie commented on her completeness in her responses, and Rose had several questions which clarified her understanding of some of the conflicts between sources, and Connie was very well informed in the differences of interpretation. Then Connie had a lot to share with her about her recent presentation and comments made by some of the faculty which had been in attendance. "They loved the directness of your response to Dr. Wellstone's question!" And Rose responded, "Well Connie you know this stuff, how else could I have responded?" Connie thought for a moment, "Well there was no evidence that there were an impending lack of food, you know, and hardly any other answer but money and greed and if there had been a drought on the way they would have hoped for a big death rate! Everybody was very impressed with your scholarship and many of these people will participate on your Ph.D. panel and granted that will not be formed for another year, but they will not forget the level of your scholarship, and they have not stopped remarking on your presentation."

They chatted a little while longer, she shared with Connie the problem with the air at night, and Connie said she has encouraged her parents not to go out at night that "the L.A. valley is like it is up where you are. I don't know if they stay in at night but I at least warned them."

They were about to discontinue their communication, and Connie gave her the heads up on the next material and the meeting date. She wrote the information down, and thanked her.

She spent the afternoon reading new material for next week, and she pulled up on her computer the assignments and the questions to read in detail with a goal of picking up on the subtle elements implied in the questions. She worked through the day and ate a little dinner and cursed the fact that the sky was really quite green and she felt anger at the environmental degradation. She flashed back to her last walk to the park in the center of the housing area, and the acrid taste of the odor in her nose and mouth came back to her and she grimaced as if she was once again walking to return home as quickly as she could. What the hell, she thought, could they be releasing into the air, it smelled like acid, a sharp brittle taste, which did nothing for the level of resentment she felt upon the retrieval of that memory. What made them think that they could just poison the population and risk the health of everyone? She on some level though knew that they probably had no real idea, they lived in places which were naturally protected from the environmental pollution, the westerly winds kept their air in the mountains perfectly cleansed. And in this moment she felt the hopelessness of any real change. They simply had to protect themselves as they could. That was that!

Rose worked in the weeks to come to complete the balance of her Master's degree, and as she approached her time to return to school for her final exam and the comprehensive exam which would be the final exam and cover all the various classes she had been exposed to over the now more than three years, She checked her vacation time which had accrued and found she would be able to go back to finish it all up in about one month's time. She had her last conference with Connie coming up in several days, and she had reviewed her notes for the entire program, and was looking forward to her Comprehensive exam as a validation of her hard work over this time of intensive learning.

Checking her e-mail, she was surprised that she had a note from Irene. She opened it to read what she least expected. "My Dear Rose, I am saddened to say I will not meet with you on your return to Campus in a month. My contract with the University has been terminated, and I must leave in two days. I have been told that some of the books in my Library have in the recent past been placed on the list which is no longer acceptable for use in research, that I have been teaching false materials etc . . . etc . . . , The Education Department has both revoked my license, and demanded I be fired from the faculty. Dr. Wellstone has protested the demand of the Government, but to no avail. I will be living with my Brother and his family on the Farm I grew up on, near Des Moines. This past two months has been an unending night mare, and so far we are unclear about how anyone found out about my personal library. For me it is important that I assure you that I feel you are such a gifted student, you should not let what has happened denture you from continuing your study and completing your advanced degree. You are a gifted student, and the simple truth is that you need to carry on whether I am here to assist you or not. I want to continue to communicate with you, I will be in your life in the future as a cheer leader and no longer your teacher, I will miss our dinners together, and I hope you heed my words of support. Your Friend, and former mentor, Irene." Rose closed the email, and felt numb. What the hell, she uttered out loud, and then she opened it once again and read it over, really not believing what she was reading. My word, she whispered, how could they have been so stupid. She is one of the most honored by her peers, and what in the world was their problem? She was now so angry and at the same time she felt a sense of abandonment. Her first reaction was to contact Lucy, so she called her communicator number, and got a response that she could leave a message that the individual she had contacted was unavailable at this time. She requested Lucy contact her, this evening if possible and disconnected. She tried to communicate with Greg, or Connie, and they too were unavailable. She left messages for them please to return her calls, and then her emotions overcame her and she sat at the kitchen table and wept. Within an hour she had a call from Lucy, and she and Lucy conversed about the uproar on campus, and Lucy had limited knowledge about a complaint that had been made but had no idea that it would have any impact on Rose, and did not know that Irene had been her primary director for her studies.

"This has an odor of something I do not like" was Lucy's comment, and she said she would poke around with people she trusted to see what she could find from the inside, and could they eat together in the downtown district at 6p.m. the next day? Rose told her about the eatery where she and Angela had met, and they agreed to meet there after work tomorrow. Disconnecting from Lucy's call she had another contact coming from Greg. "Rose, there has been a lot of trouble on campus and they have made a scapegoat of Irene, we are all sick and angry about what has happened. Why they went after her we do not know, but do not let this get in your way, she told me that she would be fine, and that I am to shepherd you forward." Rose explained that she had contacted the mentor in the government a woman she has trusted and a friend of Dr. Wellstone, to find out from the inside what the hell this was all about, and Greg responded that he needed to stay informed about whatever she could tell him and she replied that she had no reason she could not share whatever she learned, and he thanked her. "I may be calling you tomorrow evening if Lucy has anything to share with me" and Greg said he would call her after 8 p.m. tomorrow.

She put the books away for this evening, and she went to take a shower, and as soon as the hot water hit her head she began to convulsively weep, and she cried and cried until she had reached the end of her personal loss, and her tears, and the anger once again rose up in her gut, and she exited the shower, put on her robe and went back to the kitchen to find two messages on her communicator, one from Connie, and the other from Jake. She engaged the communicator and left a message for her supervisor to let her know she was ill, and would not be at work in the morning, and she called both Connie and Jake, and Jake rigged up a three way call and the three talked simultaneously about who could have been the mole, and who set him or her to do Irene in. "This has the fingerprints of the Government all over it", she said to the two of them. They agreed but they had no idea why the government cared. "Any time they think they are losing power or authority mostly because they have lost power to the Wealthy, they get uptight, and start to look for a victim to persecute." They went on talking for several more minutes, and they said they would see her soon, and disconnected the three way call.

Rose was exhausted mostly from the emotions of this night, and she went to bed and fell into a very troubled dream state, full of abandonment images, and one dream, she thought that Irene was blaming her for the trouble, and she woke saying I had no idea they were after you Irene. She had heard her words coming into a waking state, and began to cry once again. She got up and made herself some tea, and sat up for a long while. It was three in the morning before she could drop off into a sleep, but it was light and not at all restful, and she got up around six at her usual wake time, and got dressed in casual clothes, and began to give serious thought to the problem on campus to try to figure out why Irene was so important to the government to get rid of, or go after in the first place. She thought to herself that because Irene was well known it would accomplish two purposes, whatever the first thing had been and then the fact that she was both popular and well known, other professors would be more respectful of the constraints the government put out on the university communities, because they had gone after and fired one of the best and most respected of their group.

CHAPTER TWENTY

RETURN TO CAMPUS

Rose had obtained some information about Irene's dismissal, and it focused on the director of her department, a man who had one purpose and one purpose in everything he did. That was to protect himself in this system, and it was quickly determined that his 'executive assistant' was a former cop in the nearby city of Oakland, who was fired there for questionable use of force, was divorced by his wife for substantiated infidelity, one of the few legitimate reasons for legal divorce in how things were set up now, and she was awarded 70% of his account in the settlement. He was fired from the Police, and now had only 30% of his life savings to sustain himself. He had been a friend of the directors, and had been of assistance to Bret when there had been the need of someone to get rid of an up and coming departmental director in the government who had made the mistake of saying at a party one night that he was in a way gunning for Bret's job, so when there was a possibility of hiring an executive assistant, Bret, the man in charge hired Donald to be a kind of personal assistant for Bret. There had been a terrible accident at the firing range, and that up and coming departmental director had the gun blow up in his hand as he fired at a target. He was terribly disfigured, had his hand essentially blown off, and in the confusion over the event at the gun range, the gun which had been causal in the "accident" had disappeared. There were several other stories of "accidental events", all of which had elements of Donald's indirect involvement, but nothing was ever proven, and Bret had remained unscathed.

This unholy alliance between Bret, and Donald was known but rarely talked about. Rose had picked up on it early on, in fact Angela had talked about this guy who was the assistant to the Director of the department had commented that he had put the make on her on several occasions, and she had been very aggressive in reporting these events and he had been confronted by Bret to knock it off with the women. She began to dig into Bret's background and determined that he had been the son of one of the wealthy class, whose father had been drummed out of the corps for very questionable practices in his business, and she thought to herself that what were typical mores within the oligarch's he must have been a real knuckle buster. Bret had lived a charmed life though since he was kicked off the hill with the death of his father, and his step mothers taking over the family and cleaning up the business practices of her former husband and his business. It had been rumored Bret had become a governmental employee at his step mothers insistence, if for no other reason than to assuage her guilt for ditching him independent of the fact that he had no real talents in management of himself much less a huge number of departments in the state level government.

Rose was getting ready to return to School, had her vacation cleared and on a Saturday morning she mounted the train to head south to the campus. This trip lacked the hope she had felt in the past and as the train pulled into the station she saw Jake and Greg there to meet her train, and she hoped they had news about what they had found in determining the issues that had come up around Irene's dismissal. As they walked together to the eatery, they wanted to know what she had found out on her end. "Not very much" I have a little dirt on several of the men who work at the top of my division of the Government, but nothing specific. "Well we have determined that there was a mole planted here on campus to find some dirt, anything that they could use to create something to fire someone over, and it seems to have been one of the students who were admitted on a conditional basis as their records were not the best but were here because they had obtained the recommendation of someone high up in authority." She said nothing but thought to herself, that this kind of move had Donald's fingerprints all over it. Can we check those letters of reference ourselves? Greg responded that he thought if there was a possibility of finding out who was behind this awful thing, Dr. Wellstone would cooperate with us.

Rose had a cup of coffee but really had no stomach for food. The two men were ready for lunch and so they ate, and Rose sat with them while they consumed their food. She told them that she wanted to get through her tests, and then spend the next three days identifying the mole, and they agreed that Irene would want to handle it in a like manner, and so Rose went to check in at the Library, and go to her dorm. "Do not be upset by the activity in the Library" Greg cautioned her. She could feel the ire rise up in her gut with his comment, and she replied, "What is going on at the Library?" Jake explained that Irene's private library had given them the excuse that they needed and they were going through all the books in the Library to determine if there were books which had not been approved by the government for study at the University level, and so far they had pulled about 3 in 10 of the books off the shelves, and had not made it thought one third of the shelves. She with this news became enraged. "Well they terminated Irene, and now they are acting like they own the place, and in reality I guess they do." Greg replied. "They are rubbing salt into our wounds" Jake retorted, "and they are having a jolly good time doing it I say!" "When you go over just keep your feelings to yourself", Greg responded, and she said she would, "but you know it will be hard not to tell them to get the hell out of my library"! She grabbed her bag and her back pack, and walked to the dorm to pick up her schedule and then go to the library to do a final preparation for her exams.

She walked into the dorm and got her room key and schedule, and put her things into her room. The communicator was blinking which meant that she had a call waiting, she turned it to active and she saw that Dr. Wellstone had left a message, "Rose, please when you are heading toward the Library please take a moment and come into my office, I would like to see you when you come in. Thank you". She was not sure of the nature of this, she was a Masters candidate, and he was the President of the University. She put aside her feelings, and she left to go to his office, and when she walked in, he warmly greeted her and asked her to come into his office. She complied, and he shut the door.

"Since the unfortunate event two weeks ago, we have been trying to determine who was involved in the student body. There had to be a plant on campus, and we have a lead on someone that might have been the one who was the "rat". I think I know the identity, and it was the assistant director of your branch of the government who encouraged us to admit him, even though is initial work here got him expelled about seven years ago." "Are we talking about Donald Acton" she asked, and Dr. Wellstone replied "Why, Yes" "Donald Acton Assistant to the Director of Governmental Activities." She took a breath; this was coming together like well baked bread. "Dr. Wellstone, the guy is up to his neck in dirty activities for the Director of my division of Governmental Activities."

"Okay we know who our mole was then, Rose, his name is Donald T Bryant and he checked out of his dorm the night before they raided Irene's apartment. We had a list of ten suspects but the fact that you know this Donald Acton has been involved in some underhanded stuff; that is good enough for me. We will withdraw money from his account for the three weeks he was here and taking course work, and we can locate him via that account." "Can you give me his current location is that permissible? Rose asked.

I suppose I could write it down and place it on my desk on top of your purse, and you could just think it was your note and put it away, and no one would be the wiser, what do you think?" She said that would work alright for her and he did just that. She slipped it into her wallet and she walked to the door, and thanked him for the encouragement.

Over the next two days she passed both of her exams with nothing lower than a 97%. The third day on campus she put in a call to Lucy to let her know she had the name of the mole here on campus, and Lucy communicated to Rose that she, Lucy was very close to pinning this on not Donald but his boss, and she was being very careful but she thought this plan to get someone down state at the University was being talked about a lot in the upper levels of government. Lucy told her that Bret had called her and wanted to talk to her in the morning, and she would tell her what it was about if it could possibly be tied to Irene's firing. "Be near your communicator near noon tomorrow, I will need the time to get home."

At noon Rose walked into the dorm after meeting with several of the faculty who had the mole in their classes. They without exception said he was not much of a student, he was rarely prepared to discuss the material he was to have covered in his study, and he missed class a lot, and did not have a note from the infirmary to back up his excuses. She waited for the call to come through from Lucy, and she actually started to worry about her. At three she got the Call, and it was an ashen Lucy. "You will not have my assistance in the future, I have been fired today, and they refused to give me a reason. I have called my Dad who is in a retirement setting in Southern Arizona, and he is willing to put me up for a while." "Lucy you look like shit! Come down here, Dr. Wellstone will help you out and we can plan what to do next in this situation, calmly and think it through. No need to head to Happy Valley." "Yes that is where he is living, how you should know the name, Rose?" "That is where my folks were sent, and you will hate the staff they are a real drag." "Yes I have been down to see my folks before my mom died."

"Okay I will come to school" Rose followed up "it is three thirty now, get on the train that leaves at 6 p.m. and I will meet your train and get you a room here in the Adult dorm." She closed the call and then called Dr. Wellstone to tell him what had happened to Lucy, and he called to approve her Dorm status, and got her an I.D. for her stay on campus and a meal card, and it was all waiting for Lucy when she arrived late in the evening. The two women went for food, Lucy looked awful, and needed to just talk about the morning and how they handled the firing. "Both those men are sociopathic" she said as they sat down to eat and talk; "they both believe that the rules are for everyone else, but not for them". I said that they had to give me just cause for firing me and they both said that they had no such duty, and that they ran the Division as they liked and that was that." Donald then said they had enough on her to write a book, that she had colluded with employees to get around problems with not meeting their quotas, and that they had pictures of her in compromising situations that they could use if it went to court so I had better just shut up and leave. You know Rose I have never been in a situation where I could be pictured in a compromised way, so I know that they have some photos which have been doctored to look like something else." "You know Lucy they probably are just threatening you and counting on the hope that you might feel guilty!" "Well I have not been and I don't" If you can hold out for a while, down here, I think now I can get them, but it might take a while, are you okay to wait it out?" "Tell me what you have in mind" "I am not exactly sure, but I will keep you posted as the plan develops".

They walked to the Dorm and Lucy was given the meal ticket good for one year, campus I.D. an the key to her room for an unstipulated amount of time. The desk attendant then said, "I have been told by the President of the University that you have a home with us for as long as you need one." Lucy began to tear up, and Rose knew that this had been an awful day for her friend, and she put her arm around Lucy and took her upstairs to where her room would be, next to her own room. "You take a hot shower and go to bed, and I will get ahold of you and we will eat breakfast together and I will introduce you to my faculty members and friends. They will be delighted to meet you, they all know what a help to me you have been". Lucy began to unpack, and Rose, said, "Take care of you first. I am right next door, just knock on my door if you need anything". Lucy said she would and Rose went to take her shower, and go to sleep.

There was a gentle knock on her door in the morning, and Lucy was up and dressed, and with a cup of coffee for Rose. Rose took the coffee, and invited Lucy to sit while she got dressed. She grabbed some clothes, and brushed her teeth, and put on her clothes, and made up her bed, and then they walked out to the food court to order something to eat, and met with Greg, and Jake and Connie who were already there with their food half eaten. Jake teased Rose a bit, "my girl, she is relaxed finally the pressure is off. And at that the scores she made are close to spectacular. She will graduate cum laude in two days . . ." And everyone at the table clapped and congratulated Rose on her accomplishment. Connie commented that she had written to Irene with the good news about her graduation status, and had gotten back the message to give that girl a hug for her, and she got up to come to pass on the hug.

They all were happy for her and Lucy commented that she knew Rose was a gifted student, and she was sure she would do even better when she began to work toward the Ph.D. Rose began to talk to the group, about needing to take a break from school for a while, "I have to make sure this thing that has happened here on campus is put to rest in every way", and then kind of changed the subject. She and Lucy needed to go over to speak to Dr. Wellstone, and the two women got up and headed for the President's office.

As the two women walked across the grass in front of the Building of the office of the President, Lucy took Roses arm and stopped their progress. She turned to look at Rose, and said, you are just too gifted to quit, and I feel like that is what you are thinking of doing. Rose looked at her, and said, "You know you are my friend and you have been fired from a very good job for helping me, and Irene my professor is gone too. I am pissed at those two bastards, and I am looking for a big serving of justice and I intend to take those two men down. I am not sure how I will be able to do this, but I will figure it out. I need time to do this, and I will not rest until it is done. No body hurts people I consider my friends. I may come back, but not until the score evens up.

Lucy suddenly got it that this was her plan and nothing would change her mind. She had not known Rose for a long time, but she did understand the degree of her determination, and once she set her mind on something she finished. And she saw in her friend's face that look of commitment, and she let it go.

They entered the President's office, and he asked both the sit, and he circled the women and closed the door so they would not be disturbed. Well Lucy it is good to see you again. I am glad you will once again be on campus, perhaps we can find something that matches your talents for you to do while you are with us again. Lucy laughed and explained to Rose she had her first job on campus, years before after she graduated here with her Master's degree in employee management, from their business school.

"Yes she went from the frying pan right into the fire when she left us, Rose". "Dr. Wellstone I can think of many things about this school, frying pan is not something I might think of to describe it though". "She is right" replied Lucy, "you just cannot imagine the fire I did fall into though". "How many years did you put in up there"? asked Dr. Wellstone. "Let's see I think it was twelve, or perhaps now it is thirteen."

Rose then looked at Dr. Wellstone and said, "You knew exactly who to call when you thought I needed support. She has been wonderful to me, she has always been right there when I needed someone. However she would still have a position if she had not gotten tied up with me," and Lucy broke in saying "That is very kind of you Rose to think that, but they have been working hard to get rid of me, I just thought about all the issues I have tried to fight in that mess up there, and you have to know you are the only the one lonely straw that finally broke the back of the camel, nothing more."

Rose felt a mix of feeling, strong admiration for these two people, and as well a sense of responsibility for Irene, and Lucy, and she felt a strong need to make it all even to some degree or other.

The group began talking about who this Daniel Bryant was and they needed to know how he got the heads up on Irene's private library as that had been the beginning of the trauma. "We need to talk with Irene" Dr. Wellstone said, "and we also need to find the connection between Bryant and the two men up north," added Lucy. "I have her connection number we could call her now and we could ask her about this Bryant guy." Rose went to the communicator, and she logged in the proper address, and rather quickly a gentleman was seen on the communicator screen. "Franklin Acres" he responded, and Rose said "Hello, we are trying to connect with Irene Franklin is she available, and he responded "Yes. Let me call her, this might take a minute, she is out in the Cheese room, hang on I will call her." Within a few moments Irene appeared on the screen, and was surprised to see Rose on her screen. "How are you doing my dear girl, you must be a Masters, by now, have you been awarded your new degree?" "Dr. Wellstone is here and so is Lucy the woman who was my ombudsman up north. I want to tell you that we are rather quickly figuring out how this all got started, it was a plan from the higher-ups in the Bay area, and they sent a mole into your classes to get something on you to cause trouble, and get to me indirectly, his name was Daniel T. Bryant, do you remember him?" Irene thought for a moment, and she thought he was in her European history class, it was a primary class and he did not do very well and he missed class a lot as she remembered. "Why, did he have a hand in this mess?" Rose replied "We think so actually, did he ever come to your apartment for any reason"? "He brought me a paper he was late handing in and he did show up at my door, but he did not come in I do not believe. He came when I was baking and my hands were full of flour, and I did step away from the door to go and wash my hands, but I am relatively sure he did not come into my apartment. But you know I absolutely cannot be sure".

"Did he return for any reason, Irene", Lucy asked. "No, I do not think he ever returned, but there were those minutes while I cleaned my hands, he might have seen the library as I had been working at my desk and I am relatively sure the door was open." "That is the only time he came to my home, I am sure." Rose said that she thought that was enough to link him to his participation in this scam.

Irene broke into the conversation and encouraged Rose to continue with her study, but Rose was quite direct with her, she said that she had to do what she could to stop this awful mess, and Irene knowing her former student seemed to understand, and told her to come back when she was ready. Rose thanked her for her understanding, and they then all said goodbye to Irene. Lucy commented that she felt Irene in the time they had worked together really did understand the determination that Rose possessed, and let the conversation go at that point, signaling her degree of understanding.

Rose felt that Lucy would be fine here, and was grateful for that small favor, and she told them both she would try to tie Bryant to the two bosses on her return to the Bay area. Rose was eager strangely to get back and get busy with her investigation. She needed a plan, and she had no idea how she would work out contact with the two most powerful men in the Governmental complex, but she would find a way. She pondered some rather basic questions, first among them was why in hell they had to sacrifice Lucy in this process, she simply could not understand that other than it was an emotional reaction but that did not make any sense to her.

The two women returned to the Dorm after saying their good byes to Dr. Wellstone, and his parting shot was that he would see them both in the Graduate celebration. Rose was uneasy, and really wanted to leave tonight to go back north. "Lucy, give me your key to your apartment, and I will gather up your personal stuff and take it back to my place. We are close enough so I could get your clothes and personal items out and keep them for you at my place."

"Don't worry, Rose, I have boxed everything up and the manager in my section said he would keep it all, for me not to worry." "Is there anything else I can do to help" "No I think I am okay. But I do want to talk to you on a regular basis, I need to know how your detective work is going, I can help you with that I think as I know those people so well."

Rose told Lucy she wanted to take a nap, and she headed for the Dorm and Lucy went to get Lunch. Rose packed her case, and stripped her bed, and called the train station to change her reservation for tonight, and called Dr. Wellstone to let him know that he could mail her certificate to her home, and thanked him for his support and care during her time while she was here. He told her to hold it and he would be right there. Within several moments he was knocking on her door, and she opened it and seeing him standing at her door she began to cry, they walked to the second floor sitting room, and she cried and cried, releasing all the tension and frustration she had just swallowed since Irene's message to her, and her realization that the bastards had won and she had lost her dream of a life of study and teaching. He kept handing her Kleenex, and she just sobbed. He really got it that this had been a terrible loss to her. That façade of the intense unemotional person had been a façade to cover up a ton of hurt. He, as she reached the end of her tears, told her that she could work on campus and finish her degree, that he would make sure she had a home here, and would do anything to support her work here. "Dr. Wellstone you are too kind to make that offer, but I have to get those two bastards. Their behavior caused so much hurt and devastation, I just need to find some kind of justice". "Remember the offer stays open to you Rose. Please stay in touch" She agreed to stay in touch, and he left, and she finished packing and she turned in her key and walked away from the dorm, and into the food court, and after grabbing a little to eat, she walked on to the train station and waited the two hours for her train to leave.

CHAPTER TWENTY ONE

HER TRIP WITH BUCK

Buck had agreed to cook dinner for her in exchange for her fish dinner, and she had listened to his story about the community of rebels to the east of her mountain, and she had pondered in the evening the effort this group of people had put out to be able to be free. And how building under the ground was an indicator of the degree of fear they had felt. She had been fed up and angry, and it was the level of her rage that drove her over the ridge onto the Plaines and hills and valleys of her trek. She thought of the role of her anger had been far more comfortable to tolerate than the fear that drove them underground just to live in freedom.

She pondered what his words were about, he seemed to be ambivalent, he would go and work for them and he spent his time and his sweat, and he would pick up what he needed in exchange. He wanted though to live independently; he did not stay with them. She wondered why he would go in and out, and obviously the answer was that he preferred his independence. He was a mystery to her, but a mystery that she did not know how to solve. She would have to observe him, and listen, if she was to really get who this man really was.

She was intrigued by him, but it was her intellectual curiosity that got hooked. She settled the little colt and went to bed. It was a little chilly and she lit a fire and she began to try to fall asleep, but she could not get Buck to exit her thoughts. And she realized she had a number of questions she needed answers for and she gave up the process of her wondering.

As dawn began to break, she was up after a poor sleep which was punctuated by sleepless moments and then deep dreaming moments as well. As she rose she found herself to be anxious, but the reasons for that feeling were to her as yet unknown. She walked down to the trees to see if she could obtain some early ripened fruit. There was none, but she then thought she could perhaps get a rabbit and begin the jerky process and that would do for their dinner. And then she thought about the dry fruit and she said to herself that would be what she would share for the dinner tonight.

She spent the day reading and gathering a little wood, to replenish her stock. She watched the sun pass across the sky and she thought it must be near five so she headed down the hill with the pony not far behind, and she arrived at the campsite to find Buck stirring a pot over a small fire he had made for cooking. "Canned stew, and some more bread and some butter," he said," I hope that will do for you, I know it is what I typically eat at night most days". "That sounds delicious to me" she replied. "I brought some of the dried fruit I had stashed for the winter". "That sounds great, here sit down in this camp chair, and talk to me, while I finish this heating process." She agreed and she sat and they talked. "I have been wondering why you prefer to campout when you could have a little home over there with those people you seem to be consulting with?"

He tilted his head back and began to respond to her, "You know I worked 6 days out of 7 each week back at the city, and I just did not want to be called to work every day and I know that they would be doing that and I just want to be free of those kinds of demands. I want to look at the beauty of this mountain, and I want to read, and I want to do little jobs, and help them find the materials that they need to do real good repairs on their existing work. But I want some freedom, and they seem to understand. So I camp out so I can really feel free. You know I have never admitted that to anyone, but it feels like it resonates as true. Thanks Rose, you did me a favor with that question", and she smiled and said "you are welcomed."

"So tell me your story, Rose, You left because the water was awful, or what finally got you on your way".

"I planned to leave for some time but I had some business to take care of." She began to explain to him that she had really planned to finish her Ph.D. in history, and teach at the college level, but several of her friends were hurt by the government and her lead professor had been fired by the government because she had collected an unapproved library, in her apartment, and her ombudsman in the government was as well fired by the head of her division, and he and his assistant were guilty of many violations of governmental laws, and were begging to be caught up in their evil little games. She explained to Buck how after her Masters being completed she returned to her work, and received a promotion to supervisor, and then how she got into the upper echelons of her department and how she basically set them up to be discovered appropriating money for their own use, and how they had basically stolen from the government, and the episode making the voice recording of the second in command confessing, during a drunken conversation, with her, that he had given governmental money to a kid to infiltrate the university and cause trouble for the faculty. They were both fired, and the second in command was punished by losing his employment account, and he was kicked out and penniless at the end of the process.

He picked up that she had really enjoyed the process of entrapping the bastards. And she said she had been afraid at first, but she was so angry about what had happened to Irene her major professor, and Lucy the ombudsman in the government that she was able to pull it off. "Why did you not return to campus after your work was done"? Buck asked her. "I think I had just given up on people by that time, and all I could think about was getting out and finding my own way no matter if it killed me to do so. And I thought that I was close to dying when I walked up this mountain, I had not had any water for two days and before that I had only a swallow or two for several days, and I felt like I did not have the strength to get up this mountain in the hopes that I would find a little water when I got here". "You must have felt like you had an angel on your shoulder when you saw that lake" Buck replied. And she reflected on the path that was not there, and wondered why she had seen something that was making her push forward, and when she went back it was gone. She then shared with Buck the first time up the mountain, and this path was so obvious to her and then it was gone. "You know it was so obvious to me coming up and then I saw the lake, and all I could do was run peeling off my clothes and jumping into the water". Buck then said to her "I think you had an angel on your shoulder, woman, why would you see a path, which was not there?" She thought about what he said, and she had no way to think about it, no frame of reference and she just said, "I have no idea". "I was grateful for the water, but you know I did at first not feel like I wanted to do anything but stop over for a day or two, I really had to talk myself into staying, for more than a year, I had been looking for something which I could not describe to myself, much less anyone else. But since I have been here for over a year, and I am still alive, I think of this as my home".

They ate the stew out of a couple bowls he had, and they had the dried fruit, and bread and butter, and Buck washed out the bowls and the pot he had used for cooking. And as they had the dinner cleaned up they threw several more logs on the fire, and sat and talked as they had the night before. She asked him about the community and he gave her a more complete description of it, and she said she was thinking about maybe going with him when he returned in the two weeks. "What about the pony, will he be okay if we are gone a couple of days? It takes a day to get there and a day back and a day to work. That is three days; I would not want him to wonder if he had been abandoned." Rose thought about it, and thought he would most probably be okay, "I would worry about any longer, but three days he will probably be okay." She asked him about his family, and he told her about his father's anger at the water utility and how the longer he worked for them the more depressed he got, and about how when he got out of high school, how he too went to work there, and then his father decided to retire before he really should have, and his folks were sent up north to a retirement place, and his Dad got more and more depressed because he was not sure he had enough in the account to pay for heat when it was cold and finally he took his own life and left his mother there and alone. When Buck found out that his father had killed himself, he took time off to go to retrieve his mother to bring her back to live with him so he could take care of her. "She was a good woman, and deserved better than she got. When she came to live with me we enjoyed a much better life, and she even did some things which she loved to do, and I was there for her to make sure she had every opportunity. But what got her was the bad water in town, I told her to bathe rather than shower because I did not want her to get it in her mouth, and to use the bottled water for brushing her teeth, but she preferred to shower, she thought it was cleaner than bathing and I think she got some of that filthy water in her mouth. At first she thought she had gotten the flu and she could not get over it, she went to the hospital, and within about a month she was critical, and was dead in another month. From that point I raised as much hell about fixing the underground system, I even went into my Bosses office and yelled at him and called him a killer, and he shouted back that he had no okay from the mountains and his hands were tied. I brooded about that for more than a year, and then that day when I had the truck I just thought I needed out. My impotency was contributing to death in the city, and I just had to leave. I had to recognize my own helplessness. And I did not want to turn into my father and if I did not get out I was on the way to doing just that". It was clear to Rose that this was a good man, he had cared for his parents, and sent them money and then he took care of his mother, when his father died, and just the fact that he felt so frustrated by not being able to set things right in the city even after both parents were gone, she knew that he was a fine man. "You are a good man Buck and I think your mother was a lucky woman to have such a caring Son." "I loved them both, and it was a real pleasure to see that my mom could have a little peace in her life." She said that in the morning she would try for a rabbit, and he said, he had never eaten rabbit that he knew of, and she assured they were very good, and he could bring bread and butter up the hill, "and by the way don't bring bread, there is some up there, just bring the butter, and maybe another tomato, and he said he would and she walked back up the hill followed by her little buddy who had hung around Buck's camp site this evening.

Well she thought to herself, as she walked back up the hill, He seems like he was a really nice person and had really good values. She appreciated the degree of his responsibility even for people he had never known, and he seemed to be sensitive to his own needs as well and she was impressed by his comfort in talking about his feelings. In fact it made her a little jealous as she had never been able to talk much about her own feelings in fact she tried hard to escape her own emotions. He definitely had a lot more access to his own emotions than she had to hers.

She reached the top of her mountain, and she was sleepy and bedded down the colt, and went in to her little shelter and fell into a deep sleep.

The neighbors, as they had begun to refer to each other, ate one meal together each day and Buck had asked Rose if it would be okay if he worked on her shelter a bit, he felt she needed a door that could be secured, and expand it a bit so she would not be so cramped for sleep. He in addition wanted to use some of the left over bricks to expand her capacity to cook inside as the weather turned colder and she wanted to work with him in order to learn what she could about building. One evening when it was her turn to cook, and she had snagged a rabbit which she was cooking outdoors in her fire pit which he had expanded for her convenience.

A now familiar voice was heard coming up the hill, "something a little different, a Rabbit, I have never to my knowledge eaten a rabbit, but I am hungry tonight, so let's do it" he said. "It is kind of like chicken dark meat, and I got to love the taste coming across the land. It makes really good jerky too, and that is really good to have when you are traveling." "I bet that meant you could make more distance for those days." Buck commented as he met her on the hill top. "Yes, it meant that I could fetch my blanket, get a piece or two of jerky, stretch out and eat, drink some water, and let myself relax and feel satisfied."

"Rose do you know how far you walked to make it to here?" She thought for a moment and then replied, "No I don't have a clue how far it was and you know I am just grateful that I made it this far." I really do feel safe here, I can be myself; I can be free of the awful system that we have both escaped, and best of all I live here without contributing to the hurt of anyone else. You and I in that system back there if we got a raise, or a benefit of some sort, because they the Oligarch's set it up as a zero sum game, some other person lost something. When I made that little discovery I had to leave, I had real trouble with that structure of the economic system." "Rose, it is all rigged, the rich owners in that society won't let go of what they built over the years. And you know they feel like they earned that wealth, and it is legitimate, I when I was working up there on the mountain, I was talking to one of the Brown Water guards, and he said, that he has been stationed up around the community, and they talk about the working class being greedy, and that they will do whatever they can to separate us from what we have worked for years to earn. Rose they believe that we would actually would mount a raid to take their money or their stuff, or whatever. They according to the guard I spoke with, the wealth holders are very fearful. Fearful of the potential the workers would attack them, have you ever heard any one in our class talk about raiding them? I have not, and doubt they would give it a thought." Rose immediately responded that she had never heard of a person who was even interested in fighting with the wealthy, that most of her class had given up. "Yes that was what I said to the guard, and his comment to me was that Brown

Water guards is really who they need to be careful of, they have the guns".

They both laughed at the irony of such an outcome, "But Rose the guy seemed to be saying what they, the guards, really felt." And Buck had commented on the homes, and the environmental comforts that they had created for themselves up there, and he was clearly angry at the difference between the ways they lived vs. how the workers had to live. "Look Buck we have a kind of freedom that the wealthy don't have, we are genuinely free, and can read all day if we like, or we can walk and enjoy the environment, the lake and the trees, and the pony, and whatever it is we have."

She watched his face and it softened, "you amaze me Rose", he said "You have made such an amazing adjustment to this life away from people, and you have just put away whatever it was that made you angry enough to risk your life and your safety!" She thought for a moment, and then she began telling him about being so hurt and so angry about what had happened to Irene, and to Lucy, and how she got into the inner circle with the higher ups at work, and the whole story of trapping the bastards that had effectively removed her own hopes for the Ph.D. and a new career teaching on campus. She talked about Donald and his inability to stay sober at one of these "in-service" meetings that they held once a month, and how her big boss pilfered the money from the government to serve catered food and all the alcohol that they all could drink, and then the night she thought she could get a confession on her tape recorder which was a miniature bracelet that she always wore to keep track of her work, and how Donald just gushed the whole story of how they 'took down the university hot shots', and then finally how she made a contact with the legal department to get them charged with embezzlement. When that was done, I knew things were even, and I could go to visit Irene for the last time, and tell her that I had evened the score. I came back from Des Moines, left my apartment, moved to a cabin up on the eastern hills, and began to prepare to leave." She told him that when she left and began her walk away, she felt that she had settled the score, and she thought staying any longer would have put her own health at risk, and health was what was most important to her. As she walked she found a kind of peace settle in on her mind and her emotions, she told Buck that had been the most instructive experience of her life, it gave her both time and distance to put to rest the rage that had driven her during the time she worked to trap the bastards, that had so intruded in her life. "I am glad I walked, Buck because I could put the rage on the ground I covered, and as that process was going on, with each step I could feel lighter, and freer, and I would not trade that feeling of freedom for anything this world could give me". Buck was fighting back tears at this point, "I cannot tell you how I admire you and your will power". She smiled at him, and she said, "Well you wanted to know, that is the whole story." "Would you like to drive down to Des Moines and see your friend"? He asked? She thought for a moment, and said, "You know that part of my life is finished, now, I have to think about that. Isn't it a long way?" "it would take us about two or two and a half days I think, It is 8 hours to the community I work at, I think it is another two days drive, but I would want to paint over the sign on the truck before we go." She began to laugh, "You don't want Irene to think you're a common criminal huh?" "Yes, as a matter of fact, she might not understand the way you did, and I would not want her to judge either of us, in a poor way." "You know Buck I think that she would admire you for taking what you needed and thank you for coming to see her."

The rabbit was well cooked by this time and they each took some of the animal, and Buck had brought some vegies which he had cut up to make them easier to consume, and they sat near the little lake and ate, sharing with the Colt carrots which were his favorite, and She pondered how it would feel to see Irene one more time.

Buck helped her clean up and he mentioned that they would be going to the community in two days. "Is there something that I can do while you work, I do not want to be idle while everyone else is working?" I think you would be welcomed to work in the big community garden, and you could earn some credit for the commissary for things which you might like to have or need." "Well all my clothes are getting kind of ratty, and I would like to get a couple of good long pants and some shorts and a couple of shirts." "I am sure you can come home with some new duds, they have a lot of clothes in the commissary" Buck said in response and they agreed to eat at the camp site, and Buck suggested that since he wanted to leave very early so perhaps she could sleep in the tent, and he would climb into the truck cab, where he had slept as he drove across to get here, and she agreed she would be happy to facilitate an early departure, Buck headed back to his camp.

Rose spent the next day preparing for the trip, she walked with the young colt, and talked to him about her trip and she would be back in three days and he should just stay on his side of the lake and mind his own business, that she would be back and he should remember that he was her buddy. She had no idea what kind of impact she was having on the youngster, but she kept at it as she put a change of clothing into her back pack, and she took a bath in the lake to get some of the grime off her body and hair. She felt that she was prepared for the trip and she at about the mid-afternoon began the trip down the hill with the colt right behind her. She was a little concerned about his presence right behind her, but she did not change her gait, and she proceeded to Buck's campsite. She arrived to smell the odor of the meat he was cooking, ground beef, with pieces of potatoes cut up in the meat so she looked at it and commented that it smelled good and it must be hamburger stew. He shared with her that it had been his favorite supper when he was a kid, and he loved the combination. "When I go into the community I always hope they have some ground beef." Soon Buck thought it was ready to eat, and he served it in the bowls he had at the campsite, and they ate a good supper, and cleaned up quickly and he loaded the truck with several things he thought he should carry back to aid him in his work, and he brought a piece of paper that he had made a list on to share with her. "You know I asked you if I could work on your shelter, well this is a list of what I will get to accomplish that task, is it still okay with you that I do that work?" She thought that she should work in the garden to pay for some of this, and he responded, "You know that I think it is my idea and I should pay for these materials, and I will get food too, and the materials as I have a big balance in my account, and you cover the cost of the clothes you need, okay?" "Also I think that it might be helpful if you maybe just did not worry about who is paying for what." She agreed but she did become aware that she was a little uncomfortable with not paying for what she would be benefiting from. Buck picked up some of what she was worried about. He said he wanted to talk this out so when they got there she would be more comfortable with their arrangement. "Look Rose let me just do this for you, no strings attached. I have never dated, and I am frankly, needing to level with you, that I am amazed by who you are and I am as well just wanting to feel like I can do something to help you and maybe even make your life more comfortable." She listened and she responded "I am grateful for your help, but I want to let you know that I feel that one of the most painful things I have been through in my adult life was losing a man I had loved, and not acknowledged, and I am never going to go through that again. It feels like when he was killed in an explosion where he was employed, and it was so painful, that I felt like I was unable to feel anything but rage at myself for not realizing what I was feeling toward him. You know I realize that I made a different life for myself, and the fact that I could marry now and it would not be controlled in any way, but I have trouble thinking about letting myself be that vulnerable ever again, I acknowledge that I find you are a very thoughtful and kind person, you are a great guy. I though am fearful of my emotional life, and my response is to block on my feelings." Buck took in what she had shared. He put his hand out, and she grasped his hand, he put an arm around her shoulders and said, "You know I will not push you, I cannot get you out of my awareness, I am glad that you told me about your painful loss, and it hurts me that you had that loss. The first morning we met, when I came up for water, I saw your shelter, and I looked in to see you sleeping, and you were so lovely to me, I think I would do anything to protect you, and I would never do anything to hurt you. I know I cannot control how life goes, but I want to keep you safe and healthy and happy. That is how I feel, and you should know that, at least. I am very protective when I love someone, and that is what you need to know." He took her into the tent, unrolled his sleeping bag, and suggested that perhaps since they would leave very early, that she should try to get some sleep, and he said, "Rose if you need me I will be in the big truck, okay? He left the tent, and she found her mind going at quite a pace, and even though she lay down, his confession of his feelings was a shock to her, and at once she wanted to stay and run away, she was confounded by his frankness.

He called her in the morning, the sun was not up as yet, and she got up and got ready to go into the community. They drove in silence for the first part of the trip, and then Buck broke the silence and said, you look tired, Rose, did you have trouble falling asleep? She replied in the affirmative, and then said, "You know it is hard to fall asleep when someone confesses their love for you, and you react like a rabbit being watched". It was hard for her to get her head around what he had told her, that he would be her protector, her help mate, and there were, as he had said, no strings he just needed her to know his feelings. As the sun came up it was in their eyes, and they both had to shield their vision. She commented that this was the hard direction and they both laughed, and she began to feel herself relax a bit, and she shared with Buck that she had a rough night, "it was a little hard to work through what you finally shared with me last night, and I still do not know fully what to feel, think, wonder about, and I am still a bit confused". "I wondered about our relationship, you referred to us as neighbors, and friends. But you say to me that you want to keep me safe, and make my life easier, and protect me, and that is what love looks like to me, and I do not know how I feel, or if I let myself feel. When Jeff died, I got afraid because I would have had to move away from Jeff if he had lived and I just could not have married him independent of how I might have felt. I intended to be independent in the world, and work for myself and live independent in order to remain myself. I knew that my mother loved and adored my father, but gave up herself in order to be his wife and my mother. She was a natural teacher, and she gave that up and it cost her dearly. I did not want to be her. So I did the opposite. The environment of the old society had all these restrictions, and I know cognitively I no longer have to live with those old rules, and that has been a relief, and yet I have to tell you I really do feel you are a very kind and thoughtful and I am glad you live at the bottom of my hill, and it is good to be your friend, and I really can let go of some of my rules about men only being friends, I can even think about your loving me, and wanting to take care of me, and I can appreciate and even do that when I can and I think I am confused about the next step. Does there need to be a next step?" "No not if you don't feel that a next step is natural and would be something that you want" Buck replied. "We will see how things go but do not do anything that does not feel right for you." "I have always been very fact based, how will I know for sure if it should be what I feel?" she asked. "Not sure, I have always done what felt best".

He spotted a place he said he always stopped at just for a break. "There are a couple of natural springs over there, and I usually stop there, and get a big drink for the rest of the trip." They moved to the left, and pulled into a grove of trees and flowering bushes. They were green and it was a beautiful environment and she walked from the truck and dipped her hands into the spring, and drank deeply of the water which was clear and clean. She got up and walked around the spring, and turned to Buck and asked how he found this spring, and he told her that he had stayed here for some several nights, but he wanted to be farther away from the community, and he had seen the campsite near the mountain he felt more of a sense of peace. "That is interesting; it is kind of how I feel on the mountain, a sense of peace."

"How much farther to the community?" and Buck responded about two more hours. And they both climbed back into the truck, and began to resume the trip. It was about three in the afternoon, and they moved onto the black top of the road which lead directly to the community, and as he explained this was the way he found the community in the first place.

They went down the black top road, and soon they could see the first sign of the community the big water tower, and as they drove Buck spotted someone walking out to meet them, and it was the guy that was one of the leaders of the community, his name was Bill, and took a lot of the responsibility for the water system. They pulled up to meet Bill and he said, "Am I glad to see you Buck", "We have a leak and some of the underground we think is leaking a lot." "Hi miss, Buck you have a guest for us to meet?" "Yes, Bill, my friend is my neighbor and she wanted to come to work in the garden, and maybe get some credit to get some new clothes in the commissary and listen to the story too about your community." "Great there is nothing we enjoy more is a new face and a new story"

Bill got into the truck and they drove back to the underground housing, and the two men looked for the leaks with some kind of a pressure gauge which they hooked up to different parts of the lines. They located the line where the pressure was low, and Buck looked at the schematics of the original building plans. He said what they could do is shut down this section and use a kind of plastic sealant to block the line, and then they could reset the new line, and by pass the break. He said, that would be easy to get the fix, done. And they all three drove over to the community meeting hall, and Rose began to meet many of the people of the community and learn their stories. Soon a huge meal was beginning to be served and Bill stood up and introduced Rose to the community and everyone asked her to hang around after everyone ate, to meet and talk. It was an amazing evening, Rose told her story to the assembled group, and she met a woman who herself had worked in a governmental unit Rose had worked in and they bonded almost immediately and Betsy offered her a bed for the night and a trip to the garden to work with her in the morning. Betsy and Rose had so much in common, and they talked most of the night. Buck slept in a guest quarters that the community had set up for him when he was there over night, and they ate breakfast together and attended to their work for the day, and met at the evening meal.

The garden was amazing and Rose conducted a small class on composting which none of the garden group had any idea of doing. She and Betsy began working with the cooks about saving and giving compost to the gardening group and everyone voted to give Rose a supervisor standing so whenever she came to town with Buck and she could earn with her work more credits and Rose felt affirmed by the group. She sat with Buck and she shared with him her activities of the day, and he was happy about her onsite promotion in standing. "Now you can get clothes this evening and some seeds, they are very generous with credits and you will be amazed at how much you can purchase from one day's work." After their evening meal they walked to the commissary and a young man helped them get what they wanted to take with their credits and the young man showed Rose her account, and she had 12 credits for her work, given her supervisors role, and she got three pairs of pants, four shirts, and a packet of a variety of seeds and she had some credit left over. "All these seeds in the packet have done well here in our garden, but I am not sure they will do well on a mountain top" the commissary worker said, and so she got into the package of seeds and thought that the only way to really know is try them, "so I will take them as they are, and let you know how they are doing" Ed, the commissary worker said they would be interested in buying any leftover harvest if they did not eat everything that she grew.

She walked out with her new clothes, and her packets of seeds, and Buck had a bunch of lumber a new saw, and boxes of nails and other hardware. She put her stuff into the truck, and she went back into the commissary to see if she could get a hoe which would make her planting a little easier. The kid in the commissary gave her a broken shovel, and a hoe, "I bet Buck could fix the shovel handle, it is our contribution to your effort, and we look forward to your success". She was feeling very connected to the community and she loaded the two tools for her gardening into the truck, and they prepared to head back very early in the morning. Can you ask Betsy to get you up at three; I am a little concerned about the kid. And I feel we need to head back to make sure he is okay. If we leave here at three then we will get home at about 4. And we will have time to search if need be. "Okay, I will ask her maybe she has an alarm. I will be here at the truck at 3 a.m." They went to bed and Betsy had an alarm.

She shared with Betsy the presence of the colt and they needed to get back with some light still available in case they needed to find him. She slept, deeply and the alarm got her up and she had a few minutes to say good bye and thank Betsy for her hospitality.

They were on the black top road going north quickly and she commented that she had really enjoyed her visit and thanked Buck for taking her in. She commented too that she would be happy to return when she had a way to put in work and help them both with what she could earn. She somehow over the last two days had felt a kind of sense of hope, not that she wanted to move to the community but that they were there, had been so welcoming and for such a small contribution in work and knowledge she had really replenished her clothing needs and gotten a real start for her garden which she had wanted for so long. She said to Buck that she had been burying entrails and fish heads in her garden area, for years now, and she was sure now that it would pay off in great soil; and a great harvest. He said he was happy that she had enjoyed herself, but he was genuinely concerned about the pony and he was anxious to get home and find him. "Buck I am sure he is okay, he had bonded with the space up on the west of the lake, and I think he will be happy to see us, but he left the herd because his dad drove him out and there is no other place for him to go and he has all his needs met up on the mountain". "But he is bonded with you, and you are not there, and I think he will feel a lot better if he sees you."

They drove as quickly as he felt they could, and by the time the sun was high in the sky, they could almost see the campsite, and Buck felt a lot more relaxed the closer they got to the area. He pulled into his normal parking area, and they got out and they both headed back up the hill and very quickly there was a young colt standing there in the trail up, switching his tail and obviously was delighted to see them. He rose up onto his hind legs and whinnied a greeting to the returning people, and was obviously the happiest pony in the territory. The two humans were happy to see him and know that he was okay.

"I feel so much better, I was genuinely worried, but I guess you knew him better than I did." "Well I thought he would be okay but you know when it became clear that you were worried about him I just let it go, what good for both of us to be that concerned?" They unloaded the truck and Buck carried all the lumber and hardware for the construction of her shelter up the hill, and he then took down his tent and carried it up for her to occupy while he was working on stabilizing her shelter, and he brought up a very comfortable camp chair for her to use for reading or whatever and he brought up the one he had at his campsite. He brought up another package he had purchased while they were there, and it was eating bowls and some forks and spoons. And finally he gave her a real fishing pole and line, and hooks, which would not be as easily looted by the fish. She was very surprised, and thanked him and he replied, "You are the more patient of the two of us, so you should do the fishing" She was so surprised by his purchases she promised a great fish dinner in the evening tomorrow. "Good" he replied. He said that he would sleep outside the tent and she could have her privacy, and he found a place near to where the colt usually slept and he threw the sleeping bag he had brought up. He went down, and got a couple of cans for dinner, beef stew in a can, and brought it up with a pot to heat it in. She built a fire and heated the beef stew for their dinner, and they talked and ate and both were feeling tired, and they slept in the tent, as Rose felt like she did not want to kick him out of his home at this point in their relationship.

She was very touched by the surprise gifts of the fishing tackle, and pole, and the forks and spoons and bowls. They were great gifts and they made her life a lot easier. In the morning she got right to the task of fishing for their dinner and was very successful. She snagged three big ones, and she used dragon flies for bait, and she was cleaning the fish by noon and burying the entrails and heads in the far end of her garden space. She put her new spade into the ground and was delighted to see the abundance of worms and the dark shade of the dirt. She told Buck about her Grammy and her garden, and burying all of her organic garbage. It was valuable too now because she could earn more and share the learning with the community. "I bet they will see an increase in their crops after a while. They produce a lot of organic garbage down there, and by the time we get back they will have expanded the garden a lot."

"When will you need to go back" she asked him, and he replied he told them he would be back in a couple of weeks, that they had by radio, ordered some sealant to rehab the leak that they found and he would teach them how to apply the stuff, and it would be there in two weeks. "In the meantime I will do the work on your shelter, and take a couple of days to read and relax and then I can go again." They both thought it best if she stayed here next trip and Buck acknowledged he would worry about the colt if they did this too often, and she agreed.

She cooked the fish, and this time she used a little butter in the skillet, and the fish tasted so good, that she thought this was a great way to flavor the fish, and get a little of a crust on the meat. She cut up some tomatoes that Buck had brought back, and as they ate this evening she felt significantly more relaxed, she said to him that she felt peaceful like she had not felt in a long time, if ever. "I hope that is a good thing for us" and she thought she had gone through a shift as she thought about his admission of his feelings and if he could be patient she would level with him about her feelings. "There is a lot you need to know about me though", and he said "that is a lifelong process" and she agreed but then she said" if they were to have a

relationship he needed to know a lot more about her and some
of the values she had lived by that seemed out dated, and "even
inappropriate to me now."

"Like what?" "I think most men see themselves as married, or
looking if they are not, and I grew up feeling that I could never
not work. That was because the system put so many constraints
on people, and limited women if they wanted to be in a caring
relationship they forfeited their options and a lot of us just did not
want to make those kinds of deals, and I still almost think, would
I even wonder if I had not been in that kind of world, would I feel
the same way, I do not think so, you are such a nice person, and
you feel like you could live out here and be as free as I feel. I have
so bonded to this environment I see myself spending my life on this
mountain top. And I hear that is what you want. I really appreciate
that you brought your mom back to live more comfortably than
she had when she went up with your Dad. I am glad that you burst
into your boss's office and yelled about the failure to repair the pipes
that carried clean water to us all, I even think that you would have
reacted to protect the campus as I did by nailing those bastards
in government. You and I both believe in being serious about our
commitments, and doing what we say we will do. We share a lot of
rather basic values, and I really do feel very close to you, and I have
to put away those old standards that guided my life and options
for so long." She explained to him about her parents suicide, and
before she left living near the governmental office she took their
box of ashes, rented a vehicle and drove it out to the coast line and
found a place to place their ashes where no one could interrupt
her process as by the time she placed her parents into the beautiful
ocean where "I knew my mother would appreciate being placed and
my father was in no state to argue with me about it, and I waited
long enough for the government to have a law passed against placing
ashes anywhere except where people had to purchase a little piece
of land and bury ashes with a marker. I know that if I purchased a
little plot that would have totally pissed my father off." Buck had
listened and asked her why she thought it took her so long. "I was

not ready until I knew I had to leave the city, and then I needed to do what my mother wanted."

"It is kind of like you don't always know how you feel about stuff that comes along. I don't think a lot about consequences, and I just know how I feel. It makes us balanced as a couple; I need someone to talk to me about the pros and cons. The consequences of choices we can make as a couple." She thought about how he responded to her sharing her lifelong cognitive process, and she appreciated that he felt that was not only something valuable but something which he considered a strength that he needed from her.

They talked about their history for a long time. He shared that it was really very hard to live with his father's depressive state, and worried about how this affected his mother. He really did feel that if his father had been willing to take the anti-depressant that he was given by the doctors, it would have helped but his father tried to tuff it out, instead. "it was like he did not want to admit that he had an illness, that it was not all about work, but he just would not follow through, and it hurt the people who loved him the most, my Mom and Me. I have to admit that when he overdosed on his meds, it was a relief to me, at least I did not have that ongoing argument making me mad at him."

"He sounds a lot like my Dad, he would put all the blame for stuff on the owners of his plant, and he said many times when I was young that it was good that they had jobs which allowed them all to sit on their brains, I never knew what that exactly meant, but I understood that it was not a compliment". She told Buck that she used to wonder if he had been fired because he was not always careful of whom he shared his acidic comments with, and their exit to the home down in southern Arizona was about two days from the time he got the news that he did not have a job any longer. "I knew my Mom was surprised, he just came home one day, and told her to pack her stuff, that they were on their way to their assigned retirement village. Just from what my mom shared, it seemed like it was more than abrupt."

They sat up talking very late that night, and Buck showed her what he was about to do to her shelter, and she thought it would be a good thing, to have a solid door that just that would keep her warmer when the weather changed, and he told her that by that time she would relent and become his wife, and then he would keep her as warm as she needed to be. "We will see, Buck I do need some time, I will tell you what I am thinking about and what I think about us", and she agreed that she felt close to him, and she appreciated who he was, as a partner, and potential mate, and she did admit to feeling anxious about such a momentous decision. "What is it that you're anxious about, maybe if we talk about it then it will help, I really do love you, I feel it in my bones, and I have a life commitment to make to you, but only when you feel secure. I need to know what will help, and that is my only concern." "Don't you understand I do not know what that is?" "I guess I will keep talking to you and I think I can give you an answer when I figure out what it is that I feel"

They worked several days on the shelter and she dug up a portion of the garden and planted her first seeds. It was getting to be warmer at night and she thought that they would germinate if she kept the ground damp and so she looked after about a week to see if she could see any little green tops of the plants coming up. In eight days she saw her first plant coming through. It was a tomato plant and they both were excited by the new life showing its presence, and the week that passed she saw more evidence of new life coming through the dirt, and she knew that for all the entrails she had dug into the earth that her garden would rival Granny's and she felt a real pride in these new little shoots coming in and she began to feel different about Buck as well. He was doing a really good job making her shelter quite stable, and he finally hung the door, and he had put a latch on the door so it was clearly more solid and even able to be locked from either side. She thanked him for all the work he had done on the shelter, and he told her safety, was part of the reason he wanted to do the work. "I wondered about your safety if I could just walk into this space so could someone else, and I want you to have a place where you could be really safe, I could have been a bastard who might have hurt you, and the next guy who walks up here might want to hurt you. You are a beautiful woman, and I must protect you in every way I can." She put her arms around him and thanked him, and began to tear up a little, and he wiped the tears away so gently that she just stayed in his embrace, and allowed him to just hold her there in front of the shelter. She felt a stirring in her body and she knew what that was communicating to her and she stepped back and said that she knew he had to go in the morning back to the community and he should tell them all hello from her, that the garden was growing and that your woman is melting and when you get home we can talk about our relationship. I think I am getting to the point that I am ready for some talk about what we can do. I have some things that I have not told you and I need to do that but for now you have to go, and I will be here safe, and you will do what you need to do to help them". "Is there anything that I can bring you from the community?" "Can we afford a couple more packets of seeds?" "No problem, do you want particular kinds or just more in a packet" "You get what you like and it will be great". He held her close, and then went to the tent to try to get a little sleep, and she moved her stuff back into the shelter, and went to bed with a little fire in the fireplace to take the chill off the room, which now was substantially bigger than it had originally been. She had no need to bolt the door so it snapped closed, and she finally fell into a peaceful sleep, and when she heard woke she heard the colt kind of knocking on the side of her shelter. The sun was high in the sky and he had left her a note on her door before he had left to make the drive to the community. She unfolded the paper, and he had written that he hoped she had fun in the garden, and took lots of naps in the sunshine, and he would be back he thought in four days, probably there was enough in the cold chest so she would not have to go get a rabbit or fish for her supper. He signed it "I love you and can't wait to get home. Buck"

The cold chest was full of stuff to eat, and she decided to go see about the garden, and as she surveyed the environment she felt so good about what she saw, carrots coming up and lettuce, and tomatoes and even now sweet potatoes, and some onions and turnips. She checked her garden map and discovered that overnight the potatoes were coming up and she needed to create a lattice to let the leaves be off the ground. There were enough leftovers of wood and so she tied them together with wire and mounted the structure, and led the leaves up the frame. She could not have been happier, and she thought about how she had tortured herself with her defensive stance, what did she want a guarantee, which no one could give her, she did have a physical sensual urge when she was with him, and she knew what she had trouble acknowledging was that sense of passion which she felt for him. The problem is that I am not able to admit that I have a body with urges she said to herself. She had adapted to a celibate life because she felt she had no other option. And she had to tear down those defenses and she was frightened to do that. She simply had to put herself in his care and everything would be okay she thought, and that would be how she would handle it. "I trust him, and I have to trust him not just with my history, but I need to trust him to help me feel, that is what he is so good at and how I am so limited."

The day went slowly and she spent a day reading her electronic reader, and she fell asleep in the sun for a short time, and she noticed that she was needing to get out of the sun and cool for a while so she got her clothes off and went for a brief swim in the lake which attracted the attention of the colt who was into the lake before she knew it, and he swam out to meet her in the middle. His back was under water and so as she had done before quite by accident, she swung up onto his back and he proceeded to walk toward the side of the lake where it was very shallow, and she instead of getting off she let him get out of the water, and he walked around with her still astride his back and he carried her over to the shelter and then stood so still she could hear him asking her to dismount. Taking advantage of his cooperative mood she stayed and he did not move, and then after a moment she slipped off his back and thanked him for the ride, and went in the shelter to put on clothes once again, and took a nap in the afternoon.

She really spent three days of rest by and large, however as time passed her mind drifted toward the community and she wondered how Buck was doing and how his work was going, and when he felt free to leave and come home, and when he got here, how would she begin to talk with him, and what approach would he hear more accurately, and she realized that she was sitting at her desk being an editor once again, and that seemed to her new awakening emotional self the exact opposite way to think about what made her fearful about bonding their lives, she knew that the month plus they had spent together up here was from this perspective a process of growing, and trusting, and listening to the story of their lives. She had acknowledged the rage she felt upon discovering her feelings for Jeff, and how they had been close for years, prior to his death, and she had not let herself access these feelings, and even how she had recommitted to the rule of no male friends. She was such a stranger in the world of emotion, those unmanageable experiences which flowed over a person and totally disable that person as they had her in that terrible moment of recognition. She even pondered the bond between her parents which was durable unto a death in the bed together, and hoping to as she imagined walk into the black holding hands, as they always had, it was like for her, they had always been of one mind, and she could never understand that bond, most of the time from her perspective it made no sense, but there it was in front of her for the first half of her life. And yet she knew on some level of her awareness that it was a bond as strong as she had ever had seen. It seemed mystical. And she had no logical explanation to use in the face of trying to understand their Love. She felt a strong doubt she could manifest what they had seemed to feel for her and each other. And she missed in that moment having her mother to sit with and listen to, and question, and for the first time she felt a kind of empty pain in her gut, and she in her response to these feelings had come finally to the surface and tears coursed her cheeks, and she cried for the first time. "Irene said that you were no good at allowing me to be free, and that is what kept me away from you and Dad as well. I needed you to let me be me, and look at me now I do not know how I feel, I am about to take a chance, but I cannot trust me to know what the hell I feel, I know Mom what I feel right now, I feel afraid."

She sat and cried, until there were not a tear left. She felt the impact of this event and she wrapped up in her insulated blanket and she slept deeply. It was very early in the morning when she woke and she had slept for a long time, and as she cleared her eyes of the sleep she resisted getting out of the warm blanket and she rolled toward the little fire place to restart a small warming flame. She closed her eyes, and said silently to herself, maybe he will be home today. Though she did not realize it, she drifted into sleep once again, and dreamed once again of her entry into the glen here on top of her mountain, and the life giving water that she had hurled herself into. It became a metaphor for her to ponder. And she realized that was entirely an act of emotion she did not give her logical part one moments part of that decision and throwing herself into the life giving water she got it. You just jump in and trust that it is right to be there.

That was what she needed to do. Throw herself and her soul in to a process of loving him.

CHAPTER TWENTY TWO

Making a real home

She was sound asleep and she heard what she thought was the snooping little boy, in Bucks tent. She got up and opened the shelter door to see Buck's shadow in the tent. "I thought it was the pony in the tent, you must have driven all night to get back so early" she said. "I had good energy, and I had put in three days, so I had a pretty big balance, I brought back a lot of food and stuff, and I thought I just needed to get back, have you been okay?" "I have thought about my reticence a lot, and I want to talk with you about a couple of things, perhaps it will help you to understand more accurately who you have formed an attachment to, and I want to talk with you about several more things I have remembered. I am hopeful it will help you to understand me. Can I help unloading what you brought back?" "I have everything up out of the truck; my bringing the last trip is what woke you. I thought that I would let you sleep, and I was going to lie down till you woke." "Buck lie down. In fact you should come here, and we can talk and you can rest in the shelter." He walked to the shelter, and stooped to come in and lay down. He was tired from the work and from the drive as well, but he seemed to be glad to be home, and as he stretched out, she threw her pillow for him to put his head down on her pillow and he commented that it did feel good to stretch out, and finally did begin to relax. She began talking to him about her fear of intimacy, and she talked about her loss of the ability to trust almost anyone, she felt that had come from her years in the Government, and yet she could feel that waning in her relationship with him. "You have never given me a reason not to trust you. I wonder about you loving me, why, what about me made you begin to feel that even before I knew you were here. I know for me I can have trust, and if I have trust, I can love, but Buck I have only known you for such a short time, and you have shared much of your life with me. I feel that I need to share more of my self so you can really know me and it may have a real influence on how I can feel. Perhaps it is that if you know me and still love me, then I can risk loving you." Buck listened, and he said, "I would never do anything that would hurt you, and yet I hear that people have hurt you when they got too close, and I can understand why that is true for you. You have been used by people, and the folks at the college were hurt because you feel that people wanted to hurt you, and take away your program of study, and they did that. You know I understand that those things did happen to you, and I am sure you carry scars from that deviant crap. I want you to tell me whatever you need to and I will listen, so I know what has hurt you, but you can bet that you will never get that kind of crap from me. I have had that crap happen to me, I know how it feels to be double crossed, it hurt down to my soul, and I would never participate in doing that to anyone else whether I knew them or not. It's just not my style." Rose stopped to think about what she had just heard. She recognized that she knew that was his way of living: that fit for all he had said. And it was clear that was what his way of relating and she had nothing to be afraid of.

"Buck, I am clear on who you are, and I trust that, I feel I trust you to hear any issue I have or feel I might and I think that I really trust you, and I do love you, and if you and I can make a relationship and perhaps even a family, I know it is a good thing to do, one day at a time, we will talk and listen to each other and we will always be able to work through whatever presents, so I do not need to talk more it will come out in the future, and that is okay, and yes I will marry you. I love you too." He got up and headed for the tent, and quickly returned with a small box. He then said, "I bought this while I was in the community, I think it will be fitting, and will fit as well." She looked at a silver ring, with a little rose carved into the center, and she flashed on telling him about when she was born and the rose that her Father had brought to her mother. "I thought it would be very appropriate for our marriage, that it could be as loving and as successful as your parents' marriage was." And he slipped it on her ring finger and they kissed and he held her, and she felt in that moment, all the fear and apprehension fall away, and she knew that this was what she needed and wanted to do. They lay together on the floor of the shelter and Buck, exhausted from his night of driving home, fell asleep with his new wife in his arms.

Buck was sound asleep and Rose got up and went to the tent to see what he had returned with in the way of supplies. There was a rather large canned Ham among the food stuff, and she began planning a nice meal for them when he woke. She heated a couple of slices of the ham and sealed the balance of the ham in a container he had purchased for food storage, and there were some sweet potatoes she placed into the coals of the fire pit to cook, and she cut up some of the celery and carrots to eat raw. Within the hour Buck was stirring and as he came out of the shelter she met him with an embrace, and announced that dinner was almost ready, that the potatoes need about fifteen more minutes and they would be tender and ready to eat. "How long did I sleep?" He asked, and Rose replied about four or five hours she could not be sure, "and what happened just before you went to sleep was not a dream, we married each other, and I have no idea as I think about it what my new last name is? Buck quickly announced that they were Mr. and Mrs. Roberts. And she thanked him for such a lovely last name.

They sat next to the fire pit and he got up to go into the tent once again and came out with new eating utensils two plates, and silverware, and she served the ham and the sweet potatoes, put a little butter on the sweet potatoes and the raw vegies, on the side, and Buck went into the tent and returned with a slice for each of pumpernickel bread with butter. They were both hungry and finished the meal rather quickly and Buck gathered up the dishes and went to wash them in the lake, and return them to the tent.

"I am going to stoke the flames in the shelter, I am sure it has gone down since this morning, and I would feel better if we were warm tonight." Rose commented and she gathered enough wood to get through the night and have some for the morning. She sat down after putting the wood to the fire to warm the environment, Buck put his arm around her shoulders, and he simply held her for a while saying almost nothing, as he held her she more and more relaxed in his partial embrace. "I have to tell you this is the happiest day of my life, little sleep, notwithstanding, Rose. You have made me a happy man, and I want you to feel secure with me." She took a very deep breath, and responded," I feel like I have changed my life in a way that I never thought I would but it feels like when you put on a glove and it fits, exactly, it is fitting.

They sat on the edge of the top of the mountain and watched the sun set in the west. And they as the sun began its crest to allow for the dark to arrive, and the two went into the shelter, and naked they lay together, warm and enjoying the closeness of each of their bodies, and experimenting with what felt comfortable and what was supportive of their passion. Rose was surprised her body was as sensitive to Bucks touch and caresses, and he was very slow and deliberate in his making love to her, and when he could feel that she was ready he rolled her over and mounted her and just as slowly he began to thrust, and she could feel a hunger and a passion rise up in her body which would be satisfied by this wonderful man, who not too many weeks prior she had verbally attacked for being from a company she had grown to hate.

She began to groan, and then let out a muffled moan as she reached her first organism. She had not expected the depth of feeling that this night she experienced. He held her as if they were one and he cried. She asked him why he was crying and he said "Oh it is just a long time reaction to joy I have had most of my life." "Oh good, I have felt something I would have trouble describing, and I feel you sobbing in my embrace" "Oh baby Rose, I do love you, your humor, and your durability and your body, and your passion, what a surprise, your my love"

They spent the night holding each other naked in the shelter in the comfort of the warmth of the fire and their passion. Both dropped off to sleep, and as the night passed Rose would rouse to check the heat, and she had positioned herself for sleep to be close to reach the wood, and be able to stoke the flames to keep the shelter warm. It suddenly occurred to her she did not know the date of their anniversary, and she made a mental note to see if when he went back to the community he could obtain for her the date of yesterday. She needed to know the date. And on that she rolled back into his embrace and fell deeply asleep. The morning came and went with these two not really leaving their comfort together in the shelter, and after mid-morning Little Boy was gently requesting the pleasure of their presence. Rose was unsuccessful in her attempts to settle him down, and then she got a pair of pants on and a shirt and she went out to settle him down. She walked down the hill to allow him to munch in the grass that was not totally brown, and while she was there she searched the trees for fruit that she might have missed in her last trip. She found two peaches, left on the tree, perfect for breakfast she thought. So she took them back, and found Buck sound asleep. "Did I wear you out last night?" and Buck rolled over and accepted the peach, from her and asked where the alarm clock was now", "He is down the hill chewing on a little of the grass that is not too brown as yet. He seems to be content." "Come back and stay here with me" Buck requested and she was in with peach juice running down one of her arms, "These are still pretty juicy" "Do we have an agenda today?" Rose asked. Buck said, "I want to start planning our home." "You want to do what?" "We are married and we need a proper home, and I want to plan what we want so I can begin to bring home what we need, for that project." "Okay" Rose responded, "Not a lot of grass grows under your feet." "I brought home some paper and it is over in the tent, and there are some kinds of fat mechanics pencils in the small bag in the big paper bags". "I will go retrieve them, but I have a preference about where we build.

And I will explain to you why". She fetched the pencils and paper, and they sat together and Buck was very specific about the way he had thought to build, and he outlined a floor plan which looked like a misshapen "L" with a foot going the wrong way. All the water service would come from a catchment system, along the one side of the house, with a kitchen on that wall, and that would be on the east side of the proposed house, and the long part of the side, would be a living room, and a bed room at the back, and on the west wall there was a lovely stone fireplace, and she took him outside and told him the story of her original entry into the mountain top, and suggested that they have a big window in the front room and how to situate the floor plan so she could see from that window the first vision she had of the lake. "Honey, it looked like heaven to me" I knew I would live.

She took him down the hill and showed him where it was that she saw the trail coming up the only to come back and find no trail, "you know I felt like it was kind of strange, that something which was so important for me, to stay with following something which was leading the way, and showing me where it was that I needed to be, and because I was tired and really a little hopeless I seemed to need the guidance for a time. When I no longer needed that guidance, it was gone". Buck pulled her close, and thought that had she died, he would still be so alone, and he felt tears come to his eyes. He held her and simply said to her," I am so glad you found your hope, it has changed my life".

They both walked back to the wood pile and found some small pieces that could be shaped into stakes, and they paced off the outline of the external dimensions and set the stakes, and Buck began to calculate the amount of cement they would have to obtain to set the floor and establish the braces on the bottom to begin the construction of walls. He said that he could begin part of the process without any of the materials, and he told her that digging out the septic tank and digging out the area for the pipes to be laid in a way that would protect their integrity. "I have learned a lot about building, helping out with repairs in the community, so we can avoid some of the mistakes that they made in their original designs."

They began to make a list of some of the supplies, and materials they would first need, and they both agreed that it would be a wonderful thing to look forward to, and Buck thought that she should think about things which would make her life as easy as it could be made, "Honey, think about exactly what you want in a home that is ours, which will make what you do more simple, and convenient."

"We can heat water for showering and cleaning from one of the roof top solar heaters, and we can have a chemical toilet too, which will make life a lot easier, out here. And we can add anything else that crosses your mind, so let's think together before we get underway, so we can develop the structure in such a way that we don't get into the bind the community got into with add on's. That is what they spend so much sweat and time on when I go down there, and they are getting ahead of the problems but we have the option think ahead and plan ahead."

She asked him to tell her about what they needed to do to prepare and he wrote out a kind of step by step program about how to prepare the lines for the distribution of water and he told her that he was much stronger and he would do the digging and for the project so she did not have to do any of that really hard physical work. "Why don't you just let me decide what I can do and what is too much for me to handle" and he replied, "You are right, I did not have the tolerance to walk, and clearly you did, how can I know what you can do and what is too much." "That is better; I will let you know what is too much."

They talked about the house, throughout the day, and the more they talked the more excited they both became. "I want to start digging today" said Rose, and Buck replied that he felt it was jumping the gun, in a couple of days, we can do just that, but we should just spend time with each other, this is our special time, and perhaps I spoke about my dream too quickly." "No you did not speak too quickly, I am excited with your dream, and it very quickly became my own, and it is for us, not just you and it is just so exciting to think about, Buck. It will be a long time in the process, and I can wait for you, but I do not want you to think that I can't keep up with you." Buck smiled at his wife, and said to her that he would not make that mistake.

In the afternoon they walked the north side of the mountain, and picked up several large rocks that they found and Buck thought would be just perfect for the face of the fireplace and so the beginning of the process had begun.

Buck wanted to find a path that would allow him to drive up the south side of the mountain, to bring the heavy materials up into the area, and he and Rose went down the mountain toward the South, as that side seemed to have fewer large obstacles which would prevent driving the big truck up the mountain.

Buck drove the large truck up very slowly, and Rose walked in front to give him a heads up when a potentially dangerous rock was about to become a problem in his forward progress. Within the hour they were setting out marker stakes, so the trip up would have a guidance mechanism which would aid the process with getting to the top with very heavy loads.

It was afternoon, of the first full day of this new marriage, and they retired to the shelter for a nap, and they once again felt the passion that had captured the two of them in the evening, and they made love and slept for a while, and got up to quiet the hunger that they felt, and rather quickly went back to sleep completely satisfied, and happy with their new status and the goal of having a real home together.

CHAPTER TWENTY THREE

Back to the community

Buck had dug out not only the septic system hole, but Rose had made the goal of two or three rocks per day and had she thought about a quarter of the needed rocks for the face of the fireplace. The couple had discussed the possibility of a return trip to the community, and they decided to leave to make the trip within a couple of days. He made a specific list of what they needed at this point of time and part of it would require a trip in the big truck. They looked over the list, the pipes, which would set up the sewage system, and Quick set cement, to be mixed with a source of sand down in the valley. He had estimated for the structural cement he would need about fifteen or twenty feet of rock to be mixed into that concrete and he was not sure about the degree of available rocks. He then had on the list plywood to form the frame for setting the floor. so he would have it available. And in addition to the list he sat and created a work plan, for the purpose of developing some kind of a notion, about the date of completion. He tried to be very conservative, and he finally handed his work sheet to Rose. Her eyes scanned the outline, and when she looked at his estimate for date of completion as ten months, and she let out a laugh, "are you serious? Are we thinking of training the horses to help? I had a target date in my head about two years!"

"No I think I am, if not right on the dime, I am close." She re-read his list, she began to understand the step by step progress, and it did make sense to her, but she thought He was overestimating how quickly the two of them could erect a home. "Rose in the community they can get a new building up in about two weeks, and they have some mechanical aids, like earth movers, and power tools which we will not have but I am assuming we can do this, and we will have a little wager on our outcome, Okay Sweet woman?" "I will take your bet, and I promise I will not be a slacker I would promise I will give it my all."

She asked him what he would like to get done before they went into the community and he said that he needed to get down to the bottom of the septic hole, and then measure so he could get the metal liner made when they went in to the community and he could do that today.

So Rose asked what the bet would be, and she watched Buck as he thought about the nature of their wager, and he thought for a moment, and he then turned to her and said, "you need to name it", and she responded rather quickly, "If we go over one year, I can name our first child, and if I lose you can name all the children we have!" "It is a deal!" Rose responded. But honey, I may be too old to have children, I am not really clear on how old I am, but I think I am in my late 30's and most women become menopausal in their 40's. And it is my notion the older you get the less fertile, you are becoming."

"When we go to the community," Buck said, "we can determine the date and year, and use that to figure out how old each of us is, and even ask the doctor about fertility and age". Rose agreed, and they proceeded to get ready to go into the community. Buck began finishing his digging, and he very carefully measured the pit and the piping he would next set up for running water from the collection system and with this task completed from a materials perspective they were essentially ready to leave.

They went to sleep early after a quick meal and a survey of their food supply, and what food they might need to obtain for the next month.

They had slowly driven the truck down the hill, and were on the road to the community by three a.m. and Buck thought they would arrive about ten to eleven in the morning, and as they drove he was aware that the battery was high and would easily make it until the sun came up to replenish its charge. They drove and talked about the plan of their home, and Buck brought up the need to add to the design if children would be born of their union, "I designed a home for us, not really for a family, and we do need another bed room for a child, or children. Honey would you see that another room would fit with the existing design, or should we put that design I drew away and begin again?" They continued to look at options and recognized that it would not affect the part that he had worked on and they agreed to reevaluate the design when they returned home.

Before the sun was up they had passed the area where they would turn off to reach the natural spring, and were coming up on the area which just preceded the black top, and as the sun rose they were amazed that they had only twenty or so miles to the edge of the community. They drove onto the community property to the main dining room, and joined everyone for breakfast. "We hear this young woman is now Mrs. Roberts", Bill announced, and the whole community let out a cheer, for the couple and Betsy, came to sit with Rose, and said, to her she admired her spunk. "I do not know if I would be able to make the change that you have negotiated" "Betsy I had to push myself to even think about it, and I must have talked to myself for hours while Buck was away here, doing work to just give it up and trust my feelings that I could not deny."

Everyone was preparing for the day of work, and Betsy wanted to take Rose out to see the composting and what they had done with it since Rose had been in the community. "I wanted to work today in the garden, and I know they will have Buck busy with the building above ground." Rose kissed Buck and told him she would be working in the garden today with Betsy, and she would see him at lunch. Buck told her that he had made arrangements for their night, and he would show her after dinner where they would be lodging, and the couple separated to proceed to their work for the day. Rose and Betsy walked to the composting place, and Rose turned a bit of the soil and sure enough those little black bodies were present in large numbers and they were busy breaking down the organic elements in the ground to a deep black soil. "It looks great, Betsy, it will need to be moved through to the garden when it gets a bit more broken down". "What we planned to do Rose is move some of the vegetables that do not grow as well over there to here, just to see if they can be more productive and then change the garbage burial over there to begin to get the other garden to be more productive" "That seems like a great plan Betsy", and with that the two women went to the bigger garden area to hoe weeds and work the trenches to support the irrigation in the rows which were not evenly watering the growth. They worked the garden almost all morning, and they were pretty hot and tired by the midday. When Lunch was served they responded to the bell and went into the dining room to eat and have an hour off. Rose loved working in the garden, and she reported to the young man in the commissary that she would have some tomatoes to bring in on their next trip, and she thought she might be digging potatoes as well. "We are all looking forward to your harvest, Rose because we know they will be a lot tastier than what we are growing at this point."

"Jam and peanut butter sandwiches, and turkey soup for lunch" was the announcement on the black board as they walked into the big central room, and Rose went for a couple of glasses of tea, and then ate a bowl of soup, and passed on the sandwiches. Betsy and Rose quickly returned to their place in the garden, and worked to finish the two rows they had been working on. By about 4:30 they both were quite tired and they took a break and Rose told Betsy that they were up quite early to get here by morning. So she thought she needed to stop and go back to get some fluids on board, and retire early so she could put in a good day tomorrow. She shared with Betsy that they had begun to dig out foundation lines to build their own home, "We would like to have it built in a year, and Buck thinks it is possible." "But you do not?" Betsy asked. Rose for a moment thought, and then she replied that in reality she kind of knew not to doubt him, but it seemed such a monumental task for the two of them that is what causes me to wonder". "Four or five guys and gals put a house up here in about two weeks, so He may know something that we don't quite understand." "Of course, Betsy, you are right, he probably knows things that I do not really understand, and I have already been amazed by the fact that he dug out the septic tank hole in four day's work." "Pretty impressive, I'd say", was Becky's response.

They walked slowly to the community building and went in to clean up in the bathroom, and then went in to the community room to secure a table for their group. Becky had known that several of the families and individuals wanted to give the newlyweds gifts for their marriage, but had said nothing to Rose about the plan, one of the women had begun working on a quilt, and several of the others had pitched in to put together other gifts, and Becky had made up a certificate for credit from her account at the commissary for them to select what they would want, and she had been carrying the certificate in a card in her pocket all day thinking that dinner would be the celebration time. She saw Bill come into the dining room and she got up to go and check when the community would be offering their gifts. Bill said that they would do it at supper tomorrow, as he knew they would be spending the next day working.

Becky returned to the table, and Buck had come in to join them, and Becky asked him how many days more they would stay? Buck responded that they would leave and drive in the night going home, tomorrow. "Honey it might be a good idea for you to take a nap tomorrow afternoon, so one of us can be alert" Buck suggested.

She said that she would be happy to take a nap in the afternoon tomorrow, and with that comment there were announcements, and a short presentation by the community doctor about a message that he had received on the two way radio from a former colleague that there was an outbreak of flu in the population and they needed to be careful with their interaction with persons sympathetic to their cause. Delivery folks that might be carriers of the germ and not know, so the Doctor illustrated how to wash to cover any points of contact, and he suggested that perhaps it would be a good idea to use antiseptic wipes.

After they had answers for their questions, the food was served and everyone began to talk at their tables, and Bill and Buck reviewed what they needed to do in the morning so they would be able to do the rest of the work without Bucks expertise.

"Can we count on you showing up in a month?" Bill asked, and Buck answered in the affirmative. He said, he wanted to come in the next month because he would be needing about twenty or thirty lengths of six by six by twenty fours, and Bill said that was convenient because he could set those aside for Buck, because they were expecting a shipment of lumber and he was sure that they would have that with metal joints too". "I will also take all the quick mix concrete that you can spare, too, next month", added Buck to the shopping list. Bill assured him, that they had enough quick mix to cover this end of Nebraska.

Assured that the supply for their building would be available, Buck and Rose took their leave after dinner, to their logging, and to sleep. They were both tired from a long day's work, and Rose was asleep rather quickly and Buck snuggled with his sleeping wife and had gone into sleep rather quickly as well.

The work party was at the common room to eat and get busy, for the day all these people felt working with Buck present was a big help, and each time it occurred they would learn from him and feel more and more competent in their tasks.

Rose and Becky and about five more people worked in the garden for the morning and Rose and several of the other women began digging in the soil which had been composting for now about six weeks and the soil was significantly improved the quality, there were lots of worms, and the odor of the soil rich and almost black in color, very unlike that of the garden area. Rose kind of thought about how to talk about the change in the earth, and then she said to the group, "you know when we all saw what was happening to us all in the other society, our choices so limited, and so many rules to constrain our lives, I had to walk away, and so did all of you, and walking away from that environment was like trying to get to where we could to find some kind of freedom. The vegetables are like we were; they need some kind of nutrition that the stifling dry starving environment was not able or willing to give. The nutrition of the garbage breaking down is like for us the ability to exercise choices that we had lost back there." The group all took in a deep breath, and said almost in unison that the illustration was a very meaningful picture to operate from and several of the women thanked Rose for this new frame of reference. "I hope when I come back to see how it is going that I see huge 'free' veggies loving their new life and environment."

Rose worked at digging into the new area, fresh and nutrient filled dirt into the larger garden, with several others setting seeds as she finished putting in the almost black soil they had cultivated with their garbage. The women worked until lunch and then as a group went in to clean up and eat the noon meal. Rose left the group to get some sleep and have a head start on the night's drive back to the mountain, and the boy pony who they suspected would be looking out for their return.

Just as she walked back to the guest quarters, she saw Buck, Bill, and several of the younger men loading the truck with great long boards, sacks of cement and bags of sand. She was a little tired from the digging in the morning and she showered and she began to read a while before she fell into a deep sleep.

Near dinner time Buck came back to their room, and he jumped into the shower, and prepared for dinner and their exit from the community. Within several hours they would be back on their way home, and she asked him if he was exhausted from the work for the day? He said he had done a lot of the work that day along with the others, and then said to her "how do you feel about driving" and she said she thought she would be okay with it and he felt she had driven before, and it was not like there would be traffic to negotiate and he would just try to relax and not need to sleep on the trip back. "You know I am honored that you trust me to drive, and I am excited to do this". "Trust you, Honey, I need you to feel comfortable as a driver, we have two of us and two vehicles, and I need you to feel comfortable as a driver." He grabbed her in an embrace, and she laughed out loud, "Honey, I will take anything on for you." Rose said, and with that they went to dinner and to pick up a few things in the commissary before they left. When they entered the dining room they were greeted by the whole community with gifts and promises of gifts still being made, and a celebration of their union and hopes for their future.

Everyone was in a celebratory mood, and dinner was a delightful experience. They explained they needed to hit the road soon, and a group followed them to the commissary, almost everyone there, paid for the things that they were picking up as their contribution to the celebration. As they drove away from the community they felt truly blessed, and they agreed that these people would always be important in their futures.

Rose was particularly touched by their generosity, all mixed with the excitement of her controlling this huge vehicle heading home and back to her colt, with the man she loved so deeply, life was back as it had been when she had harbored that hope of escaping the government by being able to become a college teacher post Ph.D. Life had gone through the giant up's and down, and she told the whole story to Buck driving home, and she told him that their marriage and their plans were a new high for her in her life and she had him "to thank for the hope in her heart at this moment." Buck asked her to always keep the kind of communication high, "I need to know always how you are feeling Rose, either we need to share the joy, or I need to help manage the problems," and she agreed that she would always keep him informed.

As they turned toward the west and began the drive home, off the Black top road, and the sun was setting and its intensity was less and less, and she turned on the truck lights, and she found a smooth road way and they headed toward their home, with Buck now asleep in the cab, and Rose content with her new responsibility. The hours slipped by and Rose was feeling quite comfortable driving this fully loaded truck, and she was able to see the outline of the mountain after about seven hours, and she circled the end of the mountain and headed to the area where she could begin to negotiate the trail up to the area, near the foot print of the cabin. It was slow going up the hill, but she could see the markers on the side of the path, and she slowly negotiated the path, and as she drove the big truck up toward its parking place. She turned the last corner, pulled the truck into a flat place, the key turning off woke Buck, and he hugged her, and they walked over to the shelter, and both went to sleep for the balance of the night. As they entered the shelter, Little Boy acknowledged their return from his bedded posture next to the shelter, as if they had not been gone for almost four days but had merely taken a walk in the middle of the night.

Buck was up way ahead of Rose and he had begun to unload everything that he could manage by himself, and he had a large tarp to cover the bags of cement, and the pipes for the lines in the water system, and drainage, for the septic system. He had placed the smaller items into the tent, and when Rose woke up she helped him stack the lumber in a way so it too could be protected before it was used.

With the major unloading being done, and Buck made a pot of coffee, and they sat together with a pad of paper, with Buck outlining what needed to be first and second and so on. "I need to do the plumbing hook-ups, and I need to set up a way we can mix the cement and dig out the foundations, and kind of keep it very close to where it will need to be poured." "What do we need to use to mix the cement in" and Buck went to the tent, and brought out a shallow little kind of bath tub kind of object. This honey is a mortar mixer, and we do it a little at a time, until it all is mixed in, do you think you could mix and pour cement?" "Yes" she replied, "but I think it needs to be close to where it needs to be poured, because that would be too heavy for both of us to lift." "All we need to do is tip it." He replied. "I will build up the edges with framing wood and you mix the cement and we will have a full floor within about two weeks". "Today we will do some framing and tomorrow we will begin to do the floor". "I need to get some more rocks, for the fire place, and she began to feel very excited and it felt like it was indeed a potentially successful project."

"Now let's have another cup of coffee, and I will teach you to mix and pour our floor." They sat on the hillside looking in the direction of their former home, and felt the warmth of the sun on their backs, talking about what they could get done in the day, and set a goal of getting six square feet of floor formed, set, and smoothed this day. Rose thought she would work in the north east corner of the house, working through the week on getting the front part of the floor finished.

Buck pulled the mixing box up into the area that would work well for where she planned to pour the floor, and he as well emptied a bag of sand, and the aggregate into the mix, and then a bag of cement into the mixing box. She carried water from the lake, in the bucket, and as she added water and mixed by turning the mix over and over as she had seen Buck demonstrate, she really began to understand what to look for to know it was effectively ready to introduce it into the floor. Buck had set the edge with plywood panels, and as they worked away the morning, Rose could see how it would look once they made some progress through the week, and the more they worked the more of a sense of exhilaration she felt.

The first day of labor passed and at the end of the first six days of working, the water lines and septic was completed and about one third of the floor was laid and smooth with brads set into the edge of the floor which would support the wood of the walls. With six days on the job, the seventh was a day off by previous agreement, but Rose said to Buck that she thought they should work on if they were still feeling good energy. "Honey, if we do not have a break we will burn out, so trust me on that, and if you feel like you want to do something find some little thing to finish to prepare for tomorrow. Okay? And she kind of understood, but could not find anything that qualified as little, and gave up and just went gathering rocks for the face of the fireplace. Buck accompanied her on her walk, and they brought back about ten good sized rocks and placed them in the pile. They spent the rest of the day reading and lying in the sunshine which Rose had to admit felt restorative. Buck put together some dinner, and they ate and retired to sleep and were up early in the morning to begin another week.

As the week passed they had begun the base of the fireplace in the main room, and Buck showed her the mix difference for the mortar which would be used to build up the rock fireplace and she helped him build up the form for the base of the fireplace. The foot print of the home had changed, to accommodate addition of two more rooms. A door on one side of the fireplace and then another on the other, and then another cement slab which could be enclosed for two more bedrooms just in case they should be blessed. "You know Buck I have no idea if I am able to become pregnant at my age, but honey I do not want to have one without a sibling for that child. It was hard being a single child in a family too much responsibility for only one. It seems to me the first loving thing I can do in being a Mother, is to have another child so that first child is not left with so much responsibility". She shared with Buck the conversation that she and Angela had had when her parents died, about the tasks of loss and grief, being shared, was in reality, so much easier when her folks died, because she had someone to cry with and laugh as well. "Also, raising one child or two makes little difference."

Buck reflected to Rose, that he as a child had been lonely much of the time. He figured having been lonely as a kid made the prospect of being alone out on the plain's was not so intolerable as he drove away from the disintegration of the city, "you know I actually said to myself that growing up lonely was a benefit I could be with me for the rest of my life, and have no one around and it would be okay, but if I just happened to see a beautiful woman inside a little shelter it would be okay to fall in love with her, and hope for the best." She walked over to where he was, and reached up to hug him, and he scooped her up into his arms, and with that, the two had decided they needed a break.

CHAPTER TWENTY FOUR

A COMPLETION AND A BEGINNING

Buck was coming home with a lot of wood this time. Rose had stayed home for this trip, but she had sent five boxes of veggies to the community and hoped that Buck would use it for credit in the commissary for building materials, but instead Buck had asked Becky to accompany him to select some new clothes for Rose, and she had selected some shorts and tops and several other outfits for her, with underclothes, and a new pair of shoes. He had told her that over two years of working in the community he had more than enough to supply them with their needs, but she had always been responsible for all her needs and it was hard to get over feeling that she needed to help out with expenses. The shell of the house was completed, and Buck before his trip in this time commented that he planned to get a mattress for the bed he had constructed before he left. He wanted to get the most comfortable mattress he could find, and on the night before he began to return this time, he and Bill went to the commissary to find the best mattress for his needs. They had selected a goose down mattress, a mattress pad, and pillows and sheets and pillow cases, and now driving up the hill toward their home he was grinning with his selection. Several of the women had completed a quilt for them as a belated wedding gift, and he had picked that up as well, and when he drove into the back of their home, he called to her to help him bring things in. He had the pile of clothes, he and Betsy had selected for her, and he as well had the pillows for their bed. She picked up the sheets and linens, and a box of food for the next month, and on the second trip they together brought in the mattress. It fit the frame of the bed perfectly, and they put on the mattress cover, and the sheets and pillows and they both threw themselves into the new bed, and after many years of sleeping on the ground or on the inside of the shelter, this was a blessing to have a nice comfortable place to sleep.

She had noticed she had been feeling a little on edge, she felt physically more tired than usual and with the heavy labor she at first thought she was just worn out, and needed a break. And then because she had not menstruated now for two months, she was sure she was menopausal, and her opportunity to be a mom had passed. She had to admit that she was more than a little disappointed, but she and Buck had each other, and they had a home and she was happy he planned to make some simple furniture, like a table, and some chairs, and so she blew off how she felt. With Buck home she could get less focused on how she felt and pay close attention to him and what he needed and wanted. She was designing a stable shelter for Little Boy, who was not so little anymore, and Buck had brought home a bag of carrots for him from the community, which he loved, and would do almost anything to get a couple for a snack.

They worked together to unload the truck and noticed that he had purchased a flip box for the bottom of the fireplace so ashes could be put outside when they were cold, and kind of manage the waste in the fire place with just a little clean up. She wanted to bury the ashes in the garden too, she was sure she remembered that Granny put her ashes in the garden and she had looked up on the electronic reader what the values to the soil would be and she was surprised to find what she had discovered. She thought where the garden was located in a place with direct sun each day and she had predicted she would get the best results in that area, yet the facts were the west end of the garden did the least well. She looked at the areas where she got the least crop yield and thought since she had no way to test the acid base balance, of the garden, she would just experiment. She felt it those areas would be treated with the wood ash that she might get a better result.

Buck called to her and said he had something to show her. She entered their house, and he had a bunch of new clothes laid out on the bed. "Honey I got you some new duds, and a new pair of shoes. Actually Betsy helped me pick out stuff, but I think you needed a treat." She hugged him for the thoughtfulness implied in the gifts, and she tried on some of the new clothes, and he said each of the shirts and slacks and shorts etc., looked good on her.

Since the major part of the building had been completed, he set about installing things that were ready to be installed, like the sink, and set up the hand pump which came from a the lake and into a tank which had a purification system, and the final prep of the septic system, so that at the end of the day they actually had a functional toilet. She had made the bed, and in the afternoon she stretched out on the new bed to take a nap. He had previously installed a cook top on the sink, one burner which was powered by a butane tank. He heated the can of soup they had in their stock, and ate and then joined her in bed and she slept through the night. She felt much rested and much better in the morning when they rose for the day.

"I have been thinking about refrigeration, and bill showed me the units that run from bottled gas, they are huge, but he thinks we could find one which is a more normal size and he is looking around for one. Life would be a whole lot easier for us if we add that on to the design in the kitchen. And I think it would be a big help especially if we get pregnant" and with that comment she broke into tears and Buck had no idea what he had said, "Honey, I think I am becoming menopausal. I think we are just too late" she finally replied. "I have not had a menstrual period in two months, and I have just felt lousy. Sick to my stomach after I eat something and until last night I have not slept very well at all." Buck thought for a moment and then said, we need to go back into the community and have you see the Doctor, he will be able to tell what is going on with you and he can help." "You are not due to go back until another three weeks, and I will go with you then, but this is not the kind of thing I need to run to the doctor with I don't think. It just happens and that is one more thing I don't need to worry about. I am not sure what the year is but I was born in 2097". "Honey it is 2135 this year, that makes you 38, is that a typical fertility range?" "I really do not know, perhaps 40 is pretty typical for onset of menopause". "Rose I want to go in to see the doctor, independent of the work schedule, let's go in this week, I need to know that you are okay." Okay she replied but we are in no rush to find out that all my eggs have been wasted."

Buck stewed all the rest of the day, and he hovered over her until she needed to ask him to relax nothing he could do would help, and he was making her feel very anxious with his fussing around.

It was Friday morning and she had withstood, all the fussing around Buck was involved in they decided for his wellbeing they needed to head into town. They thought that they could be back by late at night, so they were on the road for an afternoon appointment with the doctor. The drive was tense, and Buck was trying to make it as smooth for her as he could. Finally she just took his arm and said, "Relax, you are like a jumping bean". He took a deep breath, and responded by saying he was just concerned and wanted her to be okay, and that he would feel better if he could just hear from the doctor that she was okay. "You said yourself that you did not feel yourself."

They arrived at the building where the doctor had his office. They walked in and one of the apprentices met them and asked them to be seated and she would let the doctor know that they were here. "I don't think you will have to wait for a long time, he is just swabbing a throat for a kid." The doctor walked out with his patient, and he was telling him he had a nasty sour throat, and he needed to drink a lot of water, and go home and get a good book to take to bed for two days." The doctor came back in and greeted the two, and asked how he could be helpful. Rose spoke up, and said she felt a little nausea in the mornings and had been tired, and was not sleeping well. The doctor told Buck to sit down and he would like to do a physical exam to rule out any other problems, and he asked for a specimen jar, and asked Rose to empty her bladder into the jar. She did that for the Dr. and then went into the exam room and the doctor did a complete physical. He took her medical history which was pretty unremarkable, and her reflexes were good, and all the rest was pretty good. He asked her if it was okay if he did a vaginal exam, and she thought that would be very important if she in fact was menopausal. After the completion of his exam, she put her clothes back on and walked to the doctor's office, and found a very worried Buck and the doctor in his private office. She sat down, and felt a little dizzy. The apprentice got her some water at the doctor's suggestion and she drank it down. "Well I have a diagnosis for you Rose. I would estimate that in about six months you and Buck will be the proud parents of a lovely and I suspect very healthy child. I would like to see you in two months, just briefly to see that your chemistry is good, and the last month I would like you to get a room in the community for you to stay in, so that you will be close by, for delivery. Your general systems review is unremarkable, you are quite healthy, and I suspect your reproductive life will be quite good and for the next 6 years will be quite viable. "So what she is feeling is pregnancy"? Buck asked. "Yes, she has typical symptoms of being a mom in waiting." "You need exercise each day, stay away from foods that do not smell good to you, and I am sending a two way radio home with you today set it up and if something is puzzling you just call." He handed her some pamphlets on the issues in pregnancy. And she shared that the thought of not being able to achieve pregnancy had made her feel sad, and that she was very happy with the news. "Doctor you have laid to rest my worst fear of not being able to have children". The assistant handed them three bottles of prenatal vitamins, and they both went to get into the truck and head home." "See I told you we should have done this even earlier", Buck said to her and he turned the truck back on the road, and checked to see if they had all the parts to the two way radio, before they got too far out of town. Rose had been quiet coming in and she could not stop talking for more than a couple of hours. "Honey we will need to have a baby bed, and a little mattress for it, you know maybe a pillow would be adequate, and diapers, I can get some cotton and make those myself, and check if they have baby food in the commissary, and I will look on the electronic library if they have any parenting stuff to read. Oh my god I am so happy with being pregnant, and to think I thought it was a foregone conclusion that I was too old and in fact was becoming menopausal. Can we hang up a line in the sunny part of the yard to hang clothes, and remember to get some clothes pins at the commissary, when you go back in to the community to work?"

"We will not have to do the rooms right away but I do think it would be good to plan on having it enclosed by next year this time, oh maybe I am rushing, who knows, but it will be nice if we can just slowly get everything ready for our family." The sun was going down, and they had the mountain in their view and knew they would be home by mid-evening.

Driving up the hill and reaching the top Buck walked her into the house, and insisted that she eat a little something, and he set up the two way radio on the kitchen counter and placed the battery into the cabinet drilled a hole to pass the cable out to the antenna which he would mount in the morning. They went to bed and Buck just had the need to hold her. They had left not knowing if their desire to have a family had a chance, and came home in a state of joy with the prospect of their first child was growing in her body and would become an individual in just seven months. Buck was just so happy and Rose was delighted. This night was magical for the two of them, and they were ready to learn how to do this as well as was possible. This was a miracle.

CHAPTER TWENTY FIVE

THE LONGEST WAIT

As the morning came they woke and Buck made coffee for himself but made tea for Rose, as she had lost her taste for coffee, she hoped for the time being.

She had her tea, and they ate little bread and butter, for which she had not lost her taste, and Rose suggested making a list of tasks, and if they were organized they could get it all done and be ready for the birth of this first child. They made their list and put it up on the cupboard door to know where they were in the process and each day they would have one of the things on the list scratched off.

She consumed copious amounts of water, and exercised daily with long walks around the environment. Rose became very sensual and would bug Buck occasionally to engage in intercourse at times which seemed to Buck, unusual but never unwelcomed. The spontaneity he watched grow in her was welcomed, and they would even wonder on their long walks if there was something in the shift in her personality was not a kind of chemical response to the growing infant in her womb. If Rose had ever been depressed through her life, she did not even see the various things that might have affected her mood before in a down direction. She was buoyant and interested in learning everything about taking good care of this little life that was making his or her entrance into this family. "I never had any idea that having a child was so delightful an event" she commented to Buck on one of their walks, and he reached around her waist and pulled her close and held her as their walk proceeded. "I understand that when this little bundle comes we might lose a lot of sleep, so naps now may help us get through those early months". They tried to keep up with the list and the tasks that were left on the list, and as time passed and Rose got larger and larger, she added to the list, figure a way to expand my clothes. On one of the trips to the community several of the women suspected that by now she would be needing maternity clothes, and had gone through their stocks and sent her a bundle home for her selection. This gift was most appreciated as her clothes had become too tight to wear and she was stretching them on, and not being able to button most of them, had to trust her expanding belly to keep her pants up. Rose planned to go to the community on the next trip, to keep her appointment with the doctor, and work in the garden and enjoy a visit with the many women who had become her friends. She was eager to talk with many of them to learn from them what their experiences had been with birth and babies, most of the families in the community had made the decision to break with the one child policy so many of the women had been able to have several children and she was sure that they had information that would be invaluable to both she and Buck. Months had passed since they had learned of the pregnancy, and it was late fall in the year, she had harvested most all of the fruit down the hill and as she was preparing to go into town with many boxes of her produce to sell in the commissary. When they gathered the harvest they had enough to put into twelve boxes, and Buck was absolutely amazed at the quality of the veggies, and the abundance. "They will think we have a factory farm out here," Buck commented as the night before the trip he loaded the twelve boxes into the back of the truck. "Well we had better, we can't totally depend on the work you do, building the credit for our needs. It might be important to think about what the kids can learn to do to help out too."

The drive into the community was uneventful, and easy, and as they drove in, Buck left Rose at the Dr.'s office and then drove on to the commissary to unload the vegetables. Rose walked into the waiting area and sat to wait for the call to go to the exam room. She had brought with her the electronic reader, and so she pulled up the material on child birth that she had been reading. The doctor called Rose in and asked about her energy and walks each day and diet, and then left so she could put on the gown to facilitate the physical exam. He placed the stethoscope on her now well expanded belly, and she noticed that he began to grin, and she asked what was humorous about her belly sounds. He looked up and said he thought two. Two what, she responded, and he asked her to give him a moment, and then he looked up at her with a smile on his face, "Rose it sounds like what I have wondered about, I think we are about to get ready for twins, do you know if twins have been born to any relatives?" She was shocked and then she said she had no idea. "I think I would have known if my aunt or my uncle had twins and I was a single birth". "Well I am hearing two distinct heart beats, but I do not have imaging technology available, so I just want you to know that there are two very distinct heart beats, your measurements are larger than I would expect if there was just one, you are a very lean woman, with little adipose tissue on your frame, so this girth must be a result of a very full uterus." She was clear that her girth had expanded, but she had not for a moment thought about the possibility of twins. "Do I need to do something different?" "Yes you will need two of whatever you need for caring for these little folks" Rose broke out in laughter.

Buck had walked back to the Doctors office, and was waiting to meet with the doctor. Rose put her clothes on and met him in the waiting room. She leaned over and announced that she was carrying two little people, instead of the typical one. "Oh My God I have to build another bed and double the other things, the high chair and all that stuff. I may need to keep the credit up via the Veggies, Well what do you think are you happy about this or what? I think it is wonderful honey, what if they are identical? How will we tell them apart? I do not want to yell at one of them if I don't for sure know who did the deed." "I think that will take care of its self as we get to know them." They both went into the doctor's office and he shared the news once again with Buck, "the two of them sound very viable, their heart beats are strong and regular and Rose is in very good shape. I want Rose to get a room here for the last month, and that arrangement needs to be done soon, I do not think that it is a good idea for the two of you traveling when she is in labor."

Buck had forgotten that Rose would need to stay for the last month but he went when they left the Doctor to make arrangements and then realized that he did not know when Rose would have completed the eighth month and would need to be here. Let's see, Rose said, I think I became pregnant near the first of June this year. Today is the 5th of November so you need to tell Bill I need lodging Middle of February. Tell him I can work in the commissary to pay for my room, and I might even be able work the garden, but you will need to check the moisture in what we have growing at that time, because I will have a winter garden in at that time. Can you do that?" Buck thought he could add that to his list of responsibilities. "Oh I hate to leave you with so much to do, and I will be so far away. Will you watch after Little Boy, and invite him to walk with you when you go somewhere?" Buck assured her he and the pony would be just fine. And he would have the big window installed by next month so she could come home to an almost air tight place to live, and then the same information became clear to both, she would not be staying here for another three months and they both broke into laughter. "Obviously, this is a big case of anticipatory anxiety. We have not been apart for months and already we are anxious about being separated."

We need to mention our need to Bill, and I need to go find him, and since we will be here two days at least, I need to find him and find out how he wants me to do to earn my keep this trip. Rose said she would see him at dinner, and she headed for the garden to work the afternoon, and meet up with her friends who had given her clothes she could wear, and announce the arrival of a matched pair in Feb, or March next year. As she came around the corner of the tool shed Becky spotted her and called out to rest to take a break they had an honored guest. Rose was greeted by six women who had sent their maternity clothes and Becky though not a mom was the organizer of the effort. She thanked them all for their generosity and "I would have had to come to town in my birthday outfit, if you all had not been so thoughtful. "Alice who had sent her maternity stuff, said it was clear there was a lot of wear left in all of the outfits, and as they sat for a visit and a drink of cold water, they all commented that she looked like she was ready to deliver, "no not until February or March, girls, and the doctor told us today he can hear two distinct heart beats, and he is sure the reason I look like I am about ready to drop, is that it is a very crowded uterus. Becky was the first to speak up, "oh my god, talk about how that feels to you, I mean I would be overwhelmed with one, much less twins." One woman in the group had twin boys and she thought it was easier to handle than she had thought. They grow up taking care of each other in so many ways. Yes at first when they were little it was a race, but as they grew they demanded less attention in the long run because they seemed to know what the other needed, it was like they could read each other's minds. That information was helpful, for Rose to ponder, and they all went back to work the garden and Rose joined in and pulled weeds and cleaned up the furrows as she went. By dinner time she was exhausted and thirsty. She and Becky walked into the community room and cleaned up and sat down with some tea which had just been brought in and poured for them by one of the kids who helped out in the kitchen.

As the kids came in with trays of food, and set up a self-serve table for people to use to take what they wanted on plates which were stacked nearby. There was a large salad and two entrée's one ham sliced, and sweet potatoes or whipped white mashed potatoes, and the other was sliced beef in lovely brown gravy. There was a large sheet cake for dessert, and homemade ice cream. It all looked good, and Rose selected sweet potatoes with the ham, and salad, and ice tea for a drink. She thought she might take some cake and ice cream and then thought better of that option, and got extra salad instead. Buck had had a labor intensive afternoon, and was tired so she got up and retrieved his food, and said to him that there was dessert, and he had both his and hers when he had finished his meal. "I do not usually eat sweets" he said, "but this is too good to pass up".

They went to their bed room shortly after the meal and visiting was finished, and Rose asked him what he would be doing in the morning and when did they plan to start home. "Do you feel like driving Honey, I would like to drive out after dinner tomorrow? But I know I will be bushed." She said she felt good and she would take a short nap in the afternoon so she would be alert. "So what have you been involved in today, you did not answer my question." I have been digging a trench for a new water distribution line they are building in a new area, and I just pitched in when I saw what was going on and I really feel the heat, here, I must have drunk a couple gallons of water, and I feel like someone has been beating me". Buck took a very hot shower and was asleep within minutes. Rose sat in bed and read until she got sleepy, and patted her two little buddies and she turned off the light, and slept until Buck roused her at 7 in the morning.

"I will see you at lunch, Honey, and don't forget to take a nap, Okay?" She assured him that she would sleep in the afternoon, and got up to dress and go out to the garden to work in the morning. She was not really hungry, but she stopped by to get a piece of fruit and coffee as she had reclaimed her taste for her normal breakfast drink. She picked up the coffee and an apple to eat on her walk to the garden, and as she headed toward the garden she noticed several men gathered around talking about something which had them all agitated, and worried. She would have had to change her path toward the garden in order to avoid these four gentlemen, and so she kept her path, and as she approached she could begin to hear what had them so engaged. "Bill has been our building Forman, for the whole time we have been here, and he has done a hell of a job, I am not interested in changing when he is so good at what he does." She knew that the community was designed to operate on the basis of consensus and it sounded to her that someone was pushing someone to take Bills responsibility. She walked on to the garden area, and she asked Betsy about the conversation she had overheard. Betsy took Rose aside, and said, "You know Rose men are funny when they think their ego has been kicked by some event. This is not the first time something like this has happened, and it probably will not be the last, the last time it happened, it was your husband they wanted to put in a leadership role, and he said he did not want to do that because he said he did not need the hassle. Men, I have decided, fight about control and women fight about being right, my solution is to not get involved. One tempest she needed not to get engaged in she thought and besides this was not the focus of her life now. As the day went on they left the garden to go over and see where the garbage was being buried, and evaluate the impact of the organic material on the ground. She was able to show Betsy how she could tell it was too soon to plant anything here, and then Betsy took her to the commissary to see some seedling trees which had come in on the last truck. "When you come next month, could you help us decide where we should set them out, we need to begin to bury garbage in those spots to develop a good healthy soil base." Rose agreed she would try to do some reading about what particular kinds of soil they might need.

The lunch bell rang, and everyone headed to the community building to eat and take a break. They noticed that the day had been relatively cool, the sky was clear but the sun was now more southerly now as she scanned the sky she noted that clouds were building and the breeze was picking up. She as they walked toward lunch, told Betsy that she was going to nap this afternoon as Buck wanted to leave after dinner, and she would need a rest so she would be able to drive back to their mountain home. She ate and visited with several of the Gardening women, and then headed to their room to shower and sleep. She was aware that she had not seen Buck for Lunch but she thought perhaps he was engaged and thought he had opted to skip lunch for some reason. She was almost asleep and a knock came on the door. It was Betsy, and she stepped in to let Rose know that Buck was taken to the Doctor, it looked like there had been an accident, and he had injured his arm, so Rose quickly put on clothes and went with Betsy to the Doctors office to see that Buck was okay.

Bill was sitting in the exam room with Buck, whose arm was bloody, and somewhat miss-sharpened. Bill had the arm wrapped in ice packs, and they were waiting for x-rays to be developed to determine their next move in the treatment of his injury. Bill usually a guy of few words, was asking Buck a lot of questions, not so much about what he was doing or how he felt, but rather what was going on when he got pinned by the supply pipe. "Bill the work crew this morning was impacted by the argument over some leadership issue. I did not pay attention, and I can't tell you much except the guy who I was working with was getting bugged by this other fellow who wanted to support another insurrection. It is my observation that you need to exert your authority with these guys, and tell them to knock it off."

Rose broke into the conversation, and asked Bill to call a meeting now to head this off. As Buck was getting a broken arm set, in the Doctor's office, Rose and Bill were ringing the bell on the community building to announce a community meeting now. Work stopped and people were en masse walking toward the building. The kitchen staff was setting out tea, and lemonade, ice and glasses, and everyone had heard that something had happened but were unsure what the issues were. They all came in and grabbed something to drink and took seats. Bill was in the front of the room and he and Rose had agreed that she would explain what Buck had to deal with and the circumstances of the accident, and he would ask the community to talk about the issues they needed to deal with.

The doors were finally closed and Rose stepped to the front of the room, and announced that her husband had a broken arm apparently because people were more interested in politics than attending to what they were there to do, safely. A man stood, and said he was the person who lost his grip on the pipe that they were connecting at the time of the accident, apologized to Rose for his inattention. Then another hand went up and said he was sorry about what had happened to Buck, but then said, Bill has not been fair about assignments, and began to bitch about unfairness about assignments. Rose stepped forward, and the group quieted, and she said, "It is my impression that around here the standard of work assignments are based on need of the community and nothing else. I used to be a supervisor for the Government, and I can guarantee that there was no fairness involved in those kinds of decision making. I do not live here, but I am a member to the extent that Buck works here and I work here when we come in and we call many of you, our friends. When I hear that something is not fair, I always remember something that my Grandmother would say. When her children would complain that a decision had not been fair, she would say in response, "Fair is where we go to buy pigs" I as a child understood that fair was a difficult standard, and fair to who or what. Always if I consider a problem within that kind of an articulation, I am setting myself up for a disappointment. I would suggest that we agree to change the focus, to what works for the larger group, the community. If you don't like it leave, if you stay change your perspective to what works for the community.

Bill got up and thanked Rose for her words, and he said," Look sometimes I feel like I have been herding cats all day. I agreed to take a leadership role five years ago, even before we left. I want you to know that I am tired of too many close calls, and now we have caused a man to endure a lot of pain and injury because you are all acting like cats instead of a unified group. I am sick of the bellyaching bull, and it must stop or we will have to disband, and I for one will never go back. Our success has been our unity, we need that back and I am asking for a democratic process here, we will have an election for work leader, and we must all, me included, go along with the results. Nominations are now open for my replacement". Hands went up and several names were suggested, Bill's first, then Ted, and Nathan. Write your vote on the ballot and put it up in the box, and Betsy you count the votes.

After every one had voted, the ballots were counted, and the results were no surprise. Bill had received 37 votes, Nathan 2, and Ted had received 1. Okay, Rose announced the numbers and the community had spoken, "If you stay you need to go along with the majority rule." Rose said to the group, and she asked if that was possible. Nathan, stood up and affirmed he would stay and he was okay with Bill, being in charge. Ted stood up and said that he and his family would be leaving. He had been the major source of the uproar, all along, and his wife stood up and announced that she would not be leaving and her children were too young to be out there alone with their father, that he would be welcomed to see the kids, but only when he would visit them in the community, and with this Bill asked Ted and his Wife to meet him in his office and they would see if there was some way to keep the community intact.

He asked Rose how her negotiation skills were, and they left together to go meet with this angry couple in the privacy of his office.

"Look Rose I was not even there when Buck got hurt, it really was not my fault", Ted said to her when she came into the office. Rose responded to Ted, that blame and a nickel were worth a nickel. "I do not care if you were at fault, or not, on the sight of the accident, I think you want to be powerful, and I have not a clue why." Ellie his wife, chimed in and said she thought that if he was in charge he would take too many chances, with the work and the people. "He gets a kind of high when he takes a risk and it works out" but she added when he takes a risk and it does not work out he denies that it was done correctly and or he says that they just did not understand the task". Bill thought for a moment and then he asked Ted to stay in the community and separate from his wife, and work as his assistant for the next six months, and if he did not want to stay after that he would be free to go. Ted agreed, and Ellie said he could move his things to where he would be staying this afternoon, and she asked him to leave her alone for a while. "Look I have not been comfortable with you for some time, and I need a break from the tension in our home. Just leave me alone, and if you can settle down, then we can talk."

Rose walked from Bill's office back to the Doctor's place, and Buck was ready to get in the truck and go home. His arm was casted, and the doctor told Rose that the bone was cracked and needed some time with the support of the cast, but it was not a break, and it should heal if he would just give it some time. She went to get the truck and drove it up to pick up Buck and then they went to the commissary to select what they might need for the next month. They checked the balance in their account, and discovered that several extra days of work had been added to the account for the injury. They picked up some meat, for their stock and a new cold box, and bread and some condiments, jelly and peanut butter, and mustard, and some flour and some soap. And they drove away in the middle of the afternoon and were home by shortly after sun down. The pony met them on the parking area, and he was a little spooked when he saw the cast on Buck's left arm. He reared up and then approached Buck and Buck let him check out the cast and he settled down so within moments he was himself and no longer spooked by this addition to Bucks body.

CHAPTER TWENTY SIX

EDWARD AND HIS SISTER ELIZABETH

Rose had opted to stay on the mountain, and let Buck go to the community after his cast was removed in early December, and the x-ray had confirmed it had healed. They were moving into a new year, and she wanted to stay home making diapers, and quilts and many of the women had baby clothes that they sent home with him, and he had made another baby bed for the second baby they would be bringing home soon. She had agreed to spend the last month in the community so when February came around she prepared to go back into the community to stay until the babies were delivered. She was also aware that her own date of birth was not too far from this date. And as she got into the truck to make that trip to the community she wondered if the kids would arrive near her own date of birth. They made the trip and because she was getting so very large, she was quite uncomfortable, riding across the plain, and said to Buck this was for sure the most uncomfortable part of the pregnancy for her, and she would be glad when these two little one's were a little more on their own. He could see that she was wearing thin, and he too wanted her to not get too invested in working for commissary credit while she was waiting. He had told her that they had a great balance in their credit account, and she needed to spend time visiting and walking and reading. She said she would but she did want to do what she could and she thought sitting in the commissary would give her something to do and that it would help the commissary staff. This was the first time they had gone in without any produce on board, but the root veggies were just not big enough to harvest and Buck had indicated he could check the growth and bring them when he came in next.

They could see the community off in the distance, and she was grateful for the end of this trip, and she stretched to try to get more comfortable. Entering the community they drove to the place where the room she would occupy for the duration of her pregnancy was located and unloaded her things, and she got out and went in to stretch out and catch her breath. This trip had clearly been the most uncomfortable of her trips in, and she was glad it was over. Buck wanted to work for a couple of days, and then return to finish up the last of the things he needed to complete before the little ones made their appearance. "I will be back in two weeks to spend a couple of days with you and work, and then at the end of the month I will come down and just wait with you and do what I can find to do here" Buck said, and she was comfortable with this. She walked with him to go and get some lunch, and they met up with Bill, and Buck asked how he was doing with his new assistant. "That kid is a good guy but he lacks a little in the department of introspection but he is getting better and he and his wife are at least talking now. And I suspect she is not letting things go like she had been doing." Rose let the two men talk and she went out to the garden to see how things were doing, with the now very active transfer of the compost, and Betsy took her to the garden area where they were going to set the little trees for their beginning grove to cultivate a variety of fruits. The little seedling trees were now about two feet tall and had been repotted so the root growth could be better supported. They walked back to the community building, and grabbed some lunch. She and Becky spent the afternoon talking and Becky asked if she was doing okay that it was just, given her size, she must feel tired. She replied that it would feel good to have her normal body back, that she got tired easily, and she just looked forward to getting to the point of launching these kids into their own lives, when she did not have to carry them around in her abdomen any more.

She was truly tired, a tiredness which she had not felt since she was walking to find, she did not know what, and she knew her time before birthing these little children, would be short. With the added pressure she was not sure she had had a deep breathe in a while, and she felt as though her lungs could not expand enough for that feeling of tightness to relieve its self. She at first thought about it a lot and tried especially on the long walks, to stand tall and breath in deeply and after a while as the babies grew; she knew she would just have to get along on what she was taking in because there was no more room to expand into. She wondered if this had been her mother's experience bearing her, and then she remembered that she had been a fairly normal sized child and only one.

She had in her brief experience of being a child never known of twins being born, none of her friends were a twin, and she wondered if the oligarchs put something in the water to stop that as a possible outcome in a pregnancy, she would not have put it past them. That would spoil their population management program.

Buck left after the two days' work, and she was sad to see him go. This was the first time together that she knew she would not be with him for fourteen days, and she cried as she waved him off as he left for their beloved home and mountain, and she returned to the room they had secured for her stay. Within moments she lay on the bed and was asleep for a long nap.

Becky was knocking for her to get up and come to dinner, and she walked with Becky to the community building. This was a surprise baby shower, men and women, girls and boys. As she walked in she was greeted by the kids who had formed a chorus, and singing a parody of happy birth day to you, there were surprises and gifts for the babies, and there had been a credits pool for the new babies so they could have a credit balance of their own, and they had a big spaghetti dinner and salad and wonderful garlic bread, and cupcakes for dessert. What a party it was and she was both surprised and elated with the support and celebration of the community.

She had help taking all the gifts back to her room, several of the women and a couple of the older kids had gotten all the gifts together and helped her carry them back to her room, and she thanked them profusely, she felt that these people were her sisters and brothers, and the kids were her family members.

Rose went to sleep and she slept, so soundly she did not wake until the mid-morning. Bill came looking for her about time for lunch and she rather sheepishly admitted to him that she had slept until ten, and was surprised she had been tired. "Rose my wife used to sleep the whole night through the last month of her pregnancies, and it was hard, but she needed to sleep. After they are born they just don't understand that the middle of the night is not a typical time to be up and crying. So don't be hard on yourself you will need the rest in a month or so." Rose walked with him, to get some lunch and then went to the commissary to sit and check people out. As she was sitting there, talking with the folks as they were checking out. She sat at the checkout desk; she felt a tension in her back. It was like the muscles began tightening, not painful just different. She stood up for a while and it felt a little better, and so she stayed in the commissary. It was about three thirty and as time had passed through the day, she noticed that it became clear that to her that a tension kind of like a pressure which had now extended to her legs and her genitals. Now that she felt the pressure was felt in her genitals, she called someone and asked if she could use the little cart to go to the doctors to see if she was in fact okay or this was a beginning of her labor. The young man walked with her to the cart, and then drove her to the little hospital which had just been finished and on the way he told someone to call the Doctor and let him know Rose was now very uncomfortable. She walked into the hospital building and did not know where to go, and the Dr.'s assistant came running into the main door, and she took her to a room and helped her disrobe, put on a hospital gown, and get up into the bed, and by that time the Dr. evaluated her degree of dilation, and commented that she had a way to go, but someone should call Buck on the radio and let him know we are on, and moving toward delivery. She

A LONG WALK TO KNOWING

asked what the date was and the Doctor responded with February 15, 2132, and she realized she would in 40 days she would be 40 years old. The word had spread over the community and many were coming to give support. The physician's assistant told the women who would have filled her room to the gills, and put them on a two hour schedule, two at a time, and so they signed up for two hour shifts through the night.

She felt the deep pressure of a contraction; it not so much hurt as it felt like a growing and generalized urge. She was surrounded by women who had at some time in the past been exactly where she found herself, with a child on the way and now totally in charge, and she was sure totally unaware. What was it that they felt, with this change in their comfort, and peaceful existence? Could they feel the switch, and were they afraid, or oblivious to this pressure, surely they were sensing on some level that something really big was about to happen and she wanted to reach them, and comfort them and say to them that Dad was on the way and she was right here, and everything would be okay. She unconsciously put her hands on her belly to try to sooth them, and this was what amounted to her first mothering act, but her consciousness of the transformation was not a sharp and a clear picture it rather was simply an attachment being experienced but not named. She then as quickly as with the response to the first deep urge to push, there was a long rest period, which was a welcomed relief for her in this beginning maternity. The physician's assistant had remained here with the group of women, and Rose, and she had noted the gentle smile appear at the same time the first deep urge to push, and she in that moment, understood this woman would be a natural protector of her children and they would be two little guys who would know they were important, and loved.

At this point the deep moments of pressure were still not particularly regular, or of increasing urgency and the women regaled Rose with the stories of their own birth process, and the joy of seeing the baby for the first time, and the responses of siblings, and the happiness

243

and anxiety of bringing the child home, with the constant reminder that this new bundle of life, was dependent on them.

Rose wanted to know what time it was and someone said it was six in the evening, and it was time to bring in the next set of volunteers, the goodbyes were attended to and the hellos' came with the next twosome of coaches, as they were welcomed in the room. The doctor dropped in and reviewed the clinical notes and said he would check in on her in a couple of hours. "This might be a very late night, and since I have a break in responsibilities now, I think I might catch some sleep, I will be in my office, come get me if you notice any issues", and he headed to get some sleep.

The time passed and as time passed both the pressure and intensity of the labor slowly increased, it was like there was an increase in discomfort, and an increase in strength of what one might think of as a pushing the babies forward and ultimately out, but it was hard to see from one episode to the next there was so little recognition of the slight increase in that it seemed to Rose no progress was being made in this task, and she found she felt trapped in a process over which she could exercise no influence and found this at best disheartening, and at worse a trap she could not escape. She said to several of the women, "How can I hurry this up?" And each in their own way replied "let go of control" or "It is about the chemistry of the process" and finally as it was in the middle of the night she simply gave in and even tried to sleep but with very little success.

At two A.M. Buck arrived and he was gowned and washed, and the picture of Rose in the midst of an increasing pressure and now some pain in the process of her laboring, he felt a deep shock in how this woman who he loved to the bottom of his being, was struggling with these consequences of their passion. She was happy to see him enter the room and then wondered if he should be here at all as she as well on some level picked up his panic at what he interpreted to be what he had done to her, rather than what they had engaged in by way of mutual passion and as she remembered mutual lust.

She asked him to go get some coffee, and take a walk, and maybe even take a nap, and of course he refused, and he asked a bunch of questions of the women who had signed up to help coach her in the process. They all tried to reassure Buck, that when this was finished she magically would completely loose the awareness of, and memory about the labor, and would feel sheer joy. This seemed fantastical to him, and he kept saying "but you don't know Rose. Her mind is like a steel trap!" And they told him to go take a nap that she had several more hours to go at this before she would be fully dilated. And of course said he was staying . . .

As the process went on the volunteers tried their best to reassure Buck that all was well and this increasing tension and the pressure was all a part of the process, and he simply could not transition into a coach, and the doctor came in, and suggested that Buck and the assistant take a short walk. The coach, being pretty well seasoned with the process, and went with Buck out to take a walk and talk him and his anxiety down. "Look Buck" she said, "this is how children come into this world. You need to stop being anxious, she will be just fine, she is perfect to give birth, and your anxiety is making this hard for her, so get a grip! She needs you to find your courage, for her and go in there and be supportive, and loving, and let her do what she is doing, and if the fear comes up you need to imagine yourself stepping on the fear, and breathe and find your courage and tell her she is doing very well." He started to cry, and they sat down and she got him something to drink, and handed him a small white pill. "That will calm you down, and we are going to sit here until it starts to work." They sat there until his hands stopped shaking, and when they got up he said he could do what he was there to do. "Did you read the pamphlet the Doctor sent home with your guys for the husbands", and he acknowledged he had only looked at it, and had not really read it through. "Okay you are a coach; do you know how to be a coach?" And she slowly taught him as they walked back what to look for and what to support. What to say to help her and then she asked him a lot of questions about how he was feeling that was different.

245

He acknowledged that he had been building the anxiety on the drive all the way in for more than 8 hours, and when he saw her that she was having to work so hard in the process and that she was in pain, he flipped out, and came apart. "If that starts again just kick me in the ass and I will straighten up." And with that they both re-entered the room, and she was pushing hard, and in the final stage of her process, the doctor had made a small cut to assist in the process and within a half an hour the first infant had crowned, and was in the process of being born. Buck did exactly what he was there to do, and did it well, and the volunteers had left this part of the process to the medical staff, and Rose. The first baby was born and he was in great shape, twenty one inches, and 7lbs. 3 oz.; she was resting and waiting for the next part of her process to begin again. Buck had seen the baby, and was just amazed at how perfect he was and how beautiful he appeared, and within a few moments Rose began to feel the pressure build up with the now present pain and the doctor said to her "okay you know what you are doing Rose, Push, Push, Push, bear down and push, we have a crown, Okay you are doing well push Rose and she could feel the second baby coming through her body and with a loud yell she pushed and the little girl entered into the first moments of her new life, and Rose was able to see this new little life, and she was amazed at how beautiful she was. They cleaned the second of their children up and weighed her and measured her and she was just a little smaller than the first, twenty inches and 6lbs, 11oz. The doctor set in two stitches, sprayed an antiseptic on the episiotomy, covered her up and congratulated her on a fine job of giving birth. And in that moment now holding her two little bundles, she understood what the women had told her all along, that the memory of the discomfort was gone and replaced by the joy of these two little babies who had come to create family for she and Buck.

Someone had rolled in two little bassinets and the babies were put in them to sleep, and Rose and Buck just looked at their perfect little babies, in wonderment. Buck sat down next to the babies sleeping and within a half an hour was asleep himself, Rose had been given a shot for what she did not know and was drowsy herself, and soon all four were sound asleep as the sun was just peaking over the horizon.

What a day and night this had been.

CHAPTER TWENTY SEVEN

Welcome home

Rose woke and was hungry for breakfast and as if the doctor's assistant could read her mind walked in with a breakfast tray that had been sent up from the community building, with scrambled eggs, and bacon and toast. There was a steaming cup of tea on the tray and some pills which she was instructed to take when the tea was not so hot. She was aware that Buck was sound asleep in the chair someone had brought in for him last night and the children were as well quiet in their little beds, and so she ate and took the pills and drank down the tea and the water on her tray. She felt very little discomfort, and in fact she began to feel her energy return to her and she wanted to get up but did not want to disturb her family so after eating she let herself relax in the bed, and within an hour she was back asleep and resting very quietly as well.

She had slept for about four more hours, when they brought her lunch, and again she ate quietly and again she dropped back into a light sleep, for about two more hours. She was awakened by the doctor's assistant, who wanted to see if her milk was coming in as yet, and she had brought a breast pump with her to see how she was doing in terms of production. Her milk was abundant, and they pumped out what they could get and it was apparent that she was producing enough for both infants, and the doctor when he came in to visit said that he had obtained some bottles and nipples and she could store her breast milk for a while in a cold box and Buck could help with the feeding, but to switch breast and bottle between the babies so they would get used to both methods of feeding. "Remember the bottles will be better received if they are not cold, and so they need to be set out for a little while."

"You may opt to feed both the babies but having a little expressed milk on the ready may at times be convenient. Two hungry babies at a time can be a little nerve racking and it is much harder on the mom than the kids. They will not take a whole lot of volume at first, just an ounce perhaps in 24 hours, at first and then they in about two or three days have a dirty diaper which looks like a squirt of mustard and that is normal." The teaching about early feeding went on for a while and while the babies were sleeping Buck was roused to listen to the process along with Rose, and he even started taking notes and asking questions.

Some of the questions they had were answered in the materials they had read, and some were answered by the physician's assistant, and after the teaching had been completed. The P.A. taught Rose how to express her breast milk, and she was almost immediately good at getting the milk down. Everything looked good, and they talked about what they needed to be able to achieve over the next week before she and Buck could return home. They had a goal, to take their family home and they spent their days getting to know their little Liz and Eddie as they had been named. Within the week they both could demonstrate competency in feeding and care. The last morning Rose was in his care the doctor reaffirmed in her mind that he was on the other end of the two way radio, that things happen and they would address any of the problems as they came up and he wanted to see her and the children in a month but she was free to head back to their home, and get the babies into their normal situation so they could adapt to what is becoming natural. They took the hospital bassinets home with them and with the load of gift's they had been given the night before the babies arrived. As they drove out of town that sixth morning of their babies lives, they were seen off by almost everyone in the community.

Bill and Buck had agreed that Buck would not be back to work for a couple of months, and the doctor had agreed that Bill would have access to the two way radio in case of a need to consult with Buck and that made everything much more relaxed for Bill given the change in Buck's schedule. So as they headed home to their mountain, with their two little new bundles, they knew that life had expanded in a way that neither had possessed the insight to see it would expand. There was a layer of expectation now which neither had any appreciation would have accompanied these two little babies, but they both felt the shift in their sense of this new life. And both saw it as hope.

After a stop at the natural springs about a third of the way home, they drove into the west heading back to their home, and as they drove up what was becoming a well-worn trail to the top of their mountain, the trail that had that day so many years before been so apparent to her and upon re-evaluation seemed not to exist, each carrying one of their new family toward the cabin that would be home for all four, they knew that they were free of over weaning rules, only the standards of fairness and equity among their peers. They could look forward to no lies, and no double speak, and a life lived in a relationship which was real and abundant and a society which was reciprocal and guided by fairness and respect of the other. As she thought about the panorama of her experience she had an urge to thank the spirit, which had been so important to the Plaines Indians, and she felt that was good. She had found this idyllic place and Buck had found her, and all of this was good. And she had now the full reality of the fact that this had been a long, but very necessary, walk to knowing.

POST SCRIPT

We find ourselves in a time when most of us, 99% of us to be exact, are walking in the shoes of people like Rose, and her colleagues who work to support the activities and needs of the 1%. Many of the 99% are like the dispossessed in this story who survive on their wit and guile. Yes there are safety nets, but there is a strong and growing inclination to do what the oligarch's in this story have succeeded in doing, set the worker against those who, in many circumstances, are frankly hopeless. There are within the human family those who have chosen to accept this process, there are however those who have chosen to protest and speak about the functional unfairness implied in rugged individualism which was a kind of permission slip for the robber barons of the 18th and 19th century which is the foundation of the equity transfer to who we see today is at the core of the legitimacy.

The establishment of Library's and the Medical Foundations was the payoff for their ticket to responsible legitimacy. Other than, The Gates Foundation, we have few if any really wealthy who take seriously the needs of the poor, or middle class who now find themselves, perhaps only now one illness away from desperation, and poverty.

It is the spirit of the 99% movement, that I wish to dedicate this small token, and I pledge to dedicate 20% of the author's proceeds and urge others to support people who are willing to draw attention to these social and ethical inequities. Every one of us can use a hand up.